THE
MOTHER
SHADOW

THE MOTHER SHADOW

MELODIE JOHNSON HOWE

Thorndike Press • Thorndike, Maine

Library of Congress Cataloging in Publication Data:

Howe, Melodie Johnson.
 The mother shadow / Melodie Johnson Howe.
   p. cm.
 ISBN 1-56054-045-1 (alk. paper : lg. print)
 1. Large type books. I. Title.
[PS3558.O8926M68   1990b]   90-42940
813'.54--dc20   CIP

Thorndike Press Large Print edition published in 1990 by
arrangement with Viking Penguin, a division of Penguin
Books USA, Inc.

Cover design by Sean & Carol Pringle.

The tree indicium is a trademark of Thorndike Press.

This book is printed on acid-free, high opacity paper.

For Bones Howe

Acknowledgments

I would like to thank Arnold Peyser for
the recommendation and the lunches;
Elaine Markson and Christi Phillips for
turning a no into a yes; and John Rechy
for teaching me the craft.

1

A low, smooth male voice infiltrated my sleep. The voice told me: "Virginity is making a comeback. Polls taken on high-school and college campuses find . . ."

I opened my eyes and turned off the radio. Sitting on the edge of my bed, staring at my unshaven legs and the chipped red nail polish on my toenails, I waited for my usual morning sadness to slowly disappear. Ever since I was a little girl I have experienced a sense of loss upon awakening. I think of this loss, this sadness, as a bridge of melancholy which I must cross to get from the comforting darkness of unconsciousness to the painful light of morning.

Since this was the morning of my thirty-fifth birthday, and I'd just been told by the radio that virginity was making a comeback, I knew my sadness was going to linger. My breasts felt heavy. How could these two little things feel so burdensome? Gravity. And how was it possible for virginity to make a comeback?!

9

The telephone rang. It had to be my mother, who lives in Versailles, Ohio, on a street called Main. She would be calling to wish me a happy birthday, and to announce, not for the first time, that I was now a mature woman who must face the fact that not everyone can be a success in Los Angeles. Please come home.

I found the telephone under yesterday's clothes. "Hello?"

"Miss Maggie Hill, please."

"Speaking."

"Ellis Kenilworth here." Kenilworth was my current temporary employer. "Would you mind coming in earlier this morning? Say, around nine o'clock instead of ten?" His cool, educated voice was frayed with tension. "I will be meeting with a Roger Valcovich, and it's imperative that you be here."

"Is something wrong, Mr. Kenilworth?"

"For the first time, I'm trying to make things right. Miss Hill, I've grown to respect you over the short period of time we've worked together. I hope that feeling is mutual."

"It is." I did respect Kenilworth. He was a true gentleman. In fact, he was the only gentleman I knew. His manners and courtesies were extended with admiration, not with a pat on the head.

"And I always felt, if need be, I could rely

on your discretion," he said.

"Of course."

"Good. Nine o'clock, then. Goodbye."

"Goodbye."

In my family, discretion meant that you kept your goddamn mouth shut. I hung up the phone. His choice of the word "imperative" was odd. For the last three months I'd been working out of Kenilworth's mansion in Pasadena. I put his handwritten inventories of his coin collection into his brand-new computer. It was one of my easier temporary jobs. There was nothing imperative about it.

I stared at my own computer. It was delicately stacked and balanced on the short, narrow bar top that separates my tiny kitchen from my tiny living-bedroom. The monitor was blank faced, the floppy disks empty. I was a writer. I had written one novel, which was published to overwhelming silence. I looked at my watch. It was eight o'clock. No time to shave my legs. Again.

Heading toward the bathroom, I flipped on the television. Jane and Bryant were sitting on the NBC sofa, looking all shiny faced and spruced up. Before I turned on the shower, I heard Jane bouncily announce that her next set of guests were Mr. J. L. Henderson, a wife beater; Mrs. Alice Henderson, his twenty-year victim; and Dr. Arnold Meitzer, psychologist. But first . . .

Warm water . . . soap . . . Maybe I could wash virginity back into my life. I shut my eyes.

There was the image of my ex-husband, Neil. He was no wife beater. I was no victim. And yet . . . all that shared pain. Why did I marry a policeman? Do not go over this again, Maggie. Oh, hell, what are birthdays for if not to review your past failures and torture yourself with those failures? Almost as much fun as picking a pimple. I married him because I thought I needed his sense of structure, his authority, his knowledge of right and wrong. I immediately rebelled against all he had to offer me. Confusing me. Confusing him.

I had liked his impersonal way of having sex. We didn't make love. We fucked. But then he had an impersonal affair, and I discovered just how very personal betrayal can be.

I got out of the shower and opened the door to let the steam out of my windowless bathroom. I heard Bryant declare that New York was going to let the local stations tell the viewers what was happening in their part of the country. I always thought that was really nice of New York. They didn't *have* to let us know what was going on.

I dried off the mirror. Serious dark-brown eyes looked at serious dark-brown eyes. High cheekbones reflected high cheekbones. My hair, the same color as my eyes, was cut just below my defiant chin. My nose avoided being cute by turning slightly down instead of up. I would have opted for cute. My mouth secretly embarrassed me: the lips were full and looked as if they were waiting for kisses. Men always looked at my mouth first. Rubbing cream into my face, which I knew didn't do a damn thing, I decided there wasn't time to blow-dry my hair.

Back in the living-bedroom, I struggled into control-top panty hose, trying not to work up a sweat. A blond young man with a smirk appeared on the TV. He told me he was David Dunn. He had his eye on L.A. But first . . .

I searched through my dresser for a forty-five-dollar French bra. I'd just bought it. I couldn't afford it. A pure white lacy strap gleamed among the twisted mass of panty hose, slips, scarfs, sweaters, and underwear. The top of my dresser was strewn with makeup, costume jewelry, paperback books, notes to myself, dirty underwear, and my grandmother's rosary. This wasn't the dresser of a thirty-five-year-old woman. This dresser looked like it belonged to a fifteen-year-old girl. My sadness was deepening into depression.

Extricating the bra, I heard the name Roger Valcovich. I faced the television. A puffy man encased in a beige suit sat behind a functional-looking desk. His round little hands were folded tightly in front of him. Except for the potted fern, they were the only objects on the desk. He talked carefully into the camera.

"Even if you have a prior drunk-driving conviction, we can help. Whatever your legal needs, the law offices of Roger Valcovich are here for you." He tilted his oblong head toward the camera. Curly silver-gray hair caught the light and twinkled. "I'm Roger Valcovich. I can help. Remember, justice does not have to cost a high price." Small lips inched into a frozen smile.

Coincidence — there had to be more than one Roger Valcovich in Los Angeles. Ellis Kenilworth used a very conservative, expensive lawyer. He certainly wouldn't be using an ambulance chaser who had to advertise. I was feeling uneasy. Kenilworth had never involved me in a meeting before, imperative or not.

I turned off the television and finished dressing. Black skirt. Pink shirt. Black patent sling-backs. Black-and-pink tweed jacket with big shoulder pads. Shoulder pads make me feel less melancholy. They also make me

14

look like I don't have a neck. You can't have everything.

I grabbed my grandmother's rosary. She's eighty-five but thinks she's a hundred and helps Willard with the weather on the "Today" show. I took a paperback of *Madame Bovary* and, along with my rosary, dropped it into my leather sack of a purse. I was reading *Bovary* for the third time. I understood why she had to kill herself. But I kept hoping.

I turned on the phone machine, a small lamp by the bed, and the radio. I found the classical station. It was the only kind of music my landlady let me play all day. Maybe if I get robbed the classical music will soothe the burglar and he won't vandalize the place.

I stepped outside my tan stucco apartment. The architecture was third world. Locking my door, I made the mistake of taking a deep breath. The smell of burritos, swimming-pool chlorine, exhaust, and early-morning coffee brewing at the 7-Eleven across the street, violated my body. I had not come out to Los Angeles to live in the San Fernando Valley. That was not part of the dream. But the rent was cheaper on this side of the hill, and that was part of reality. Another failure to torture myself with.

Maneuvering my Honda east on the Ventura Freeway, I rolled back the sun roof so my hair could dry. The radio rocked. I loved being alone in my car. I loved driving. My Honda was the only thing in my life I had control over.

I kept thinking about virginity making a comeback. What form would she take? She wouldn't dare return in the bowed and draped form of the Blessed Mother. Virginity wasn't coming back because she was sacred or moral. No. Virginity was traipsing back into our lives like an old ex–movie queen. Big tits jiggling. Flabby hips swaying. A thin halo of platinum hair. Diseased pink flesh stuffed in hourglass white.

"I'm back in town, big boys," she'd coo, scared to death.

2

The poor and the old wealthy are living closer together in Pasadena — at least what remains of the old wealthy. Most of their mansions have been crushed by quick money. Condominiums, gated for the safe life, have been erected in their place. The surviving mansions grace wide, shady streets which run parallel to wide, shady streets dotted with shabby bungalows and disintegrating apartment houses. But no matter how the city changes, Pasadena has a highly polished Calvinistic shine that will never tarnish. It produces Rose Queens with the same hardworking enthusiasm with which it produces a new civic center.

I turned down a street lined with aged oak trees and parked in front of the Kenilworth home. It was a large two-story white house with an elegant veranda sweeping across the entire length of its façade. Steps cascaded from the center of the veranda onto a spread of lawn that made me think of picnics and croquet and ladies in white linen dresses. Nine chimneys jutted from the roof. Smoke drifted from only one: the fireplace in the mother's bedroom always burned. A narrow strip of asphalt ran alongside the house under an ornate portico. The driveway was a begrudging afterthought to the endurance of the automobile. No iron gates, no attack dogs, no video cameras protected this house. The Kenilworth mansion displayed itself openly to all who passed by. I admired this unguarded house. It wasn't boldly displaying wealth; it was defiantly displaying continuity, survival. I didn't know the Kenilworths well enough to know what survival had cost them. But at this moment in my life, when I was contemplating the return of virginity, why shouldn't I believe in the basic goodness of big white houses?

I made my way up to the veranda and the giant square of a solid mahogany door and rang the bell.

Holding a bone-china coffee cup splattered with red roses, Sutton, Ellis's younger brother, let me into the white marble foyer. Pale blue eyes widened. "My, you're early this morning!"

I smiled.

"Who's in there with Ellis?" He tried to look disinterested, but his reddish-blond brows arched.

I wasn't sure if my discretion included the

family, so I changed the subject. "How's your mother?" I asked.

"In her sitting room, by the fire, drinking tea and warm milk. Beautiful as an angel. You're looking even more attractive this morning, if that's possible."

"Thanks." Our eyes flirted.

Sutton had once been a very handsome man. His hair was still wavy sun-blond, and he carried himself with a certain specialness that beautiful people possess. But time had smoothed the jaggedness of his features, turning his beauty soft. When he smiled, as he did now, the sharpness of youth shone through. Sutton and I had a relationship based on flirtation. The boundaries were tacitly understood: winks, innuendos, admiring looks, and the touching of hands on arms were allowed; nothing more. I don't know how that sometimes happens between men and women, but it does. And it's fun.

Cupping his hand under my elbow, he made a grand display of promenading me across the foyer toward the office door. The heels of my sling-back shoes made tippity-tap noises on the marble floor. Tippity-tap. It was a vulnerable sound. Tippity-tap. A female sound. Tippity-tap. Tippity-tap. The sound of thirty-five.

"It's my birthday," I blurted. Oh, hell,

someone should know that it wasn't just another day.

"I hate birthdays. They always make me wish I'd never been born," he replied.

As we passed the open double mahogany doors to the library, Judith Kenilworth, sitting on a rose damask sofa by a silver tea set, raised her blond patrician head from the *Los Angeles Times* and stared at me. I smiled. She didn't. She had never smiled at me in three months. But I kept trying.

Sutton deposited me in front of the office door. Leaning close, he whispered, "Happy birthday, Maggie. If I were my own man I'd spend my nights trying to seduce you."

"Whose man are you?" I asked, half seriously, half flirting.

"You know where sister and I are breakfasting if Ellis needs us," he said, ignoring the question. "But he never does need us, does he?" He turned and sauntered away as the large, shadowy American clock, which stood in the gliding curve of an august stairway, began to discreetly chime nine. I always felt that the clock was embarrassed to break the silence of this stately home by its boorish mechanical need to tell time.

I opened the door to the office. Ellis Kenilworth stood as I entered the room. He performed his manners as easily as my ex opened

20

a beer can. He had never been as handsome as Sutton; he had also not gone soft. His features were hawk-like. In contrast to their sharpness, his hazel eyes were gentle and seemed to focus more on what he was thinking than on what he was actually seeing. His lean body was clad, as usual, in gray slacks, cashmere blue blazer, button-down shirt, and muted striped tie.

"Miss Hill, this is Mr. Valcovich."

It was him — the star of law and television. He didn't get the hint from Kenilworth and stand. Instead, he nestled his rump back into a green leather chair and waved a round, chubby hand laden with two huge gold rings at me. The rings had not appeared in his commercial.

I sat at my desk, which was opposite Kenilworth's. He sat down, not looking at Valcovich. There was an awkward silence which I'm sure only Kenilworth and I felt. Finally I spoke.

"Saw you on television this morning."

"Which commercial did you see?!" I thought he was going to leap up and demand I let him sign an autograph.

"Something about drunk driving."

"That's a great one. 'Justice doesn't have to cost a high price.' " He beamed. Kenilworth's cheeks flushed. He still couldn't look at him. And I couldn't figure out what he was doing

21

here. Kenilworth's faraway eyes attempted to focus on mine. He ran his hand over his ash-blond hair. I was in the land of the blonds — the real blonds that come in various shades.

"Mr. Valcovich has just helped me draft a codicil. I want you to type it and then witness it."

"I've never typed a codicil."

The star of law and television grabbed his legal-size yellow pad and slapped it onto my desk. "Just type it as I've written it. If you can't make out a word, don't guess. Ask."

"And when you have finished, Miss Hill, please pay Mr. Valcovich three thousand dollars, cash, from the safe."

"Three thousand dollars!" I don't like to see people get taken, no matter how much money they have. I couldn't help myself. I turned on Valcovich. "I thought you said justice was cheap!"

"This has nothing to do with justice. And I think you're out of place, little lady."

"Little lady?!"

"Miss Hill, please," Kenilworth said.

"If my secretary talked like that she'd be out on her ass."

"Ass?!" It was my turn to slap the legal tablet on the desk.

"Mr. Valcovich, that is enough!" Kenilworth almost raised his voice. "Miss Hill, please proceed."

"Do I make a copy?" I asked.

"No."

Valcovich leaned forward. "I should have a copy."

"No."

"That's very unusual. . . . "

"I have paid you an outrageous sum because I want you to do exactly as I wish. You will not have a copy. You will not talk to any member of my family. And when you leave here, that is the last I will see of you."

Valcovich leaned back and crossed his legs. "Whatever you say, Mr. Kenilworth."

As I put the paper in the typewriter, Kenilworth swiveled around in his chair and stared out the floor-to-ceiling arched window that overlooked his beloved sculpture garden. The garden ran the entire length of the property. Hedges and bushes were cut and sculpted into clapping seals, jumping fish, diving birds. A dark green dog walked on his hind feet while a bushy green cat curled into sleep. There were even a unicorn, a Pegasus, and the American eagle carrying an unfurled flag in his beak. Being all in green, the eagle and the flag lost some of their patriotic stirring. But the garden itself was awe inspiring.

I read Valcovich's writing very carefully. I

felt his eyes on me. They looked just as small as they had on TV. But what the TV didn't show was their greediness.

The codicil was short and to the point. Ellis Kenilworth was leaving his entire collection of rare and ancient coins to Claire Conrad, who resided at Conrad Cottage, the San Marino Hotel, San Marino, California. If she should die before she could take possession, the collection would go to auction but never revert back to his family. I wondered who Claire Conrad was. I also wondered why Kenilworth didn't want his mother, brother, and sister to share in the profits of his collection.

As I began to type, Valcovich turned and looked out the arched window. "Must cost a lot of money to keep up a garden like that," he said.

"Unnecessary things are very expensive," Kenilworth said sadly.

"Who's the kid?"

"Excuse me." Kenilworth went out the French doors to the garden.

Valcovich repeated his question to me. I looked out the window. Kenilworth was picking up a red ball as a small male form, arms akimbo, lumbered toward him.

"He's not a kid," I said. "He's probably in his late twenties. Suffers from Down's syndrome. I think his name is Jerry."

"Kenilworth's?"

"No."

"How did he get into the garden?"

"I don't know. You see, it's none of my business," I said pointedly. Actually, it had never occurred to me to ask. In the last three months I had seen the young man in the garden maybe six times. He would appear, then disappear. Sometimes Kenilworth would play ball with him. Sometimes he would just stare at him from the window.

Valcovich leaned over my shoulder. "You've made three errors. Type it over."

"You know, you're much looser in person than you are on television."

"Thank — " He stopped; the small eyes narrowed. He was trying to figure out if he'd been complimented or put down. I gave him a sweet smile.

There was a quick knock and the office door opened. "Where's Ellis? We're going to be late," Judith demanded, looking around the room.

"In the garden."

She shut the door behind her. Her honey-blond hair was tied back with a black ribbon. Her thick hair was her only good quality. She had Ellis's aquiline features, which should have given her an angular strength and beauty; but because she was so uptight they made her look pinched and strict. Her mouth was fixed, as usual, in a straight line. Folding her arms across her bony chest, she peered at Valcovich. "You look familiar. Do I know you?"

"Probably saw me on TV."

"Oh. You're an actor." Unimpressed, she moved toward the French doors. Then it dawned on her. "What's an actor doing here?" she demanded.

"I'm a lawyer. I advertise on television," he said proudly.

"You have business with my brother?"

"Me," I heard myself saying. "I mean . . . he's my lawyer. I had an accident with the car and he's helping me out," I babbled, trying not to look at the paper in the typewriter.

"Just like Ellis to let you do it on our time," she said, going out to the garden.

Valcovich smiled at me. He had small teeth. They were the best feature of his smile. The worst feature was a calculated intimacy, as if he and I had just shared a sexy moment.

I took the paper out of the typewriter and put in a fresh one.

"You better tear that draft up. We wouldn't want sister to know she's not getting any of the ancient jingle-jangle." Again the intimate smile. "By the way, do you always lie so easily?"

"You seemed so enthralled with your TV

persona I was a little worried about your ability to remain confidential." I tore the draft into shreds.

" 'TV persona.' " He repeated the words softly, lovingly.

Judith followed Ellis back into the office. "I have been working months on this symposium," she said. "You promised you would go!" Her bluish-white skin flushed red with anger.

"I said no."

"Brian Waingrove is expecting you."

"I am conducting business. And you know you're not supposed to be in here while I'm working."

Judith's mouth trembled. "Waingrove could help us."

"You are not supposed to be in this office. Please leave."

I had never seen the Kenilworths argue. It was disturbing to see Ellis treat Judith like a little girl. It was even more disturbing to see Judith act like one. Her lower lip pushed out into a pout. Hazel eyes filled with tears. I guessed Judith to be in her forties, but right now she looked like a middle-aged child. How could she give up those hard-earned years so easily? Her whole life reduced to a pout. I looked away. It's not easy to see another woman reduced to a child — maybe because we all live on the edge of a pout.

There was a knock. The office door opened. This time it was Sutton. "Are we all ready to go?" he asked cheerfully.

"Ellis isn't coming." Judith's voice quivered.

"You promised her," Sutton said, looking steadily into Ellis's eyes. "You really must stop breaking promises."

It was strange, but of the three it was Ellis who looked the most betrayed. Sutton extended his hand to Judith. I waited for the door to slam, but it closed quietly behind them. In my family the door would have slammed so hard the framed family photos would've fallen from the walls.

I put a fresh sheet of paper in the typewriter and began again. Ellis slumped back in his chair, his faraway eyes staring at a spot on the wall just over my head. Valcovich kept a steady watch on my typing, which made me nervous. I could hear Sutton's car backing slowly out of the narrow drive. When I finally got a clean copy, Kenilworth decided there was a problem with some of the wording. After much talk they revised the codicil. An hour later I sat down to re-type it. Valcovich looked out the window. Kenilworth burned the other drafts in an ashtray, then dumped the ashes into the wastepaper basket.

I handed him the clean draft. Both men read it. Kenilworth signed, then asked me to sign. I did.

"Pay him, Miss Hill." His voice was heavy with fatigue. "I went to the bank yesterday. The three thousand dollars is in the safe."

I unlocked the safe and took out three neatly wrapped bundles of money and handed them to Valcovich. He counted through the money with the quickness of a Las Vegas dealer. "It's been a pleasure doing business with you, Mr. Kenilworth," he said, trying to look professional instead of devious.

"Show the gentleman out, Miss Hill."

We crossed the foyer to the sound of my shoes beating out their tippity-taps. Valcovich's all-knowing smile was firmly in place, the greedy eyes on my lips. Slowly, they moved down my body to my feet. By the time we reached the front door his eyes were back on my lips. Even after liberation and the sexual revolution there are still men who can make me feel cheap. Valcovich was one of them. I opened the front door. He swaggered outside, turned quickly around, and gave me another once-over. I squared my padded shoulders, readying myself for the sexual pass. My hand firmly gripped the door handle. I was going to let him throw his remark, then I was going to block it by slamming the door in his face.

"Funny a man like Kenilworth would hire a lawyer like me," he said. I hadn't anticipated the truth, but my reaction was already prepared. I slammed the door in his face.

I went back to the office. An envelope, dove-gray with my name written on it in blue ink, lay on my desk.

"What's this?" I asked.

"The codicil."

"It has my name on it. What's going on here, Mr. Kenilworth?"

His eyes slowly focused on my face. "You have spunk."

"Okay, I have spunk. Why is my name on this envelope?"

"Actually, you have guts — a quality I lack."

"Mr. Kenilworth . . . "

"Do you know how much my coin collection is worth?"

"No."

"A little over four million dollars."

"You mean all those names I've been entering into the computer — Livincius Regulus, 42 B.C. — are worth . . . "

"Yes, Miss Hill. My father willed me his coin collection. At the time it was probably worth ten thousand dollars. Mother was given everything else. Nobody cared about his old coins. But I did. It was one of the few things in life for which I had an ability and a passion." Pale lips formed a sad smile. "Now, the family is very interested in my collection. They need my money."

"You don't want them to have it. Fine with me. But why is my name written on this envelope?"

Kenilworth moved from behind his desk and picked up my purse. "I want you to keep it for me while I'm at lunch."

"Oh, no. Put it in the safe."

"The combination is well known in this household."

"Nobody's here."

"Mother is."

"I can't take the responsibility."

"Whether you like it or not, Miss Hill, you are a responsible woman. I'll just slip it in this sack you carry. I have a feeling it will be very safe in here. . . . You're reading *Madame Bovary*." He pronounced it with a French accent. "I always felt very deeply for her. I suppose that's Flaubert's triumph. But in my case I think it was just one bourgeoisie identifying with another."

"Mr. Kenilworth, listen to me. I do not want to be responsible. Please, take it back."

"After lunch. I will make arrangements then."

"But what if something should happen?"

He looked sharply at me. "Like what?"

31

"I don't know . . . anything . . . "

"Whatever happens, Miss Hill, I do not want my family to get their hands on this. Now, will you keep it till I return?"

I took a deep breath. I always do before I give in. "Yes."

He gave my hand a fatherly pat. And I felt like the good daughter. A disturbing feeling: I learned very early that daughters can never be good enough.

"It's none of my business, but do you love her?" I asked, feeling a little foolish.

"Love? Who?"

"Claire Conrad."

"I've never met her."

He moved toward the office door, paused, then turned and faced me. "I do know her by reputation. I probably should have made it clear that the coin collection is a form of payment to her. Payment for the truth — a truth I am unable to deal with. If anything should happen, Miss Hill, tell her that."

"But nothing's going to, right?"

"Right. I will see you after lunch." He left the office.

Feeling totally confused and wondering what kind of truth could be worth four million dollars, I began to compute, with a new respect, old inventories and list new ones. The hall clock prudently chimed one, and like

Pavlov's dog I automatically looked out the window to see Aiko, the houseman, setting up my lunch tray in the garden. He waved. I waved back. Commanding the computer to save, I headed toward the French doors. I stopped, turned, and stared at my bag. I usually left it by my desk while I ate lunch, but today I picked it up and lugged it outside.

Aiko always placed me at a large table on the stone veranda overlooking the garden. The table was shaded by a fringed umbrella. This afternoon I was having an onion tart with a small mixed-green salad lightly flavored with mustard dressing. A glass of Chardonnay, so he informed me, glistened in the sunlight. I leaned back in my chair and sipped the wine, which tasted like green olives, and thought about Kenilworth's sad eyes . . . Valcovich's greedy eyes. Why did I lie to Judith about Valcovich? Why didn't I just keep my mouth shut? Why did I always get so involved? What was this need I had to protect people? Rescue people? What business was it of mine? In other words, why did I have Ellis Kenilworth's codicil in my purse?

But the sun was warm, the wine was making me lazy, and all the green little animals had been trimmed to perfection. A fish arched. A rabbit crouched. A seal balanced a ball. There was the smell of freshly cut grass, and there was a bird, a real one, perched on the rim of the umbrella, tugging at a cord of twisted fringe. This bird was going to have a very well decorated nest, I thought, shutting my eyes.

A gun exploded the silence. The bird screamed. I stood up, knocking over the wine. And then I was running. Down the veranda. Through the French doors. Into the office. Silence. Out into the foyer. Aiko and the maid stood frozen, looking toward the top of the stairs. I ran up the stairway. Stopped. Listened. Only my breathing. I walked slowly down the wide hallway. All doors closed. Both sides. The smell of gun. One door. Open. White tiles. White rug. Lysol clean. Blue cashmere blazer. Gray slacks. Blue button-down shirt. Striped tie. Neatly folded. The shower. Glass door open. He was there. Sitting. Naked. Shotgun between his legs. Pieces of his head. Blood. Bone. Ash-blond hair. Skin. Splattered on white tile. Not one piece of him on the white rug. I turned away and leaned against the bathroom wall. I was going to vomit. I was going to faint.

"What was that noise? That noise? Ellis? Sutton?" the mother's frightened voice called from the hall.

I groped my way toward the door, swallowing my saliva, blinking away bright yellow dots lined in black. I tripped over his clothes.

34

An ebony fountain pen rolled on top of a white note card. His writing.

"Ellis? Ellis!" She was almost to the door.

"It's me, Mrs. Kenilworth. Maggie." I grabbed for the note and lunged out into the hallway, shutting the bathroom door behind me. As I looked at Eleanor Kenilworth, I realized all I had in my hand was the pen.

Tall and frail, she leaned against the hallway wall. Aquamarine eyes searched my face. She clutched at a pale green bed jacket slipping from her shoulder.

"That noise . . . what was it?" Her skin was as white as her hair.

"It was nothing . . . a car backfiring." I took her thin hand — a circle of diamonds turned loosely on her wedding-ring finger — and guided her back to her room.

"I used to hunt pheasant. I was a very good shot. We had grand hunting parties. Our land went for miles and miles then. Pheasants flew up from the bush. Their beautiful feathers caught in the sun."

Her sitting room was pale green. I helped her to a green chaise lounge by the fireplace. The flames cracked.

"So you see, I know that sound," she said, leaning back, studying me. Her eyes narrowed. "What are you doing up here? You don't belong up here."

The room was hot and smelled of perfume, roses, and face powder. I backed away from the fire, feeling dizzy.

"I came up to get Mr. Kenilworth's pen." I held out my hand to show her. She shut her eyes.

"Oh, God . . . oh, God . . . You must get me tea now. I need to be soothed. That noise . . . I need to be soothed."

"I'll tell Aiko," I said, backing out of the room.

"See that you do." She dismissed me with a wave of her hand.

I hurried down the stairs. Aiko and the maid, their eyes waiting for an answer, looked very small standing in the large foyer.

"Mr. Kenilworth is dead."

The maid's hand flew to her mouth. Aiko put his arm around her, repeating, "No, no, no."

"Aiko, I want you to call the emergency number, the police, and I guess the family physician. Maria, I want you to go in and fix tea for Mrs. Kenilworth. Take it up to her and stay with her." I was amazed how calm and assured my voice sounded.

As they hurried off, I slowly went back up the stairs. I looked down the long corridor. It ended in a small glassed-in rotunda. A Victorian table centered in the rotunda held red garden roses. In the dim lines of sun the roses looked black. I walked down the hall. Taking deep breaths, I opened the bathroom door. Everything was exactly the same. Ellis Kenilworth was still there, head smeared over the shower walls. His clothes . . . I stared down at his clothes. The suicide note was gone. I searched his jacket and trousers. There was no note. And then I felt it. Fear. Inexplicably, I was afraid for my own life. I whirled around to face the door. It was just as I had left it. Closed. I looked at another closed door. I opened it and peered into Kenilworth's bedroom. I shut my eyes. Get hold of yourself, Maggie. I walked out of the bathroom and down the hallway and stood by Mrs. Kenilworth's room. Her door was closed. Just as I had left it. There was the smell of perfume mixed with the smell of roses in the corridor. But there would be — she had been in the hallway with me.

"Excuse me."

I spun around. The maid stepped nervously back, almost spilling the tea.

"Maria, you frightened me."

Opening the door for her, I looked into the room. Eleanor Kenilworth was just as I had left her. She was on the chaise with her eyes closed.

As I went back down the stairs, I could hear

the sound of sirens in the distance. I crossed the foyer. My heels clicked tippity-tap, tippity-tap. The hall clock discreetly chimed two times. I made my way through the office and out into the garden. My purse was right where I had left it. I grabbed it and started back into the house. In the foyer I stopped and opened my bag. The dove-gray envelope with my name written on it was there.

Just as I reached for it, the front door flew open. Sutton stood there with a large bouquet of pink and yellow flowers. "Happy birthday!" he said, thrusting the flowers into my arms. "I know it's a surprise, but a simple 'thank you' would do."

The paramedics, fire trucks, and police cars turned onto the street and began lining up in front of the house. Sutton stared out at them.

"Good God, what's going on? It's not Mother?" He was halfway up the stairs.

"Ellis. Suicide!" I yelled.

He looked over the banister at me. "Ellis?! Does mother know?"

"I'm not sure."

It was eight o'clock when I finally drove into the underground parking lot of my building. The smell of Mexican food wafted through the garage from one of the apartments. I had spent the rest of the day and the evening repeating my story over and over to the police, the plainclothes detectives, the firemen, Dr. Granger, the family physician, Sutton, and Judith. My story started with the sipping of my wine and ended with my accepting Sutton's flowers. Like a good daughter, I never mentioned the amendment to Ellis Kenilworth's will. I thought of telling the police, but I was afraid they'd turn it over to the family. Instead, I talked about what I thought was a missing suicide note. But it was finally decided with the doctor's help that I had been in a state of shock. It seems I had wanted an answer, an explanation to Ellis Kenilworth's actions; therefore I had imagined a letter. But it wasn't a letter. It wasn't paper. And when pressed, I could not honestly describe what I had seen, except it was white, and looked like the back of a photograph, and I knew I had seen it. Ellis Kenilworth had written something on the back of a photograph. Sutton was the only one who seemed to believe me.

I got out of the car and walked up dirty cement steps into the cool, damp courtyard. The swimming pool glared baby blue in the night. At the end of the pool was a small area of grass where one shaggy palm tree grew. A bright yellow light bathed it in sunshine glow. I started up the stairs to my apartment.

"Where have you been? You're late."

Now I knew why I'd divorced him: always the accusation in the form of a question. He was sitting in a deck chair, holding a beer can in one hand and a bottle of champagne with a ribbon around its neck in the other. The pool light reflected dark ripples on his wide, handsome face. His thinning black hair was flecked with gray. The dark, assessing eyes never looked away. The mouth tilted up at the ends, making him look as if he were smiling at a joke that only he understood.

"What are you doing here?"

"Celebration."

"You mean now that we're divorced you finally remember my birthday?"

He stood up, smiling even more. He was developing a slight paunch, but he still had the build of a man who relied on his body to protect himself.

"Did it ever occur to you I might've had a date?" I asked, going up the stairs. He followed.

"I took a chance."

I unlocked the door and pushed it open with my foot. We went in and he kicked the door shut with his foot.

"I brought you something," he said.

I threw my purse in my only chair and turned off the radio. "The beer? Or the champagne?"

"One of the WB's in the apartment downstairs gave me the beer while I was waiting. This is for you." He handed me the champagne. His lips curled. I loved those lips. But I'd never trust them again.

"Thank you. He's not a wetback. He's legal."

"Do you have a corkscrew?" He downed the last of the beer and tossed the can in the bathroom wastebasket.

"This is champagne. You don't need a corkscrew."

"Just like beer." The dark eyes studied my face. The lips stopped smiling. "You're not going to like me for saying this . . . but you look terrible."

"My employer blew his head off with a shotgun today."

"God damn!"

He was there. Arms around me. And I began to cry.

What else are big shoulders for?

3

Virginity was not having her comeback in my life. My breasts were tender from making love, and my morning sadness was overwhelming. Ellis Kenilworth was dead and I had gone to bed with my ex-husband. Cause and effect. Death and sex.

Last night, I had wanted passion to obliterate the image of Kenilworth's shattered skull. It had nothing to do with Neil — or so I kept telling myself. I had told Neil to leave. Obediently, he sneaked out in the early-morning hours as quietly as a burglar. I didn't want to fall asleep in his arms and be jarred awake by the moans of his unconscious cries; body jerking, feet moving as if running. I didn't want to witness his vulnerability in sleep. And I didn't want him listening to my night murmurs — watching my body, a trembling shadow, fragile in sleep. A man and woman needed to trust one another for that.

Trust. The word, like a magnet, pulled my thoughts away from Neil across the room to my purse. It was in the chair where I had tossed it last night. Kenilworth had trusted me. I turned my purse upside down, spilling out its contents: car keys, makeup kit, wallet, hair brush, comb, Filofax, checkbook, overdrafts, aspirin, bank statements, Tampax, *Madame Bovary*, pens, sunglasses, my grandmother's rosary. The large dove-gray envelope was there. I opened it. The codicil was gone.

My body cold, I sank back down onto the bed. Pulling a pink kimono around me, I tried to organize my thoughts. My mind raced over possibilities. Neil. But he didn't know about the codicil. Even if he did, he wouldn't take it. What he stole from me was never tangible.

I went into the kitchen. I began brewing coffee. Think, Maggie, think. I had heard the shot. Ran into the house, leaving my purse in the garden. For how long? I made the coffee strong. I had gone back to the garden, gotten my purse, and looked in it. The envelope was there. But I never looked inside the envelope. Think, Maggie! Maybe it was taken later, when I was talking to the police. Did I leave my purse somewhere? Think! But all I could remember was Kenilworth's body, zipped into a cocoon-like purple bag, strapped to a stretcher. The wheels of the stretcher squeaked on the white marble floor.

After three cups of coffee and pacing in a small circle — all my apartment would allow — I decided to call Valcovich. He was the only one who could back me up about there being a codicil. I got the phone book and flipped through the Yellow Pages. I found the magic word: Attorneys. He had a quarter of a page. Roger Valcovich, Attorney-at-Law. Green Cards. Disability. No-Fault Divorce. Vets Welcome. He did it all.

I searched for the telephone and found it wedged between a box of half-eaten pizza and the empty bottle of champagne. I dialed.

A husky female voice answered, "Law offices."

"Roger Valcovich, please."

"Who's calling?" She smoked; I could hear the rattle of phlegm. Her kind of voice, once considered sexy, was now a sign of death.

"Maggie Hill."

"Please hold."

In a few seconds he was on the line. "Yes, Maggie?"

"We met yesterday in Ellis Kenilworth's office."

"How could I forget?" His voice was too cheerful. "Yesterday was when I got lucky. I'm the luckiest guy in the world. What can I do for you, Maggie?"

"You helped write a codicil for Mr. Kenilworth."

"Codicil?"

"An amendment to his will."

"I know what it is. But that wasn't why I was in his office. I was there because of you. You were in an auto accident."

"What's going on, Valcovich?"

"If you wish, you can make an appointment."

"Listen, you son of a bitch . . ."

"Now, now . . ."

"How did you get lucky, Valcovich?"

A long pause, then a grating chuckle. "I looked out a window."

"What window? What are you talking about?"

Another grating chuckle.

"The police might be interested in your luck."

"What will you tell them? You have no proof of anything. I heard on the local news this morning that Kenilworth killed himself. You're unlucky, Maggie."

"Listen, you bastard — "

"And you're out of work, too. I'd hire you, but I just couldn't take your lip." He slammed the phone down.

He was right. I had no proof. I decided to call Neil; he was a policeman. I dialed.

A sleepy female answered the phone. "Hello?"

45

I tried to control my voice. "Is Neil there?" I didn't do too well. It was shaky with rage.

"Working." Pause. "Who's calling?"

I recognized the sound of suspicion. I could've eased her fears. Told her just the ex-wife calling. Only a business matter. I didn't. I hung up without answering.

I wanted her to worry. I wanted *him* to worry. Son of a bitch! Betrayal was a habit with Neil. My reactions to his betrayals were habit. I knew my emotional knee-jerks as well as a woman knows which fingernail she likes to gnaw on. First there's pain — the kind that takes your breath away. Then there's a sense of abandonment — the kind that makes you feel like a lost little girl, the kind you hate yourself for feeling. Then there's anger — the kind that makes you feel righteous and power-ful, the kind you never want to let go of. Why did I still feel these emotions? Why was I still thinking of him? Oh, hell, I'd only wanted passion.

Think about another bastard, Maggie. Think about Valcovich. How does a man like him get lucky? He takes advantage of other people.

I decided to pay the Kenilworths an unannounced visit.

My Honda smelled like a funeral chapel. I had left Sutton's flowers in the backseat. I threw them in the apartment dumpster. But even with the sun roof down I smelled dead flowers all the way to Pasadena.

It was the kind of Los Angeles weather I detested: perfect. A strong, warm spring wind had blown all the haze, fog, smog, and clouds into a brown bundle and thrown it out over the Pacific. A relentless sun burned down, distilling the subtle hues of nature into a blinding glare. Every car, every home, every human I passed made me squint. The lawns of Pasadena looked as if they'd been glazed with green enamel. The sidewalks reflected like paths of chrome. But I was safe. I had on my designer shades. Sunglasses protect my soul against perfect weather.

I pulled up in front of the big white house. A hunter-green Jaguar was parked behind a blue van in the driveway. The Kenilworths drove only American. As I made my way toward the house I took a look at the van. A large hunk of a man in tight jeans, holding a phallic-looking rug cleaner, was painted on its side. Printed over the muscle-bound head was the name CHUCK'S and a phone number. I guess Kenilworth got a little of himself on the white rug.

Aiko answered the door. He looked tired but pleased to see me.

"Hello, Miss Hill, you come in."

"Hi, Aiko." As he shut the front door I could hear the sounds of Chuck's machinery cleaning away upstairs.

"I need to talk to Judith and Sutton. Are they here?"

"Miss Kenilworth in library. Follow me."

Before I could do that, Judith appeared in the foyer.

"We didn't expect you, Maggie," she said, closing the library doors behind her. In the three months I had worked there, I'd never seen the library doors closed.

I studied her face for some sort of reaction to my presence. She was as unsmiling and austere as ever. "That will be all, Aiko." She buttoned another button on her gray cashmere cardigan. "Did you come to clean out your desk? You didn't pick a very appropriate time. We are a family in mourning."

"I came to talk to you and Sutton."

The library doors opened. A woman, draped in lavender suede, stood staring at me with tilted green eyes. "Sorry, I thought it was Brian."

Her skin was wedding-gown white. Pinkish-blond hair curved seductively around a face that had been pulled and tightened into the never-never land of agelessness. She was probably in her late fifties. Her breasts were higher and firmer than mine. She wasn't bad looking if you liked man-made women.

"Go back and finish your coffee," Judith told her. "Maggie was just leaving."

"Maggie?" She stepped forward. Diamond studs the size of my thumbnail were embedded in her earlobes. She looked more like Rodeo Drive than Lake Avenue.

"The secretary?" She said it the way some people say "the wife" or "the girlfriend." Why have these words become permanently disabling?

"Temporary secretary." Oh, hell.

"You found the suicide note?"

"I saw it."

She looked at Judith, then back at me. "I guess Judith isn't going to introduce us. I'm Patricia Kenilworth. Ellis's widow." Mauve lips pushed against tight skin, trying to form a smile.

I slowly closed my open mouth, then opened it again: "I didn't know Mr. Kenilworth was married."

"I'm the family secret. Have been for years."

Judith blanched. "You're his *ex*-wife," she snapped.

"His *only* wife," Patricia said defiantly. "The Kenilworths don't like outsiders. Maybe you've noticed?" She studied me. "Did you read the note?"

"No."

49

Her eyes were as shifty as a cat's. "If I found a suicide note, I'd read it."

"I didn't have time to read it. And when I went back for the note, it was gone."

The eyes were trying to decide if I was telling the truth. "It must've been terrible seeing him . . . a shock."

"Yes."

"Maybe you just thought — "

Judith interrupted. "That's what we were trying to explain to Maggie last night. It was a shock. She imagined a letter. Or she saw a piece of paper in his jacket that was unrelated to his suicide. Why don't you come back next week and clean out your desk, Maggie, when things have calmed down?" She took Patricia's arm and they headed toward the library.

"The suicide note wasn't written on a piece of paper. It was written on the back of something like a photograph. And I'm not here to clean out my desk. I'm here — "

I didn't get to finish. Patricia broke away from Judith and moved quickly to me, sliding a hand as soft as velvet around my wrist. Her eyes were frightened.

"Photograph? What photograph? Do you have it?"

"Patricia!" Judith snapped.

"I need a drink. Suicide is terrible . . . a terrible tragedy. Ellis is dead. He doesn't have to suffer anymore. But the rest of us . . . " She disappeared into the library.

"Judith, I need to talk to you about Ellis's will," I said.

"His will is none of your business."

"I think you'd better get Sutton. There's something else missing besides the suicide note."

She studied me for a moment, then headed for the library. I followed. She went to a leather-top desk, picked up the phone, and pushed the intercom button.

"Sutton? Maggie Hill is here. . . . No, she hasn't come to pay her condolences. She's here about . . . just a minute." She looked at me. "What did you say it was?"

"A codicil to Ellis's will."

She spoke into the phone. "Ellis and his will or something. . . . I have no idea what she's talking about. Would you come down? . . . For God's sake, you can leave her alone for a few minutes! . . . Well, tell the cleaning crew to turn off the machine if it bothers her." She carefully put the phone down. "Mother is very upset."

"Eleanor is finally old now. I always thought her power would diminish with age, but it hasn't." Patricia poured straight scotch. The sun angled in through the opening of the rose damask drapes and glanced off her thick gold bracelet. She moved out of the line of the sun and sat on a beige silk chair next to a wall of leather-bound books. By the slow way she crossed her legs I knew she thought she had the best pair in the room. She sipped. Ice tinkled.

"You didn't tell me anything about a codicil, Judith."

"I don't know anything about it. I don't even know what one is." Judith took her usual place on the rose damask sofa. She sat with her knees pressed tightly together.

"And you don't know anything about Ellis leaving a photograph either. It seems Maggie has all kinds of privileged information. Did he mention me in his codicil?" The cat eyes turned coy.

"No," I said.

"Always thinking of yourself," Judith said.

Patricia laughed. Ice tinkled. Perfume wafted. Diamonds flashed. She was the kind of woman that permeated a room.

"I've *had* to think about myself, Judith. You've never been thrown out. Abandoned. I have. Eleanor saw to that."

"You were paid," Judith whined.

"A monthly pittance for five years. And in return I signed over any claim to the Kenilworth estate. Are you sure he didn't change that in his codicil, Maggie?"

52

I shook my head.

"It was a long time ago." Judith's hand tightened into a fist.

"The past is more real to me than the present. That's one thing your mother and I have in common, Judith."

Sutton came into the room. His eyes were red and he looked older. If appearances count for anything, he seemed to be the only one grieving for Ellis.

"Hello, Maggie." He patted my hand and looked into my eyes, flirting as if it were just any other morning. Patricia saw this and pounced on it.

"Don't tell me, Sutton, you've finally met a woman who stirs the old loins! I didn't think they could be stirred."

"Must you talk that way?" Judith glared at her.

The cat eyes turned innocent. "What did I say? 'Loins'? My God, Judith, you probably blush when you order a loin of beef. If it makes you happier, I'll say 'cock' from now on."

Judith pressed her lips white.

"I take it you've met the widow," Sutton said to me.

Patricia downed the last of her scotch. "You should've seen Sutton thirty years ago, Maggie. A true beauty." The last words were spoken with sadness.

Ignoring her remark, Sutton smiled at me. "It was nice of you to come. What can we do for you?" He settled on the sofa next to his sister.

"Yesterday morning Ellis had me type a codicil to his will. He put it in an envelope with my name on it and placed it in my purse until he could find a safer place for it. Then he . . . killed himself. When I got home I discovered the codicil was missing." They were looking at me like I was crazy. I didn't blame them.

"I'm sure if there were an amendment to his will old Proctor would know about it."

"He didn't use your lawyer. He used Roger Valcovich. You met him in the office yesterday."

"You mean that seedy fellow?"

"Yes. Has he contacted you?"

"The only lawyer I met in the office yesterday was yours, Maggie," Judith said. "He was helping you because you were in a car accident."

"Yes . . . but that wasn't true. I mean . . . "

"You lied?"

"No . . . Ellis didn't want you to know about the codicil. I was afraid Valcovich was going to say something, so I made up a story."

"And we believed you. Why wouldn't we?"

54

"He didn't want the family to know?" Cat eyes blinked at Judith and Sutton. "My, my. What did he want to keep from the family?"

Brother and sister said nothing. I wondered if Valcovich had already gotten to them. And for how much? I decided this was no time to be discreet.

"He left his entire coin collection to a woman named Claire Conrad," I said. "He made it quite clear that it was never to go to anyone in the family or connected to the family."

"Ellis was such a bore with that collection." Patricia studied Sutton and Judith. "Why wouldn't he want you to have it?"

Judith sat frozen. The angry-little-girl expression I had seen on her face yesterday was back. Sutton looked thoughtful. Neither one answered.

"He told me the collection was worth over four million dollars," I said.

Patricia sat forward, uncrossing her legs. Then she threw her head back and laughed. "Poor Sutton! Poor Judith! Poor Eleanor! Now it's your turn to be disinherited. If you need to borrow money, don't hesitate to ask!" She stopped laughing. When she finally spoke again, her voice was serious. "God, he hated us." There were tears in her eyes. I couldn't tell if they were from laughter or sadness.

"He hated *you!*" Judith challenged.

Sutton put his hand on hers. "Please. We're all in an emotional state."

"Who is this Claire Conrad? Friend? Lover?" The green eyes turned seductive.

"He didn't know her," I said.

"Really, Maggie." Sutton smiled warmly. "You can't seriously ask us to believe that Ellis would just give away his collection to a woman he didn't know?"

"The name is familiar," Patricia said. "I think I read about her in *Time* or *People* or some other magazine. They referred to her as 'the Great Woman . . . Something' — you know, one of those genderless names like 'doctor' or 'writer.' I can't remember. I'm so preoccupied with my own life, how can I remember what other people do?"

"Ellis said that Claire Conrad might help with the truth or something like that," I said.

"What truth?" Patricia's perfect white teeth bit at her lower lip.

"I don't know. But he was willing to pay a lot of money for it." I turned on Sutton and Judith. "What are you willing to pay Valcovich?"

Judith's strict eyes took me in. "As far as I'm concerned, I met a man in Ellis's office who was introduced to me by you as your

56

lawyer. A codicil was never mentioned. Now, unless you can produce it, I don't think we have anything to talk about." She stood, clutching at her sweater.

"She does have a point, Maggie," Sutton said.

"So he is blackmailing you."

Patricia stood. "Blackmail. A family tradition. If you will excuse me, I came here to pay my condolences to Eleanor." She moved toward the doors.

"I'll go with you," Sutton said quickly.

"Don't you trust me alone with her?"

"Sutton," Judith said. "Let her go see Mother."

"She's very upset. Don't stay too long," he warned.

"I'm sure she's very upset. Mothers always bear the guilt." She left the room. I could hear the tippity-tap sounds of her high heels crossing the marble floor.

"I'd like to see if Ellis wrote Valcovich's name and number in his appointment book," I said.

"What would that prove?" Judith asked.

"Ellis would never write one of my personal appointments in his book. It would prove that Valcovich came to see him, not me."

"I'm not exactly sure where he keeps his calendar. Probably his desk," Sutton said.

"I know where it is," I said.

"Shall we?" He offered his hand. I took it. Our eyes weren't flirting.

Judith folded her arms protectively against her bony breast. We followed her to the office. She opened the door.

"Brian!" she gasped. "We've been waiting for you."

Her arms unfolded. She reached out for his hand. He waved it just out of her reach. His other hand held the telephone. He leaned back in Ellis's chair, feet on Ellis's desk. Putting a manicured finger to his lips, he warned us to be quiet.

Judith obediently fell silent. A look of possessiveness filled her eyes. I knew that look. There was no other person in that room for Judith. She was gazing on the man she loved.

"At least he could get his feet off the desk," Sutton said under his breath.

I was a little shocked at Judith's taste. This guy's eyes were the color of onyx and hard to read. Each strand of dark hair was arranged carefully over his scalp and sprayed into its proper place. I'm suspicious of men who try to hide their baldness; I always wonder what else they're hiding. His lips were thin, unyielding. I tried to imagine pressing my lips against his; I didn't get very far. I tried to imagine Judith pressing her lips against his; I got a little further — after all, they had the same kind of lips. His nose curved down, then suddenly tilted up at the end, giving him the strangely superior look of someone doomed to smell out the rottenness of life. I decided I didn't like him. I didn't like the way he was usurping Kenilworth's desk. His left foot, shod in a highly polished shoe, rested on Ellis's appointment book. I jerked the book out from under it. His foot slammed back down on the desk. Judith gasped again. He never missed a beat. And he never looked at me. He just continued to say "Yes . . . yes" importantly into the phone.

I took the book and sat down at my desk.

"Yes, yes. Good news. See you tomorrow night." He put the phone down. "We've had so many registrations that the hotel's moving the symposium to the International Ballroom — the biggest room they've got." His nose twitched.

"Oh, Brian, that's wonderful!" She blew him a kiss.

Intimacy made Judith look awkward. But then, maybe she looked awkward because he ignored her kiss.

"This is Maggie Hill, Ellis's secretary," Sutton said to Brian.

"The secretary? Here to clean out your desk?" Brian asked.

59

A lot of people wanted me to clean out my desk. He stood, hands in the pockets of his expensive navy pin-striped suit. Sutton began a rambling explanation to Brian about the entire situation.

I opened the appointment book. But I knew there wasn't going to be anything about Valcovich in it. Kenilworth always kept his book in his bottom right-hand drawer. It was never left out on his desk. Sure enough, the page containing the date April 22 was neatly cut out of the book.

"Yesterday's date is missing," I said. My statement was greeted with silence. I crossed my legs and hit my knee under the desk, snagging my $5.95 panty hose.

"I'm Brian Waingrove." He sauntered over and offered me his card instead of his hand. The paper-sack-brown card told me, in shiny darker brown lettering, that Brian was an expert at managing money.

"Whose?" I asked.

"I beg your pardon?"

"Whose money are you so good at managing?"

"I help people who are in debt. I help people who have millions. I make no distinctions."

"I don't need any money managing," I said.

"I do think you need some clarity of thought." His nose twitched. He was on the scent of something. "If I understand Sutton correctly, you are accusing them of something . . . well . . . illegal."

"She doesn't mean it that way," Sutton said. "If Maggie says there was a codicil, then I'm sure there's . . . an explanation."

"Since you were given custody of the codicil, the explanation is Maggie's burden," Brian sniffed. "It must be a heavy one." He peered down his nose at me. "So heavy you want to draw in two innocent people. If you would only think, Maggie, you would see that my two dear friends could not have taken the codicil. First of all, they would have to know there *was* one. Then they would have to know that Ellis put it in your purse — an unlikely place, you have to admit. And lastly, they would have to know that Ellis was going to kill himself yesterday afternoon, putting the codicil into effect."

"I wasn't accusing them of stealing it. I'm accusing them of letting Valcovich blackmail them so they can keep a four-million-dollar coin collection."

"But how could he have possibly known it was in your purse? Why don't we call this so-called lawyer?"

"Fine." I picked up the phone and dialed his number.

"You know his telephone number by heart,"

Waingrove observed.

"I'm very good with numbers, too," I said.

The Smoker answered. "Law offices."

"This is Maggie Hill."

"He's not in."

"Tell him I'm with the Kenilworths and they would like to talk to him."

"Just a minute." Suppressed cough.

"Here." I handed the phone to Waingrove, picked up my purse, and went and stood by the window. What had Valcovich seen? I saw only Kenilworth's beautiful garden. I headed for the door.

"Don't you want to hear what he has to say to us, Maggie?" Sutton asked.

"Why should I sit here and listen to you and that jerk lie to each other for my benefit?"

I was out of the Kenilworth house and was heading to my car when I heard my name. Patricia stood by the Jaguar. Parked behind it was a silver Mercedes, the color of small change. It had to be Waingrove's.

"Maggie." She came toward me, her hand shading her eyes.

In the white glare I could see her fleshy neck. You can tell the age of a tree by counting the rings inside the trunk. You can tell a turtle's age by counting the dots on its belly. If you want to know a woman's age, just look at her neck.

"I wanted to talk to you alone. Do you mind?"

"Why should I?" She followed me to my car. Her skin was translucent. In the relentless sun Patricia looked more ghost than woman.

"I loved Ellis. When I was young, I gave up everything for him. So you see, it's only natural that I would want to know his last words."

"I've already told you. I don't know what his last words were. I didn't read the note."

"What is it you want?" she asked.

"Nothing. I want nothing."

"You mean like Christmas when we all say we don't want anything. Yet we all want to open a gift . . . receive a present . . . on Christmas day. We all eventually think of something we want." In the heat her mauve lipstick was bleeding into the lines around her mouth, lines even the plastic surgeons couldn't remove.

"I've never been bribed before," I said.

"You shouldn't think of it that way. I'm a generous woman. I love to give gifts. It makes me happy."

"It wouldn't make me happy."

Her velvety hand was around my wrist again. Nails sharp in my flesh.

"Eleanor said you came out of the bathroom with his pen. That means you went through his things. You saw the photograph, didn't you? You took it. I swear to God, if you have information that will hurt my family . . . I . . . will — "

"Patricia!" Sutton yelled from the veranda. She slowly loosened her grip on my wrist.

"I've written down my phone number. No questions asked. I'll give you a nice big present." She pressed a piece of paper into my hand and hurried across the lawn to the house.

I got into my car. I stared at the perfect imprint of her nails on the inside of my wrist.

I put on my sunglasses.

4

I headed for a gas station that I knew had a working pay phone. Turning east on Colorado Boulevard, I passed the Norton Simon Museum, a big, brown, manly-looking building, shaped like a giant humidor. It always amazed me that one man collected all that art and stored it at just the right temperature, like cigars. I thought of Ellis Kenilworth. If he didn't want his family to have his coin collection, why didn't he leave it to a public place like a library or university? Collectors have egos. They like to have their names on wings of buildings and museums. They want public recognition for all their years of spending money. Why did he leave his collection to a woman named Claire Conrad? It was time to find out.

I pulled into the self-service gas station and parked in front of the pay phones. An American flag about the size of my hometown flapped and snapped in the wind over my head. I slipped into a phone booth. A pimply-faced kid leered lasciviously at me from his security-tight cashier stall. We stared at one another from our little boxes. I decided to take his leer as a compliment; there are so few compliments in this world. I smiled back. I punched up Information and asked for the number of the San Marino Hotel. A computerized female voice, sounding like a teacher with a speech impediment, clicked on. It patiently told me the number. I thanked it and dialed.

A voice husky with chic announced, "San Marino Hotel."

"Claire Conrad, Conrad Cottage," I said. The voice connected me.

A woman with a very thick accent answered, "Conrad Cottage."

"I'd like to speak to Ms. Claire Conrad, please."

"May I ask what it is regarding?" Maybe the accent was Hungarian.

"I'm Maggie Hill. She doesn't know me. It's a personal matter. Confidential."

"A personal matter! Excellent. You come now?"

"Well . . . I . . . yes . . . I'm near you . . . "

"Good. You come. Work will do her good. Goodbye."

"Wait! I need directions."

She gave me confusing directions to the San

66

Marino Hotel and the cottage and hung up. I wondered what kind of work this woman was talking about.

Always looking for something a little extra, I stuck my finger into the coin return. I felt something cold, slimy wet. Some ass had spit into the slot. I stepped outside the booth, frantically wiping my finger with a Kleenex. I saw the pimply-faced kid leaning out of his box giving change to somebody in a Datsun. He looked at me over the roof of the car. His head bounced with laughter on his scrawny red neck. So much for compliments. Oh, hell.

San Marino is just like Beverly Hills except it's not as desperate for attention. I drove my Honda through streets dappled with shade and sun. Lacy trees effetely extended their branches over expensive homes. The area was populated with men in polo shirts and plaid pants, children in private-school uniforms, and women who have settled for short hair, cotton skirts, espadrilles, and one big solitary diamond.

Doing as I was told, I turned left on Marino Road. In the distance loomed the San Marino Hotel. Six stories of Gothic orangy-brown plaster reached upward toward the heavens and curved outward ready to embrace all who entered her. Windows of various shapes and sizes looked out like black possessive eyes over the vast grounds. I approached a long narrow road. An elegant sign declared that this was the entrance to the hotel. Black paint shredded from the base of the sign. Turning down the road, I was uneasily aware of weeds bullying up through cracked asphalt. On each side of the road were islands of brown grass. The road merged into the grand sweep of a circular drive — a drive designed for Bugattis, Bentleys, and Rolls-Royces. But there was only the wind twisting a pile of dusty gray leaves around and around the tarmac. Golden arches shimmered on a rolling plastic container which had once held a large Coke. The wind scuttled it against the hotel steps. Its companion, the paper bag, had been blown flat against the glass doors of the hotel, doors that were chained and padlocked.

I got out of the car and stared up at the hotel. It rose above me, struggling for grandeur, trying to defy its darkness. Tattered white drapes, sucked from open windows by the wind, quivered against their casements. Some windows were shattered, others just empty like dead eyes. I was alone with this corpse of a hotel. Not only humans die.

Walking up the unswept steps, I peered through the smeared glass doors into the lobby. I could make out a high vaulted ceiling, a gold leaf balcony, a long, dark wood reception desk like a giant coffin. Leaves, in place of Oriental rugs, scattered on a vast pink-and-gold marble floor. There were no chandeliers and no furniture. This grande dame had been stripped of all her possessions. I whirled around. Footsteps! No. The only movement came from a shaggy sunflower, flourishing in the burnt grass, nodding its heavy yellow head in the breeze.

I looked out over the grounds. The hotel had been built on a plateau. On the west side the land dropped off into what looked like a ravine. I went down the steps and across the grass. It was stiff beneath my feet. Trying to keep the heels of my shoes from sinking into the powdered earth, I stood on the edge of the ravine. Below me was a tangle of brush, a mass of wildflowers, and weeds. On the other side a whole new world shone brightly. Sparkling white bungalows and cottages gleamed in their nests of dark green ivy. Geraniums frothed red, pink, fuchsia. Pathways and narrow streets connected these dwellings in a maze-like network that went on for acres. Conrad Cottage had to be down there somewhere. I could see an Olympic-size swimming pool and hear the faint laughter of pale, wet bodies. In the far distance, beyond San Marino and Pasadena, the L.A. Basin spread out toward the shimmering curve of the Pacific. I noticed that a covered wooden bridge connected this shiny new world to the side of the hotel. From where I stood, there seemed to be no way to get to the bridge except from inside the hotel.

I made my way back to the car. Studying the directions, I tried to make out where I had gone wrong. I felt as if somebody were watching me. I looked around. Nobody. Only the hotel and its empty windows. I put the car in gear and sped away.

I turned back onto Marino Road and saw the sign. It was much smaller than the original. Newly planted flowers surrounded freshly painted white wood. Written in black script were the words TEMPORARY LOBBY. A black arrow pointed the direction. I followed the arrow back the way I had come. Another sign pointed me onto a side street. Following arrows, I made my way through the maze of narrow streets and into a parking lot. A low white building glistened in the sun. I parked where it said GUEST.

Poking my head in the doorway of the building, I asked, "Is this the lobby?"

A man standing behind a small fake-wood reception desk flicked a piece of lint off his freshly pressed green jacket and snapped "Yes" at me. Gold braid decorated his shoulders. Brass buttons flashed with polished perfection. He looked like a general who had lost his command. Busy brown eyes looked everywhere around the room but at me. This was a difficult feat, since the room was small and he and I were the only ones in it.

An antique Oriental rug intricately patterned with yellow, greens, and pinks filled the floor. Opposite the reception desk sat two high-backed chairs covered in threadbare pale-green velvet. There was something shabbily beautiful about the chairs. Between them was a round Victorian table displaying a large arrangement of garden roses. Photographs and hotel awards filled the walls.

Stepping up to the desk, I said, "Ms. Claire Conrad, please."

"Do you have an appointment?" Impatient fingers tapped.

"She's expecting me. I got lost over in the other — "

Pale eyelids lowered with boredom. "Your name?"

"Hill. H-i-l-l." I spelled it carefully for him.

Checking some sort of list, he said, "I just don't want Miss Conrad in a snit. It's not my fault she can't stay in the hotel. We even named a cottage after her and allowed her her own front door." He flipped his hand toward the wall in back of him. "Go through the ar-

71

bor next to the parking lot. Turn left on the street and you'll see the sign 'Conrad Cottage.' "

"Thank you."

He looked away. He was bored again.

"You must miss the old hotel. What happened to it?"

For a moment he looked human — but only for a moment. "I thought the whole world knew. Earthquake standards. The poor old thing wasn't up to code," he said, looking out the window toward the hotel as if it were a lost lover.

"Going to tear it down?" I enjoyed watching him blanch.

"I don't know. The last I heard, the Japanese or the Arabs may buy her and . . . I'm not sure." He turned his back on me and began doing busywork.

On my way out the door I stopped and looked at some of the photographs. They appeared to have been taken in the hotel's heyday. Men and women dressed in white lounged in wicker chairs while others played badminton on islands of lawn in front of a bustling new hotel. In another photo a tall, lean, angular man, dressed in a dark suit and tie with a panama hat shading his eyes, dug a hole in the ground with a ribboned shovel. A typed caption explained that this man was

Mr. Elisha Kenilworth breaking ground for the new hotel, 1916. Another photograph showed a group of young women standing in a semicircle in one of the public rooms of the hotel. They all had white corsages pinned to their dresses. One young woman stood triumphantly in the middle of the semicircle, holding a small bouquet. A cloche cap fitted snugly to her head. Blond curls poked out. A strand of pearls graced a long neck. Eleanor Kenilworth confronted the camera with a defiant confidence. The caption read: MRS. ELEANOR KENILWORTH ELECTED JUNIOR LEAGUE PRESIDENT, JUNE 1925.

The general of the lobby was watching me. He said forlornly, "I wish they still owned her."

"Who?"

"The Kenilworths!" he snapped.

"They owned this hotel?"

"They built her. They never would've let this happen to her," he said, staring out the window, his gold braid catching the sun. He cocked his head to one side. He had a second thought. "Of course, you never can tell. I mean, the son did kill himself."

"How do you know?"

"My dear, anyone who watched the eleven o'clock news last night knows." He drew himself up to attention and sneered. "I bet he killed himself over money. In families like that the cause of death is always related to money."

I stared at the pale-green chairs. They were the same color as Eleanor Kenilworth's sitting room. "Did Ellis Kenilworth ever come by the hotel to visit Claire Conrad?"

"I never talk about our permanent guests."

" 'Permanent guest.' I like that phrase. That's like always being a temporary secretary." He failed to see the irony. I moved closer to the desk. "Would you talk about her for twenty?"

"Twenty what?"

"Dollars." I took out my wallet.

He shrugged, but his eyes were hard on my wallet.

"Well?"

"Honey, if you're going to bribe me, you're supposed to show me the money first."

"Oh." I opened my wallet. All I had was nine dollars and change. I could've sworn I had twenty. . . . The pizza! I paid for the pizza last night! Damn Neil!

Putting my wallet in my purse, I said, "I'm really shocked you'd take a bribe. I mean, in a classy place like this! You should be ashamed of yourself."

"I never said I was taking your money." He lowered his voice and hissed, "You bitch!"

74

"Now don't get nasty," I said, moving quickly toward the door.

"I should report you!" he yelled.

"I should report *you!*" I slammed the door.

Leaving the disgruntled general to dominate his tiny fiefdom, I felt a little sheepish as I made my way up stone steps to the arbor. Oh, hell, it *was* the first time I ever tried to bribe anybody. I had the feeling Patricia Kenilworth would've handled it much better.

The arbor was covered with thick, gnarled vines dripping with purple flowers shaped like miniature bugles. I felt pretty walking under it. I could almost feel what it must've been like to be the young Eleanor Kenilworth. For a moment. My life, my background, was so far removed from that kind of power. Money. Quiet money.

I stepped out of the arbor onto a street that curved around near the ravine and the covered wooden bridge. The words CONRAD COTTAGE were painted on the curb in front of a white wood cottage that was set down from the street with its back facing the hotel. It was one of the older, bigger cottages. To me it looked like a nice-sized home.

I made my way down brick steps to a highly varnished front door. A crown sprouting wings and supporting a cross was carved on it. It looked like a family crest. When I was growing up, there was a word that all young middle-class girls feared. The word was "conceited." One of the most devastating moments of my high-school life was being called conceited by a beautiful cheerleader. She always seemed to be in midair. I always felt I was slogging through mud. Being accused of conceit was a way young girls kept each other down and in their proper place. A way of developing a lack of self-worth. I don't remember a boy ever calling me conceited. It's a word I never use. But now that I am thirty-five and a mature woman, I think I'll give it a try. This was a conceited door.

I rang the bell. The wings moved. The crown slid sideways. I was staring into dark glass. I couldn't see through it, but I had the feeling someone was seeing me. The crown slid back into place. The door opened.

"Miss Hill?" The man had an English accent.

"Yes."

He wore a gray jacket over black-and-gray striped trousers. A full head of chestnut-brown hair swept back from a high, intelligent forehead. Watchful brown eyes moved slowly over my body. There was nothing sexual in this action.

His eyes came to rest on my purse. "Do you mind?" He took my purse from me and looked quickly in it. He handed it back. "One can never be too sure nowadays."

"Too sure of what?"

He didn't answer. Instead, he said, "This way, please."

I followed him down three tiled steps into a large room with a cathedral ceiling. I couldn't help noticing that his shoulders were broad, his waist and hips narrow. I wished I had a butler like him. He turned around and caught me staring. I blushed. That's another thing liberation and the sexual revolution haven't been able to prevent. His demeanor didn't shift an inch. Well trained.

"Would you mind waiting here?"

"Not at all." I sat down in a white high-backed wing chair with legs that looked as if they belonged to an eagle.

"Excuse me, would you mind sitting here?" He gestured toward one of the two sofas. "The Queen Anne is Miss Conrad's chair."

I got up and sat on the sofa, crossing my legs. There was the rustle of my skirt, slip, and nylons. Female sounds. The brown eyes flickered quickly over me again. He wasn't checking for weapons this time. I felt a slight triumph. Female sounds are not always vulnerable.

"May I get you something to drink?" His eyes were on my mouth.

"Coffee."

He walked crisply from the room.

Since I wasn't able to take my eyes off the butler, I hadn't really looked at the room. It was large, airy, filled with books and paintings. White linen slipcovers fit snugly over the sofas. The furniture had been arranged so people could talk. Burgundy-colored pillows were tossed onto the sofas like big drops of wine. Side tables were piled with books, ashtrays, and objets d'art. At the end of the room was a big round table covered with a green felt cloth. Books, papers, a magnifying glass, a pair of white gloves, and a pair of black gloves were scattered on it. Near the table was a globe as big as a beach ball. Behind the table were doors leading out to a garden. In the distance was the hotel. Staring at it, I became aware of the sounds of a woman sobbing. The sounds seemed to come from behind a closed door next to the tiled stairs.

A heavyset woman carrying coffee slouched through the foyer and down the stairs. Her hair was gray. Her skin looked as if it had never been touched by the sun. The pristine skin contrasted sharply with the stark black dress and sensible black shoes. Putting the coffee on a table by the fireplace, she asked, "You take cream?" She had a thick Hungarian accent.

"Thank you."

She handed me the coffee. I sipped. "It's very good," I said. She studied me with knowing gray eyes.

The sobbing got louder. Unperturbed, the woman clasped her hands prayer-like over her motherly breasts and beamed at me.

The sobs turned into a whiny voice. "But he took all my money."

A clear, firm female voice replied: "It is not a crime if you willingly gave it to him. Alas, neither is stupidity."

The woman in front of me looked with disdain toward the closed doors, then back at me. She gently rocked her clasped hands and continued to beam. I was feeling uneasy. This woman was behaving like my mother when I go home to visit: the constant proud staring . . . the hands in prayer. I sipped my coffee and smiled at her.

"I . . ." sobbed the voice. "Loved . . ." Sob. Sob. "Him . . ." Sigh. "What will I do?"

"Learn the difference between a worthless man and a worthy man before you give him all your money. That will be a hundred and fifty dollars."

"What?!" Screamed.

"I value my time."

"I don't have . . . He has . . ."

"Leave!" Disgusted.

A bell tinkled.

79

"But I loved . . . him." The whine was back.

"Love is no excuse."

The Englishman appeared and opened the door. He went in and quickly returned with a young woman on his arm. I had pictured her thin and mousy. She wore magenta tights. Large rhinestone earrings shone from under hennaed hair. Her face was all eye shadow and lipstick. Silver loafers shimmered on her feet. I thought she would've known her men as well as she knew the brand name of her cosmetics. But you can never tell about women. We're always in disguise, so it's difficult to pick out the victims from the victors.

The Englishman ushered her out.

The woman who was in the disguise of my mother "tsk-tsked." "She did not have a good personal matter." Her eyes scrutinized me; her voice turned confidential. "Make your personal matter . . . complex. She likes complexities."

"Thanks for the tip."

"A personal matter that is complex is just what she needs," she said, as if she were discussing the medicinal values of chicken soup.

The Englishman returned. He extended his hand toward the closed door. "You may go in now." The watchful brown eyes looked right through me as he opened the door. The door closed so quickly behind me I felt as if I'd been pushed into the room.

Claire Conrad was all in white, propped up by large white pillows in a large white bed. A white canopy draped down from some sort of Egyptian or Grecian cement molding. On the forefinger of her right hand was a chunk of lapis the size of a small jagged rock. Her eyes were as dark blue as her ring. They were the only color she seemed to allow in the room. She tilted her elegant head toward me. Thick silver hair swept back from her face like the folded wings of a bird. It was hard to tell how old she was — early fifties, I guessed.

Holding a bottle of pills in one hand, she fixed me with disturbing, intelligent eyes. "I am recuperating from the loss of my last ovary. Forced into menopause." She unfolded a long, graceful hand, revealing a pill. "Now, I must take liver-colored hormones on certain days, yellow hormones on other days. Do you think this is what *Time* magazine meant when they referred to me as a *woman* detective?" Refined lips smiled.

"You're a detective?"

"What's left of me." Lake-blue eyes narrowed. "Where is your table . . . your equipment?"

"What kind of a detective?"

"The kind that knows you are not a masseuse.

81

And that Boulton and Gerta have tried to trick me again. This time it will not work." She grabbed a sterling silver dinner bell and began ringing it.

I could feel the wayward two on the other side of the door, holding their breath, listening. Unable to get their attention, she slammed the bell down on the bedside table. "Damn them!"

"I'm Maggie Hill," I said quickly. "I worked for — "

"I don't care who you are or for whom you have worked. I will not put up with these childish pranks. Do you hear me?!" she screamed at the closed door. Then she turned on me. "First I am sent that poor twit of a girl with her pathetic story of rejection and deception. How could they think her tawdry plight would entice me from my recuperation?! She'll just be taken advantage of again and again. Earn more money and give it away to the next man who comes along."

"She was in love," I said.

"Oh, God." She collapsed back onto the bed. "Go away. I'm tired. I'm going to sleep."

She closed her eyes. I watched. Not a finger twitched. I waited. Not an eyelash fluttered. Silence. I no longer existed for her. I stood there thinking about Kenilworth's shattered head. About a suicide note I saw but wasn't there. About Patricia Kenilworth's nails digging into my wrist. About a codicil I'd been given to keep and was now gone. I thought about this woman lying smugly in her bed. I thought about how I had driven all the way out to San Marino to let her know that four million bucks had been taken from her. And unless we did something, she wasn't going to get what was legally hers. I thought about her conceited front door and how casually she shut people out. I decided I didn't like this woman. I decided to sit down. I decided to tell her all about it.

"I'm Maggie Hill. And I've been dealing with a lot of pompous people lately. And you're just another one. I was Ellis Kenilworth's secretary. That is . . . before he blew his head off with a shotgun." There was no flicker of movement.

I continued. "Yesterday he had me type a codicil to his will. It stated that after his death you should receive his entire collection of rare and ancient coins, valued at over four million dollars." Not a twitch, not a tremor crossed that quiet, sculpted face. "I came here to tell you that the codicil has been stolen. But you and your front door are so conceited, so self-centered . . . so . . . hell, I'm sure it doesn't matter to you. But it matters to me." No reaction.

83

I doggedly went on telling the entire story, remembering details I had forgotten. I suppose a half-hour had gone by when I finally finished. My throat was dry, my voice slightly hoarse. I couldn't look at her anymore. I watched the breeze billow white gauze curtains over open windows. Maybe a minute passed. Her eyes remained closed. Only her lips moved when she finally spoke.

"Why didn't you look in your purse when you got home last night?"

Of all the questions she could've asked, that one surprised me. I had remembered a great many details. I had purposely left out the detail of Neil. He wasn't any of her business.

"That's a very large purse you carry. I think there would be things in there you would need in order to prepare for bed." She opened her eyes and stared at the top of her canopy.

"I just went right to sleep. To be honest with you, I forgot about the codicil."

"You're not being honest with me." She sat up. Hard eyes burrowed into me.

I tried to equal her stare. But I was losing. She was right. I wasn't being honest with her. But I didn't want to talk to this woman about knocking off a bottle of champagne. I didn't want to talk to her about going to bed with my ex-husband. I didn't want to talk to her about a sleepy female voice. I was protecting again. But who was I protecting? Myself.

5

Claire Conrad sat up. Lines carved deep on
the sides of her mouth and across her forehead. These lines, instead of detracting from
her beauty, defined and strengthened it. She
tapped the bottle of liver-colored hormones
against a bedside table bleached the color of
dried bones.

"You've called me pompous and self-centered. You've based these observations on
your reaction to my front door. A front door
can be opened. It can be closed. It can be
wood. It can be glass. It cannot be conceited.
You have projected emotion onto an inani-
mate object — a form of childish behavior
which muddles the adult's perceptive pow-
ers."

She stared at the pills in her hand. "Women,
contrary to the opinions of doctors, are indi-
viduals. A few of us are unique. I assume
there must be an appropriate time in the day
to take one of these — a moment when my
body and my mind are ready for a shot of the

old female juices. You'd think the doctors would know that moment, but they don't."

Tossing the hormones down, she threw back the bedclothes and stood. She was tall, about six feet. White-belted pajamas covered a long, graceful body. The pajamas were creaseless. How did she stay in bed and not wrinkle her clothes? She grabbed an ivory walking stick that leaned against the back of a chair and strode across the room, looking perfectly healthy to me.

As if reading my thoughts, she slowed her pace, leaned on the cane, and shot me a defiant glare over her shoulder. "I have a right to malinger. And you have invaded my right."

She disappeared into a walk-in closet and reappeared wrapped in a long white velvet bathrobe. She looked like an angel of judgment. And I was the one being judged.

She swept across the room, walking stick in hand, and threw open the bedroom door. Gerta and the Englishman began busying themselves. Gerta grabbed a pillow and frantically shook it. He picked up a silver ashtray and held it to the light — checking for fingerprints, no doubt. Claire brushed past them and arranged herself in the Queen Anne chair.

"Stop flapping that pillow, Gerta. You're spreading dust and goose feathers everywhere. Shouldn't you be fixing lunch? I'm starved."

Gerta hurried out of the room, but not before she beamed another proud smile in my direction.

"Boulton, you will remain," Claire commanded. "You were listening at the door. Did you hear everything?"

"Yes, madam."

"Are there any questions you would like to ask Miss Hill?"

"You mean other than what she was doing after eight o'clock last night?"

She tilted her head slightly. He fixed his watchful brown eyes on me and asked, "Why do you think Eleanor Kenilworth took the suicide note?"

"I didn't say she did."

"You implied it," Claire said, tapping the finger with the lapis rock on the head of her stick.

"She was the only one there. She had the opportunity when I went downstairs to talk to the help and order her tea."

"You said the maid came up behind you in the hall and frightened you." It was the Englishman named Boulton.

"I was standing at Mrs. Kenilworth's sitting-room door, which is near the top of the stairs. I thought I would've seen the maid come up the stairs, but I didn't. Of course, I was intent on —"

"Servants' stairs," he said. They looked knowingly at one another.

"Servants' stairs?" I repeated dumbly.

"Most houses such as the Kenilworths' would have them," Boulton explained.

The shared secure look of people who have it made irritated me. "I was raised in a house where we made our own tea and had only one set of stairs. They were so narrow we couldn't pass each other on them. So I'm not familiar — "

"Miss Hill, your story is not going to raise Boulton's social consciousness. Like you, he is a snob." She smiled for the first time. "Our intention is not to make a class distinction but to point out that servants' stairs can be used by the help or by people who do not want to be seen by the rest of the house." She turned to Boulton. "Any more questions?"

He looked me up and down and shook his head.

"Still checking for weapons?" I asked a little too defensively.

Claire laughed. It was a good, solid, warm laugh. Boulton stiffened into a proper butler, and his watchful brown eyes turned discreet. A slash of red formed on each cheek. I liked that.

Claire leaned back in her chair. "What did Valcovich see from the office window? And this vision, whatever it was — how could it lead him to the codicil in your purse?" Eyes flashed with the excitement of thought. "I find this Patricia Kenilworth interesting. Divorced all those years and suddenly returns worried about what her husband might've said before he killed himself. You're sure it was a photograph?" she asked me.

"As sure as I can be. So what do we do?"

She stood. "Nothing."

"What do you mean, nothing? You could call Valcovich."

"How do I know you and Valcovich are not in this together?"

"In *what* together?"

"*You* could've taken the suicide note. *You* could've taken the codicil. *You* could be involved in extortion along with Valcovich. Until I feel you've been honest with me — until you tell me why you never looked in your purse last night — I see no reason to trust you."

"I came here to tell you that somebody has stolen a four-million-dollar coin collection that is legally yours and *you* don't trust *me?!* Fine! Fine!"

I made my way to the front door. I'd told the truth. If it wasn't good enough for her, there was nothing else I could do. The door was locked. They moved slowly toward me, the lady and her butler: a Gothic couple. I wanted nothing to do with them. I wanted out.

"Unlock the door, Boulton," she commanded.

He did as he was told. I stepped outside and started up the steps.

"One final comment, Miss Hill. If you are telling the truth, you could be in danger."

That stopped me. I turned and looked at her. She stood in the doorway leaning on her walking stick as if she were at Ascot. Boulton stood just behind her. And just behind him was the half-open door with the family crest.

"If you're telling the truth," she continued, "then the person or persons who stole these documents know that you know they exist. In the case of the suicide note, they may even think you've read it. If they were willing to steal to keep these papers from being discovered, they may be willing to go further."

The phrase "you could be in danger" was as abstract to me as the phrase "virginity is making a comeback." I was tired.

"I've had it with Pasadena." I turned and went up the steps. I heard the family crest close behind me. Some family.

I was on the Arroyo Seco Freeway going sixty-five miles an hour away from Pasadena toward Hollywood. If Claire Conrad didn't believe me, what the hell. I don't know how telling her I'd gone to bed with my ex-husband was going to make her trust me. I did what I had to do and that was that. I didn't want to be responsible for the damn codicil anyway. I'd told Kenilworth that. What right did he have forcing it on me, then going upstairs and killing himself? What right? I was through. It was time to get involved in my own life. I headed for the New Woman Employment Agency, formerly the Girl Friday Employment Agency. Times change, but the jobs don't. And I needed one again.

My radio blasted. A group of male voices screamed at me over their synthesizers, screamed at me to give it to them. Give it to them! It was a love song. Rock 'n' roll was middle-aged, but it had never grown up. The male voices sounded shrill and desperate. I turned them off. Silence. *I* was almost middle-aged. *I* was shrill and desperate. I was in danger. I wondered what form danger would take. A male form, of course. He'd be dressed in black and always have a gun in his hand and a hard-on. Unlike virginity, danger would never have left town. Oh, hell.

I got off the freeway at Highland and drove down to Hollywood Boulevard. The New Woman Agency was near La Brea just before Hollywood Boulevard turns into a street of houses and condos. The agency was in one of those high-rise buildings that look as if they were made out of wraparound sunglasses. Across the street, men, balancing cameras on their shoulders, circled and captured *an event* for the six o'clock news. Either someone was having his star put in the sidewalk or he had been murdered. I parked the car in the high rise's parking lot.

The New Woman Agency was on the seventh floor. The agency consisted of three small offices, two hard-working women named Corinne and Phyllis, and a lot of telephones.

I went in. Corinne was sitting at her desk talking to a young Mexican woman. "Do you speak English?" she asked.

"*Sí* . . . yes."

A little boy clung to the woman's leg. She nervously stroked his shiny-clean hair. Corinne looked up at me. She was dressed in a three-piece green suit. Thick red hair curled in all directions.

"Maggie! Phyllis, it's Maggie," she yelled into the next room.

"Out of work again," I said.

"Be with you in a second. Go in and see Phyllis. She's got something to show you." Corinne turned back to the young woman. "Can you type?"

Averting her eyes from Corinne's, the woman

nodded. The boy buried his face in his mother's lap, pulling her skirt up around his cheeks and exposing her prim cotton slip. Embarrassed, she pulled the fabric from his hands and smoothed her skirt.

"I'm going to have to test you."

"Test?"

"To see how fast you can type."

"Oh . . ." The young woman's voice trailed off into hopelessness. She stared at the boy. He seemed to sense her fear and patted her hand. That simple meaningful gesture made me feel something I wasn't prepared for: envy. Mother and child. I could feel the envy in my womb. A swift jab. I looked away and told myself it was just my body clock reminding me of my age. What a lovely term, "body clock." So mechanical sounding. So impersonal. Like a clock connected to a bomb, ticking, ticking, ticking till it explodes. I looked back at them. That little boy's gesture wasn't going to put food on the table. That little boy's gesture wasn't going to help her learn to speak English or to type. What good was that little boy's gesture? My envy was gone. Now I was feeling the proper emotion: despair. I walked into Phyllis's office hoping that what she had for me was another job and wishing that minorities would stop having babies. This is America. Don't they know about the

94

freedom of abortion?

Her hair was dyed raven today. The last time I saw Phyllis she was a redhead. The time before that, a brunette. The time before that . . . I can't remember.

She was peering out the narrow band of dark window allotted to her street-side office. "Did you see her?" Phyllis lisped through the retainer she wore on her teeth.

"Who?"

"Victoria Moor!"

I looked out the window. The dark glass made Hollywood appear as if it were in mourning. I watched the huddle on the sidewalk spread apart, revealing a thin bleached blonde kneeling as if in prayer. Venus had her half-shell; Victoria Moor had her star on a dirty sidewalk. She rose from her knees. Her breasts tilted upward toward us, the Hollywood sun, and God. The circling, dipping, jabbing camera shadow-boxed around her every move. She waved and slithered into a long white line of a limousine.

"Isn't she beautiful?" Phyllis lisped, forming a tiny bubble of saliva on her retainer. It popped. She had straight teeth, but not straight enough for Phyllis.

"She starves herself and has her breasts enlarged and you call it beauty?"

"Oh, Maggie, you don't like anything. Do

you think she killed him?"

"Killed who?" The question startled me. And again I thought of that word "danger."

"Junior Paddingworth! Oh, God, I hope they don't send her to prison. Then she has to wear one of those drab gray dresses all the time and we don't get to see the beautiful clothes."

She sat at her desk and began going through piles of folders and papers looking for something. Her stubby nails were painted the color of bubble gum. Furry stuffed animals about the size of my fist hung from her desk lamp and balanced on stacks of files. They smiled stupidly at me. A can of some nutrient diet mix teetered on the edge of her desk.

"I hope in all that mess you're trying to find a job for me," I said, placing the can so it wouldn't fall off.

"You have another month to go out in Pasadena."

She didn't know. I didn't feel like telling her. "Finished."

"Here it is!" Triumphantly, she plucked a bright yellow book from the pile of papers and held it up for me to see. In bold green letters was the title, *Cornsilk*. Under it, in much smaller print, was my name. A round red price tag declared my book was worth ninety-nine cents.

"And you told Corinne and me it was out of print," Phyllis chided.

"It is."

"Autograph it for me." She thrust the book into my hands as she picked up the ringing telephone.

Phyllis tried to calm an angry temporary employer. I tried objectively to study the photograph of me on the back of the book. I couldn't. I looked so young. So earnest. So innocent. I felt the same swift jab of envy I had felt when looking at the mother and child, but the pain wasn't in my womb. It was under my heart, where I always imagined my soul was hidden. I quickly autographed the book and tossed it onto the desk.

Phyllis was now talking to an angry temporary employee. I stared at a stack of telephone books on the floor next to her desk. I wondered what would happen if I showed up at Valcovich's office. Come on, Maggie, you've had it with Pasadena. You weren't going to think about the Kenilworths. I turned and looked out at the Hollywood Hills. They were cluttered with houses. It was easier to think about the Kenilworths than to think about that young writer on the back of a book. It was easier to think about why somebody would steal a codicil than about why I had never written another book. I lifted the Yellow Pages onto my lap and flipped to the *A*'s. I took a piece of paper from Phyllis's desk and wrote down Valcovich's address.

Corinne stood in the doorway. Her green suit gave her body the curious look of a sturdy stem. The unruly red hair made her head the flower. "She couldn't type, let alone run a computer. I told her to go to one of the local colleges — a night course to learn some skills and English. I mean, what else could I do for her?"

I wasn't thinking about the mother and child anymore. I was thinking about Valcovich. "Listen, if you get anything for me, let me know," I said, heading out of the office. " 'Bye, Phyllis."

"That's what we get paid for," Corinne said, following me to the door.

"See you later."

"Maggie." She put her hand on my arm, stopping me. "That woman didn't want to be a maid. What is it *you* don't want to be?"

"What are you talking about?"

"What are you doing here, Maggie? Why are you taking jobs you could perform in your sleep? I read your book."

"I gotta go, Corinne. Call me."

I was out the door and down the hallway.

"It made me cry," Corinne yelled after me. Why do women think it's a good book if it's made them cry? Why are tears so important to us?

Valcovich's office was on Pico Boulevard in a four-story building wedged between one-story shops. The building was designed to always look new, so it always looked cheap. He was on the third floor. The elevator was busy. I took the stairs and came out into a hallway of office doors. The sounds of Muzak collided with the sounds of rock 'n' roll. The rock music bellowed from an open office. Three young men who looked as if they belonged in the sixties stared at a computer. Antinuclear posters covered the walls. A large sign urged people to pay five dollars and march for peace. It was difficult to get people to spend money for peace when they weren't sure where war was. Around the corner from the antinukes and on the street side were the law offices of Roger Valcovich. I took a deep breath and breezed in.

The reception desk was empty except for an ashtray filled with butts. In the small waiting room an old couple held shaky hands. A young woman, tears streaming down her face, sat twisting her wedding band. A bearded man pounded his fist on his knee while he read *People* magazine. A woman of about fifty appeared from behind a row of filing cabinets. I could tell by the burning cigarette in her hand that she was The Smoker.

"Do you have an appointment?"

"Yes."

"Name?"

"Maggie Hill."

"I don't see you on the list."

"Just tell him my name. He'll see me."

She studied me for moment, taking a drag on her cigarette and letting the smoke out through her nose. When she spoke, it was in a whisper: "He's not in."

I turned to the group in the waiting room. "Do you know Valcovich isn't in his office?" I asked them.

The old man glared at The Smoker. "I've been here an hour. Waiting! What do you mean, not in?"

The young girl began to sob loudly. The old woman looked bewildered. The guy with the beard continued to read *People* and pound his fist.

The Smoker moved swiftly toward them. "Don't worry, Mr. Valcovich will see you."

"Have to get a lawyer for the lawyer!" the old man yelled at his wife.

"What?!" she yelled back.

The Smoker turned on me. "Wait here."

She hurried down a narrow hall to a closed door. I smiled at the old man and his wife. I thought about telling these poor people what a creep Valcovich was until it dawned on me that I shouldn't just be standing there. I ran down the hall and threw open the door. Valcovich was standing behind a large white desk, looking puffy and mean. The Smoker was drawn and nervous.

"Maggie! What a nice surprise," he said sweetly, settling himself into a white leather chair.

I had the peculiar feeling that somebody had just left the room in a hurry; there was the lingering smell of another person. I saw only one other door. I opened it and peered out into the hallway. Other than the sound of Muzak and the sound of the Grateful Dead, it was empty. Closing the door, I turned back to Valcovich.

His greedy eyes watched me. He placed his hands on his desk just as he had in his television commercial and turned to The Smoker. "Ellen, get the accident forms for Maggie to fill out."

"You're a terrible actor," I said.

He looked hurt.

"I want the codicil, Valcovich."

He shook his head sadly. "Maggie, Maggie. Why do you keep on about that? You're beginning to sound a little crazy."

"How much money did you get out of the Kenilworths?"

"I think we have a nut on our hands. Call the police, Ellen."

The Smoker picked up the telephone as if she had never seen one before.

"Don't bother. I'm leaving. I'm not going to let this go, Valcovich."

I walked out the private entrance into the corridor, slamming the door shut. Then I stood quietly, listening. I heard The Smoker go into a coughing fit. I could hear Valcovich talking; but between The Smoker's gasps for life, the moans of the Grateful Dead, and the sweet slurpings of Muzak, I couldn't make out his words.

Oh, hell. I was strapped back in the Honda, curling my way through Laurel Canyon to the Ventura Freeway and home. Moving slowly in rush-hour traffic, I thought about my uneventful visit to Valcovich's office. What had I expected him to do? Tell me the truth? I found out what I already knew: he was in this up to his fat neck. And so was I.

I unlocked my apartment door to the sounds of Prokofiev's *Romeo and Juliet*. I shoved the door open with my foot. Frying pan. Sheets. Toaster oven. Clothes. Mattress ripped. Dresser drawers dumped. Dishes scattered. Chair on its side. Cushion split. Pillow feathers everywhere like snow. The smell of day-old pizza. I leaned against the wall, trying to take in the chaos. Television. Phone machine blinking. Computer. Tape deck. Radio — the Montagues and the Capulets marched. All there. So this was danger.

I found the telephone and dialed.

Boulton answered.

"This is Maggie. I want to speak to her."

She came onto the line. "Yes, Miss Hill?"

"Call me Maggie. We're going to pretend we're best friends and I'm going to tell you how I fucked my brains out last night with my ex-husband so I wouldn't have to think of all the different pieces of Kenilworth's face. That's why I never looked in my purse. I made him leave early in the morning because I don't trust him enough to wake up next to him. He didn't know about the codicil. He never looked in my purse. When I found it was missing, I called him, because he's a policeman. A woman answered. I hung up. Any questions?"

"No."

"Your turn to be honest with me. Did you send your butler over here to ransack my apartment?"

"No."

"Well, somebody was looking for something and has made a terrible mess, and I don't like it one bit."

103

"Don't touch anything. We'll be there as quickly as we can, Miss Hill."

I gave her directions and hung up. I made my way to the refrigerator and got a bottle of white wine. I took a glass and went and sat down by the baby-blue pool. Hands shaking, I filled my glass and leaned back in a cheap plastic lounge chair. I drank and refilled the glass. The sun was going down, burning the tan walls of the apartment complex red.

The codicil had been stolen from me, my apartment ransacked, and I'd just confessed my sex life to a woman I hardly knew. I gulped and poured myself another. My hands still shook. The pool light went on. I could hear a woman bitching in Spanish. Another one bitched in English. A man belched. The palm tree's spotlight clicked on. A baby bitched. I poured more wine. Oh, hell, if I wasn't confessing, I was protecting. I drank and shut my eyes. I smelled meat frying. Grease crackled. Dishes clattered. A man and woman laughed. Homey sounds . . . comforting sounds . . .

6

"Glass containers are not allowed by the pool. You speak English. You can read the rules. Do you hear me? Wake up!"

Froman's eighty-proof breath filled my nostrils. I blinked. Boozy, belligerent eyes bore down on mine. Behind her face apartment windows were yellow squares of light in the darkness.

"Drinking by the pool. Men leaving all hours of the night. I will not tolerate such behavior," Froman yelled. She was the kind of drunk who never slurred her words; her voice just got louder and louder.

"I rent to mi . . . nor . . . ities. I believe in e . . . quality. And what has it got me? *You!* Sleeping it off around the pool!"

My head pounded. My neck was stiff. I closed my eyes and tried to figure out how Froman's renting to minorities and believing in equality had brought us together by the pool. I knew there was an important reason for my being here outside at night, if only I could think of it.

"Wake up!" Froman bellowed.

I turned my head away from hers and slowly opened my eyes again. There, within reach, but dangerously near the edge of the pool, was my half-empty bottle of wine. Fear slowly crept back into me, jarring my memory. I was in danger.

"Waiting for someone," I mumbled. My mouth tasted like Froman's smelled.

"Your friends are already here. I know what you're up to." Her watery eyes narrowed. "You stay down here while they have the use of your apartment."

She snapped her head in the direction of my apartment, a movement that suddenly propelled her backwards right into the lone palm tree. Wrapping her arm around its bumpy trunk, she steadied herself. Bathed in the jaundice glow of the floodlight, she checked her rigorously sprayed brown hair for loose strands. There were none. Froman was a neat drunk.

I looked up at my window. Shadows crossed the square of light. Struggling awkwardly to my feet, I grabbed the wine and hurried toward the stairs.

Froman swayed after me. "Living in an apartment complex is a group effort. I must look out for the rights of the group. And you are threatening those rights by your ab . . .

aber . . . rant behavior."

I could never figure out if Froman was a communist or a fascist. Whatever her politics were, they didn't allow for human frailties or human delights. I felt a perverse sense of triumph when I threw open my door. I wanted her to see that my apartment had been ransacked right under her big red nose.

Claire Conrad, dressed in white trousers, white blouse, white jacket belted at the waist, stood leaning on her ivory walking stick in the middle of my life's possessions. She was reading my novel. More people had been interested in my novel in one day than when it was first published.

Boulton stood by the box springs of my bed. He held my radio by its cord as if he were holding a dead rodent by the tail. He dusted it with a white powder. Was it only yesterday that my radio had told me virginity was making a comeback?

Froman bumped past me into the room. She jerked to a halt. Her mouth sagged open. No words came out.

Claire peered over the book at me. "You're awake. Who is this?"

"Mrs. Froman, the manager. How could you let me sleep?"

"You obviously needed to. You should never use the word 'corn' in a title. The critics might use it back at you."

"They did."

She turned to Froman. The dark blue eyes filled with loathing. "Mrs. Froman, did you see anybody go in or out of Miss Hill's apartment this afternoon?"

Froman wagged her head.

"Do you think any of the other tenants might — "

"Everyone keeps to themselves here," I said. "I can predict nobody saw anything."

"I need a drink," Froman moaned.

I handed her the bottle of wine. She sucked from it like a baby.

Putting my radio in a plastic bag, Boulton said, "There are two sets of prints in the apartment. One set I assume to be Miss Hill's. The other prints are only on the champagne bottle, the glass, the night stand, and . . ." The watchful brown eyes moved quickly up my body and came to rest on my lips. I felt as if he could see the unique spidery pattern of Neil's hands on my arms, my breasts, my hips, my thighs, like stains.

"I assume these prints belong to the policeman." Boulton held up the radio. "There is one lone print that doesn't match. It's on the dial of this."

"Good. Then we have what we need," Claire said.

"Have what?" I asked.

"A clue." The refined lips smiled.

Froman quit sucking and bawled, "What's going on here? Are you the police? You don't look like the police." Her voice was gaining strength.

"Boulton, give her one of my cards."

From inside his coat he produced an ivory-colored card. Froman read it carefully and sneered.

"I don't need a private detective to know what's going on here. You don't fool me. I told her to quit playing that music. I had to come all the way up here this afternoon and pound on the door!"

"When?!"

"You tell *me*. You were here."

"And did Miss Hill turn off the music? Or did she put it back on the classical station?"

"She knows what we agreed to."

"I wasn't here this afternoon!"

"I heard you in here making this mess. I know what you're up to. You want out of the apartment without paying the security deposit. I've seen it all before. Pretend you've been burgled . . . " Froman was booming.

"Wait a minute," I yelled over her. "I *don't* want out of my apartment, and I *have* been burgled! *You* let it happen!"

"You're going to get out, all right. Now!"

"This is my apartment. You have no right . . ."

"You are a monthly. I decide when this is your apartment and when it is not your apartment. It is *not* your apartment."

"You *are* a fascist!"

"How dare you! I have fought the good fight." She swayed primly to the door and opened it. Standing on my thin balcony, she pulled herself up to attention and screamed, "Out! Out! I want you out! Now!"

"I'm not leaving!" I yelled back.

"She's right," Claire said. "You can't stay here."

"This is my home."

"Out! Out! Out!" Froman chanted.

"Shut up!" the man next door yelled.

"This is Mrs. Froman!" she bellowed back.

"Up yours!" he replied.

Froman slammed my door in my face.

I turned on Claire. "This may not look like much to you. But I live here. She has no right to throw me out."

"Look around, Miss Hill. What do you see?"

"I don't have to look around. I know. Chaos."

"Exactly."

"To be honest with you, my apartment doesn't look much better than this even when

110

it's in order. I'm staying."

"Miss Hill, you may love to wallow in your own private chaos. But this is not your chaos. This has been created by somebody else — by somebody who has a great deal of anger and rage in them. Look at the unnecessary destruction. It's not safe to stay here, Miss Hill. You can stay with us until we resolve this . . . situation. Pack some clothes, and be sure to include a proper outfit for a funeral. Ellis Kenilworth is being buried tomorrow. . . . This should do." With her stick she lifted a beige dress off the floor. It hung limply from the ivory cane like boned flesh.

"I hate that dress."

"Then why did you buy it?"

"Haven't you ever bought an outfit you didn't like?"

"No. Did you make some sort of agreement with the manager about your radio?"

"While I'm gone I can leave it on the classical station."

"Then our intruder must not have liked classical music. He or she turned the dial, probably to rock music, and the manager heard it and began pounding on the door. So the intruder turned it back."

"But why didn't the person leave his gloves on to do that?" Boulton asked.

"I'm sure one could get very warm destroying another's possessions. He probably had his gloves on when he changed the station. But what if he took his gloves off to wipe his forehead or just cool himself, and Froman begins to bang on the door demanding he change the music? Afraid he'll be discovered, he changes the station back, forgetting to put on his gloves. Do you know anyone, man or woman, who detests classical music, Miss Hill?"

"Not for that brief a time."

"While you pack, do you mind if I listen to your phone machine?"

"Be my guest." I began to gather my clothes from the floor. Boulton opened my two suitcases. My mother's voice filled the room.

"Happy birthday, Maggie. Why aren't you answering? Oh, hell, come home."

I folded my jacket with the big shoulder pads. His voice made my stomach tighten. "Neil," he said, then hung up.

"Was that his name or a command?" Claire asked, half-smiling.

I glared and stuffed more clothes into the suitcase.

"Call him back," Claire said.

"I don't want to talk to him."

"I'd like you to ask him to run a check on that fingerprint. See if it has a name. Boulton can meet him at the police station with the radio."

112

"You mean you want me to ask him for a favor? I won't!"

"Miss Hill, to me love is an adolescent disease. By the time you're an adult, you should already have had it and be immune to it. I obviously hold a minority view. But I have very little patience for people who are in the thick of love. I am here to work. If you are going to get all tangled up in your emotions, you will be absolutely no help to me. Now, try to look objectively at your situation with this man and you will see that Neil owes *you* a favor."

"Oh, hell."

The Englishman handed me the phone; it was covered with white dust. I dialed. He answered.

"It's Maggie."

His voice lowered to a whisper. "I can't talk now."

"Then why did you call me?"

"I . . . don't know."

"Don't worry, you're safe. It's business. There's an Englishman named Boulton — he's going to meet you at headquarters with my radio. He wants to know if you can put a name to a fingerprint that was left on it. Don't worry, it's not yours."

"What's up?"

"Nothing. I just want you to do this for me."

"I can't. Against the rules."

"You owe me one."

His voice lowered. "You wanted it last night."

"Does *she* know I wanted it?"

"Jesus Christ! How did we end up like this?"

"Boulton will be there in about twenty minutes." I hung up the phone.

"Well?" Claire asked.

"I feel like shit."

"Is he going to meet Boulton?"

"I don't know. Give it a try."

Boulton turned to Claire. "What about you?"

"Miss Hill can drive me back to the cottage."

"Do you think that wise?"

"I'm a very good driver," I said, zipping up my suitcase.

"But Miss Conrad is a very bad passenger," he replied.

I went into the bathroom and stood for a moment leaning on the sink. Tears formed. I threw cold water on my face until the tears stopped.

Boulton appeared in the doorway. "Would you mind leaving me the key to your apartment? I'll come back and collect the telly and the computer and anything else you'd like."

I wiped my face with a towel. "My books. Thanks."

The front door was open. Claire stood on the balcony waiting. I stepped over bedclothes, shattered dishes, and other possessions. How quickly my life had come to look like debris!

In the dim light of the garage I unlocked the car.

"Is this *you?*" Claire asked, peering down at my car.

"No, it's not *me*. It's a Honda."

"If I drove a car, I would not drive such a small one."

"You don't drive?! I don't know anybody who doesn't drive."

"I have a fear of automobiles. Boulton thinks my fear comes from my parents' having died in a car crash."

"What do you think?"

"I think I would prefer not to die in a Honda. My parents died in a Bentley." She strapped herself into the car.

On the long drive back to Pasadena I told her about my visiting Valcovich and the peculiar feeling I had that someone had just left his office.

She never spoke until we were out of the car and going down the brick steps to her house.

"It's important I meet this Valcovich. Obviously, if I use my name he will try to avoid me. You said he was very concerned about his TV persona."

"I think he fancies himself an actor. You have an incredible memory."

"I have a phenomenal memory. Tomorrow Valcovich will receive a phone call from a theatrical agency wanting to put him in a movie or a television show. Think up something clever."

"Me?"

She unlocked the door. "Yes, you. I never use disguises. It's the one thing Sherlock Holmes and I do not have in common."

Was she kidding?

"Personally," she said, stepping into the foyer, "I think he used disguises because he could play at being lower class. Very Victorian."

Gerta hurried into the hall. When she saw me, she blurted, "I knew you would have a complex matter."

"That's me. Filled with complexities."

"Gerta, show Miss Hill the guest room and fix her some dinner."

"Oh, no . . . I don't want to put you to any trouble," I said, while Gerta tugged my suitcase from my hand.

"You will put Gerta to trouble if you don't

116

let her do this for you. I'm tired. I'm going to bed. Good night, Miss Hill. Oh, by the way, I took your book with me. Do you mind if I read it?"

"No."

She strode across the living room and disappeared into her bedroom. I followed Gerta down a hallway opposite the living room. We passed a small formal dining room. At the end of the hall was a door and, across from it, stairs that led down. Gerta opened the door and ushered me in.

Chunky beams criss-crossed the ceiling. The wood floor was a warm yellow-brown. Stucco walls glowed a soft candlelight color. A faded rose comforter enveloped the bed. Across from the bed was a small fireplace. Two chairs, in old chintz slipcovers, faced one another by the open hearth. The slipcovers looked as comfortable as old sweaters. Bookcases were built around a mirror and a dresser. A seductive room.

"You like it?" Gerta asked.

"The kind of room I've dreamed about."

"That's the reaction Miss Conrad wishes from her guests."

"Does she have many guests?"

"Depends. Not lately. Of course, she has not been working. That's why it's so good to see you. You've given Miss Conrad something

117

to do. Work makes her happy."

"Glad I could make Miss Conrad happy."

"I fix you something to eat. Come into the dining room after you unpack."

I thanked her and began hanging up my clothes. I opened the window next to the bookcase and stared out. The hotel, unfit for humans, was a black hulk in the moonlight. I closed the window and went back down the hall to the dining room.

A spotless linen cloth had been draped over the end of the dining room table and set with sterling silver and china so thin I felt I could crush it in my hand.

Gerta watched me eat her spinach soufflé. "Won't you sit down?" I asked. "I'd love some company." I sipped the red wine, which tasted like smoke and earth. Gerta shoved herself into a chair.

"How long have you been with Claire Conrad?"

"A long time. I knew her father first."

"The man who died in the Bentley."

"Such a tragedy . . . such a waste. I came to her after the tragedy. She had no one."

"Did the accident happen here?"

"In England. Soon after the war."

"Vietnam?"

"That was no war. The *real* war! The one we all understand. She was just a young girl."

"She's not English, is she? She sounds American."

"Very American. I'm American, now." Gerta beamed.

"Congratulations."

"You eat. Go on." She pushed my plate closer to me.

"Where are your rooms?" I asked, swallowing.

"Right off my kitchen."

"Has Boulton been with Claire many years?"

"Not so many."

"Where does Boulton sleep — I mean, stay — I mean, his rooms?"

"Boulton's rooms are downstairs." The sound of his voice made me hit the crystal goblet against my plate. It let out a thin cry, as if I'd hurt it.

Gerta leaped up. "Boulton! Why don't you make noise like other men? You're supposed to come into a house and yell 'I'm home! I'm home!' so the women can stop gossiping about you!" She turned and left the room.

His jacket was unbuttoned and his tie loosened at the neck. He was looking less and less like a butler.

"What else would you like to know, Miss Hill?" He went to the sideboard and poured himself a brandy.

"Was Neil there?"

119

"Not a bad bloke."

"And does the fingerprint have a name?"

"I am employed by Miss Conrad. I'm to convey all information to her first. Anything else?"

"Yes . . . I can't believe you got that body by polishing tea sets."

"Tea services are quite heavy. By the way, my room is not far from yours. Just down the stairs."

"In case I need help."

"Of course."

"You're rather far away from the woman you're supposed to be protecting. You're not a butler. You're her bodyguard, aren't you?"

"I am highly trained as both, and my rooms extend from the stairs to her bedroom. There is a private staircase between her bedroom and mine."

"Convenient."

"It is, rather. Well . . . good night, Miss Hill."

"All this 'miss' and 'madam'! Do you and I have to be so formal? I'm not used to it."

"To quote Miss Conrad: 'Formality is structure. Structure is civilization.' And I am a butler."

He swallowed the last of his brandy and walked quietly out of the room. I stuck my head into the kitchen and thanked Gerta for the meal. She gave me a motherly pat on the cheek and I went back to my room.

My computer, telephone machine, radio, books were all neatly placed. While I got ready for bed, I decided to call Neil and find out about the fingerprint. *I* wasn't paid by Miss Conrad. The phone was on the nightstand. I sat on the bed and dialed his number. While it rang, I was sure I heard the click of another phone being picked up. Somebody was listening. Or was I paranoid? She answered.

"Hello?"

"Is Neil there?"

"He's working."

"Oh."

"Who is this?"

"Maggie Hill. The ex."

"Oh."

"I was having him check on something for me at the department."

"Oh."

"I'll call there."

"We're getting married."

"Oh."

"I just thought you should know."

"Thank you."

"You're welcome. I'll tell him you called."

"Thank you."

"You're welcome."

She hung up. I didn't. I waited to hear if there was another click, if somebody else was hanging up. I held my breath, thinking of Neil holding the champagne bottle in his hands, the bottle tied with silver ribbons. He had wanted to celebrate.

"Good night, Maggie." Boulton spoke softly into the phone.

I heard the click.

7

It was the next morning, and I was dressed in my beige number, sitting at the dining-room table, finishing the last of my coffee. Claire sat across from me. She wore a black shirt, black slacks, and a black jacket. Her large, pale hand rested on the handle of an ebony walking stick. The chunk of lapis shimmered darkly. She read from a piece of paper.

"His name is Bobby Alt. He was arrested a year ago for prostitution. At the time he was twenty-five, weighed a hundred and thirty pounds, five feet seven inches tall, brown hair, brown eyes, and no distinguishing marks. He gave a Glendale address — 4081 Wedgwood Street. Sound familiar?"

"No."

"You must thank your policeman for us."

"He's getting married."

"Again? Men and women will never learn. It's eight forty-five. The funeral's at eleven. We'll go to Glendale first, see if he still lives there. I doubt that he does, but it's a beginning."

123

"Does Boulton always listen in on phone conversations?"

"I allow him to use his own judgment in that area."

"Does that mean I'm still under suspicion?"

The dark blue eyes assessed me. "I'll tell him you're to be trusted. One more thing, Miss Hill. I'm not used to having a client who doesn't pay. My fees are quite high."

"If you're as good as you say you are, you're going to get four million dollars!"

"Miss Hill, if I am to trust you, you must trust me. I don't want the coin collection."

"What do you want?"

"To do what I do best. Sleuth. Now, when did Ellis pay you last?"

"The first of the month."

"A week ago."

"Yes."

"In other words, he has paid for your services for another three weeks. Due to circumstances you cannot fulfill those services."

I nodded and brushed toast crumbs from my dress.

"Since you have been paid for an entire month, I see no reason why you couldn't perform similar services for me."

"Be your secretary?"

"I will take your services as my fee. You will

perform your duties at the big table in the living room."

"Perform my duties! You've got to be kidding! I'm not going to sit here answering the telephone while you're out having all the fun!"

"Fun?" She repeated the word as if she didn't know its definition.

"What I mean to say is . . . the codicil was stolen from *me*. It was *my* apartment that was broken into. I want to be there when you find out who did it, not banished to the big table because Ellis Kenilworth happened to pay me before he died!"

She leaned back in her chair. "Miss Hill, if you are to be involved in the art of detection, the first rule to learn is that you mustn't leap to conclusions. I have no desire to deprive myself of your secretarial skills. Nor do I have a desire to deprive myself of your quick mind and confrontational spirit. Which reminds me, you can call Valcovich from the car phone."

She plucked a small pill from a silver tray and downed it with the last of her orange juice. "Please, write down the time I took this dreadful hormone."

"It doesn't matter when you take them just as long as you take them."

"I am reduced to being dependent on a substance that is a chemical imitation. Depen-

125

dency and imitation are forms of behavior I do not admire. This is my way of asserting control. Humor me."

I got my Filofax out of my purse and wrote down her name, the date, and the time.

"I've told Boulton to bring the car around. Are you ready?"

I followed her down the hall and out the front door. I had the feeling that being a secretary to Claire Conrad was going to be a lot tougher than being a secretary to Kenilworth. I also felt that I was somehow being taken advantage of. I just couldn't figure out where.

We went up the steps and there was the car, big and black as a hearse.

"It's a Bentley!" I blurted.

"Correct."

"Don't you think you're tempting fate?"

"I challenge fate."

Boulton came around the car, opened the back door, and helped her in. He turned to me, bowing slightly. "Good morning, Maggie."

"I'm to be trusted. Now you won't have to stay up late listening to my phone conversations."

"Pity," he said, helping me in.

The car door closed with the authority of a bank vault's. The seats were well-worn gray leather. Highly polished burl wood framed the windows and the very narrow dashboard. Crystal bud vases, in sterling silver holders, were connected to the side paneling near the passenger windows. Each vase held a small bouquet of fresh wildflowers. The car rolled forward and we lumbered down the narrow street. I felt as if I were inside a dinosaur.

Claire handed me the car phone. "Make Mr. Valcovich an offer he cannot refuse."

I punched in his number.

"You remember his number," she observed.

"I only have an incredible memory."

The Smoker's voice filled my ear. "Law offices."

I took a deep breath and clamped my fingers over my nose. "This is Edith Wharton from the Arts and Stars Theatrical Agency calling Mr. Roger Valcovich."

She coughed and asked me to hold. Valcovich must've been standing on top of her. He breathed greedily into the phone.

"Yeah? This is Roger Valcovich."

"Mr. Valcovich? This is Edith Wharton from Arts and Stars Theatrical Agency. I saw one of your commercials and thought you'd be just right for a role in an upcoming miniseries we're casting."

I had to look away from Claire. She was staring at me as if she were witnessing a bad accident.

127

"Of course, being a busy, successful lawyer, I don't know if you'd be interested in such a — "

"I'm interested. Lawyers are actors at heart, you know."

"Yes. Well, I'm not going to be in my office today. I'm calling from my car phone. I hope you can hear me. Maybe we could meet at your office."

"My last appointment's at six. How about six thirty?"

"Fine."

"I have photographs. Do you want photographs?"

"Photographs? Oh, yes . . . of course. Six thirty then. Look forward to meeting you."

"Thank you for calling. Thank you for seeing my commercials. Thank you for thinking of me," he gushed.

I hung up the car phone.

"Edith Wharton?!" Claire gasped.

"He fell for it."

"What if the man reads literature?"

"He's a jerk."

"There are jerks who read literature."

"Not this one."

"Let's hope your perceptions are as acute as your sense of irony. Which reminds me, I read your novel last night. You're a very promising writer."

"Thank you."

"After a *certain* age, Miss Hill, it's not a compliment to be just a promising writer."

"Look, I didn't ask you to read my book."

"You did not." She turned and looked out the window.

"What kind of comment was that anyway?"

"I merely suggest that writing about yourself growing up in Ohio is charming, especially the section on the nuns in full habit, sitting at your mother's table, nibbling on baked chicken thighs, but — "

"They weren't nibbling, they were gnawing. And it was fried chicken breast, not the thigh."

"I think 'thigh,' as a word, has much more — "

"Look, my book has been published and buried and I've never written anything else, so why are we going on about it?"

"I am not a wasteful person and I hate to see waste in others — especially if it's intelligence and talent which are being squandered."

It was my turn to look out the window.

"It seems to me you haven't found the right subject," she continued. "You need a subject that goes beyond mere charm. You need a subject that is highly intelligent, sophisticated, complex, and yet has a touch of mystery mixed with danger. In other words, unique."

I peered back at her. "And who might that subject be?"

"Me, of course."

"Oh, hell."

"That wasn't exactly the reaction I had hoped for." She tapped Boulton on the shoulder with her stick. "That's the address across the street."

As Boulton aimed the Bentley into a parking space, between a dented pickup and a Chevy on blocks, she smiled benignly at me.

"Forget my idea, Miss Hill. I succumbed to a moment of whimsy. I was thinking about Holmes and Watson . . . Johnson and Boswell . . . Vance and Van Dine. Notice how equally famous they all are. You can't talk about Holmes without talking about the good doctor. But where are the women? You don't see that kind of strong, classical relationship between women. Women go off by themselves, like sick animals, and write pathetic little diaries in rented rooms. Poor women. Please, forget my idea."

"Sure." Boswell and Johnson. *Sure!* And who the hell were Vance and Van Dine? They sounded like a pair of figure skaters. Just get the codicil back, Maggie, and leave.

Glendale could be any small town in any state in America. In California it just happens to have popped up between Pasadena and

Hollywood. Wedgwood was a working-class street lined with small Spanish bungalows. The tile roofs gleamed a warm earth red in the sun. The lawns were neat and the sidewalks bumpy from the roots of old trees. Worn compact cars rested in some of the driveways.

Three small children stared in awe at the car through a chain link fence surrounding their yard. Next door to the children an Asian woman squatted on her square of lawn as if she were in a rice field, her claw-like hands plucking at weeds only she could see. She rose; ancient eyes took us in and lodged us in the vast history of her memory. It was the kind of neighborhood that made me feel embarrassed about being in a Bentley.

"Good morning," I said to her. She scurried into her house.

"You're not used to being the intruder, are you?" Claire asked.

"I think it's the car."

"It's the profession. The detective is always the intruder," she said flatly.

We walked across the street to the house.

"Wait out here," she commanded Boulton.

He stood guard on the little slab of lawn, looking every inch like Secret Service. Claire rang the bell.

"Do you really need him?" I whispered.

"I pay him to prove his masculinity so I don't have to prove mine."

The door opened. A middle-aged woman, in a pink knit dress and a valentine-dotted apron, peered through the screen door at us.

"Yes?"

"Excuse me," Claire said. "We're looking for a Mr. Bobby Alt."

The woman shifted uneasily. TV news droned, with artificial urgency, in the room behind her.

"Who are you?" she asked timidly.

Claire handed her a card. The woman wiped her hands on her apron before she took it.

"I don't understand."

"If we could just talk with you . . . Your son is not in any trouble. Bobby Alt is your son?"

"Yes."

Claire opened the screen door. The woman stood passively as we edged our way into the living room. Beige walls matched the beige rug which matched the beige sofa. The young blonde in lime-green shorts lying on the sofa didn't match. She dangled a chunky leg, her big toe digging at the sand-colored carpet. Brown eyes were riveted on the TV. She was maybe twenty.

"My daughter Robin."

Robin didn't look at us. Robin didn't move, except the one leg. She continued watching the news, one instant clip of disaster after another.

"Robin?" The mother tentatively approached her. "Robin?"

Robin was transfixed, her pupils large. Robin was stoned out of her head.

"Robin's concentrating. It's all right. We won't disturb her." She motioned for us to sit in two beige chairs in the corner of the room.

"I'll stand. No rest for the weary," she said. "Would you like some coffee? Tea?"

"No, thank you," I said.

We didn't take the chairs. Claire leaned elegantly on her walking stick as if she were watching a cricket match and asked, "Does your son still live at home?"

"No. I don't know where he lives. There's nothing wrong, is there?"

"When did you see him last?" Claire asked.

"About six months ago. He came to get his things. He got a new job. He's a very good boy."

Robin moaned and giggled. It was hard to tell if it was in reaction to her mother's observation, the television, or just a thought she'd never remember again.

Claire asked, "Did he tell you where he was working?"

"No." She looked hurt. "I pleaded with him to tell me. But he wouldn't. He just kept saying . . . he's got another . . . " Her eyes focused on her daughter, who had pulled herself up into a sitting position. "It's so difficult to raise children now," she sighed.

"There are places you can take her," I said.

"Places? I don't know what you mean. She's just watching television. As soon as she figures out what she's going to do with her life, she'll be fine. Things aren't like they used to be. Did you see the people in this neighborhood? Boat people! I'm living next door to boat people!"

Claire's voice was soothing. "Your daughter will do just fine. What did Bobby mean . . . he got another? Another what?"

Mrs. Alt nervously wiped her hands on her apron again.

"Mother! Another *mother!*" She spat out the word. Resentment glistened in her eyes. "I hate that word. I hate it! I wish to God I'd never been a mother!" She moved to the door and opened it. "I can't talk anymore. Please go."

I took one last look at Robin. On the table next to her was a large brass-framed picture. In it a bright-eyed Robin leaped toward the heavens, waving pom-poms and smiling victoriously in the sun. Now she stared dumbly at some revolutionaries in the Philippine jungles. The beige walls and the beige carpeting felt like quicksand.

We were back in the car and headed toward the Pasadena Presbyterian Church.

"Great," I said. "We found out Bobby Alt has acquired another mother."

"Not an easy thing to acquire if you already have one," Boulton said.

"I wonder if he would break into an apartment for his new mother," Claire mused.

8

When I was eleven, I did twenty Hail Marys for whispering to my girlfriends that Jesus's blood — painted dripping from his hands and feet on our church's cross — was the same color as Revlon's Love That Red.

There was no blood on the gold cross in the Pasadena Presbyterian Church. No Christ figure writhed in pain or ecstasy, those two emotions so interrelated in my religious upbringing. This cross was as clean and as sleek as a new hood ornament. Below the unadorned cross was the closed coffin of Ellis Kenilworth. Draped in a blanket of flowers and surrounded by enormous bouquets and wreaths, it looked like a float in the Rose Parade.

Claire and I sat in the back of the church. While an organ heaved and sighed sad chords, I pointed out the Kenilworths to her. They sat in the first pew. Sutton had his arm around Eleanor. Her thin shoulders quivered with grief. Judith sat as close to Brian Waingrove as his ungiving body would allow. The family doctor, the family lawyer, Aiko, and Maria sat nearby. None of the other mourners looked familiar to me. Most of them, meaning the men, had an air of functional importance like city bureaucrats.

"You don't see Patricia Kenilworth?" Claire asked.

"No. I had the feeling they wouldn't want her at the funeral — or anywhere else, for that matter."

"Why don't they get on with this? Or are they trying to give us an example of the limbo of eternity Ellis Kenilworth is experiencing?" she moaned, moving her long body uneasily in the hard, puritanical pew.

A woman sitting in front of us craned her head around, screwed up her powdered face into a knot of disdain, let Claire take a good look at it, then turned back to the cross and the coffin.

I concentrated on a stained-glass window. A white-robed saint with the most heavenly blue eyes and sexy, blond, surfer's hair cuddled a fluffy lamb in the crook of his arm. He looked like a veterinarian I knew who lived in Malibu. I'd dated him for a while. Nothing serious.

The minister appeared between the coffin and the pulpit. He wore a dark blue suit and a maroon silk tie. His thick, wavy hair was as white as Weber's bread. I like my men of God to wear collars and funny hats and kingly robes, like the Pope. I want to know that I'm in the presence of a man of God. I want to know whom I'm talking to.

When he spoke, his voice was as flat as the Midwest. "Those who trust in God shall understand the truth."

The oak doors opened. Sunlight plunged into the church, and with it came Patricia Kenilworth in tight-fitting black. A veil waved over her face like a dark mist. The diamond studs flashed. With her was a woman in a dove-gray suit; a wide-brimmed hat swooped down and covered her profile. Patricia hesitated, her body wavering, like an actress who has forgotten her lines. The woman in gray took her hand, and together they walked defiantly down the aisle. There was something familiar in the woman's undulating walk. I was sure I had met her before.

Claire whispered, "Patricia Kenilworth?"

"In the widow's weeds."

I had to give it to her — she walked all the way down to where the Kenilworths sat. The mourners stretched their necks for a better view. Whispers grew louder. The woman in gray forced the Kenilworths to stand as she and Patricia pushed into the pew.

The minister managed to continue: "We

cannot judge a man by his death. But we can judge a man by his life."

As the woman in gray moved into the pew, she turned and faced the congregation. I recognized her. I had spent many a lonely Wednesday night sitting on my bed, eating pizza, watching her on "Family Rites."

"Victoria Moor," I gasped.

"The actress?" Claire leaned forward.

"I saw her yesterday getting her star on Hollywood Boulevard."

Slowly the whispers turned to coughs, as the minister gave a glowing account of Ellis Kenilworth's life. Patricia Kenilworth was never mentioned. I sat and wondered what Victoria Moor was doing at Ellis Kenilworth's funeral. The minister's voice filtered into my thoughts.

"And now we must surrender Ellis Kenilworth into Your tender, wounded hands, O Lord, where You can comfort and listen to his moaning soul. Let us pray. Our Father . . ."

Moaning soul . . . I stared at the casket and I knew it was up to me to put Ellis Kenilworth to rest.

When the service was over, I started to get up. Claire stopped me. "We wait till the family leaves."

The mourners moved cautiously down the aisle toward the coffin and the Kenilworth family. One by one they paid their last respects and filed out. Some took a last look at Kenilworth. Most took a last look at Victoria Moor. Soon they were gone, and only the minister, the Kenilworths, Patricia, and the actress remained. We stayed in our pew in the back of the church, watching.

Eleanor Kenilworth rose shakily to her feet. Hard aquamarine eyes stared at Patricia and Victoria Moor. "How dare you come to his funeral! You have no right here!"

Patricia took the actress's hand. "I told you we shouldn't have come. Let's go."

"No, Mother. I have every right to see my father buried." Victoria Moor's voice was firm.

Surprised at what I'd just heard, I turned and looked at Claire. She slouched down in the pew, her hand resting on the handle of her walking stick, her face expressionless.

"Please leave," Judith begged. "Get out of our lives."

"That's impossible now, isn't it? Eleanor's made it impossible," Victoria said.

Anger transformed Eleanor's frail body to one of vigor.

"You killed him! You killed him!" she repeated fiercely.

"His own guilt killed him," the actress snapped back. "And I'm glad it did."

Eleanor raised a black-gloved hand and

slapped Victoria Moor across the mouth, knocking her hat off. Bleached-blond curls bounced voluptuously. Sutton and Judith didn't move.

The minister turned and looked at the coffin as if Ellis could see how unseemly his funeral had become. He mumbled, "Tragedy makes us do things we may — "

"Stop using euphemisms! My son blew his head off," Eleanor screamed.

Waingrove leaped into action. "Take her out through the rectory. I'll have the car brought around," he commanded Judith.

But she didn't go near her mother. Brian looked at Sutton. He didn't move, either. And I realized Sutton was afraid of his mother. As if reaching out to a snarling dog, he slowly, carefully, put his arm around her.

"If only you could have just left him alone! If you could have just let him be mine," Eleanor sobbed as the minister guided her and Sutton through the rectory door. Judith followed at a safe distance.

Brian picked up Victoria's hat and handed it to her.

"Thank you, darling," she said.

"You could at least have told me you were planning to attend."

"Don't talk to me the way you talk to Judith."

They stared at one another.

"You'd better go and tell the driver to bring the car around. If I finish shooting in time, I may see you after the symposium," she said.

Brian sniffed the air and went out the side door of the church.

The two women turned and faced the casket. Their backs were to us.

"You were born out of love, Victoria. You must believe that." Patricia took her daughter's hand.

"I was born — no, was *created* out of your anger."

"My despair. You'll at least give me that."

"I wonder if Frankenstein created his monster out of despair."

"Stop it! You are a beauty. You are *my* beauty."

"I want to go, Mother."

The two women turned away from the casket and started up the aisle. They saw us. For a moment they froze, heads tilted at right angles. Both had their left hands raised to their throats. They looked alike. But it was more than a family resemblance — it was a surgical resemblance. Their tiny noses had been sculpted by the same plastic surgeon. Noses designed for display. Breathing was secondary. The green eyes, wide and lifted, gave them both a sly, startled look. The only difference was age.

"Oh . . . it's Ellis's secretary . . . isn't it?" Patricia said, peering nervously up the aisle at us.

Claire and I stood. "Maggie Hill," I said.

"That's right. So nice of you to come." She took her daughter's hand and moved toward us. "Do you have something for me?" she asked innocently.

"We would like to talk to you," Claire said, handing Patricia her card.

She read it, then handed it to Victoria.

"I usually know when I have an audience." The actress handed the card back to Claire.

"Did you ever find your codicil?" Patricia asked me.

"No."

"You have had a run of bad luck."

"Somebody else told me that."

"We'll talk with them in the limo, Mother."

As we went outside, I took one last look at Kenilworth's coffin. I thought I heard the moaning of his soul.

The sun turned everything white. The few remaining mourners blurred in the glare. I put on my sunglasses, and slowly the world came back into focus.

"People are looking at me, Mother. Hurry," Victoria said nervously.

"I'm trying, darling."

The mourners herded together and began

to move slowly down the slope of lawn toward Victoria. Their somber gray faces brightened with the hope of touching a star. One woman already had her printed funeral service folded and ready for an autograph. She waved a pen at Victoria as if it were a magic wand.

The long white limousine was parked in front of the Bentley. Boulton leaned against the side of the dinosaur, watching.

"Follow us if needed," Claire said to him. He nodded and got into the Bentley.

Victoria's chauffeur held the door for us. He reminded me of the muscle-bound guy painted on the rug-cleaning van. Mounds of biceps pushed against the dark sleeves of his jacket. Peroxided hair was cut perfectly. I could see only my own sunglasses in his reflective sunglasses.

Patricia curled into the corner of the limo. Claire sat next to her. Victoria took the other corner. I got the jump seat.

"Let's get out of here. Drive till I tell you to stop," Victoria commanded the chauffeur.

We moved slowly away from the church. Facing the back window, I watched the Bentley follow us, and the mourners, teetering on the edge of the curb like tightrope walkers, stretching their necks for one last look at Victoria Moor.

"I have a two o'clock call at the studio, so I

don't have time to wander aimlessly around Pasadena. What do you want?" she asked. The green eyes were as hard as emeralds.

"Miss Hill's apartment was broken into," Claire said. "Nothing was taken. We think they were looking for Ellis Kenilworth's suicide note. Your mother made her interest in that note very clear to Miss Hill."

"You're accusing Mother of breaking and entering?" Victoria laughed. "Look at those nails. She can hardly open a refrigerator." She held up Patricia's soft white hand, displaying the long, pointed, mauve-colored nails.

Claire smiled. "Yes. I see what you mean. It's just that your mother made it clear that she would reward Miss Hill if she knew where the suicide note was."

"And does Miss Hill need rewarding?" Victoria asked, staring boldly into Claire's eyes.

"Call me Maggie," I said. The three women ignored me.

"I think it's possible that by tomorrow or the next day at the latest we will be in a position to discuss the matter with you," Claire said.

I tried to keep my face passive while I wondered what the hell she was doing.

Patricia leaned toward me. "You did take it. You had to. Even Eleanor said as much."

"Mother!" Victoria glared at her. "Why

145

don't we wait and see if they have it."

Patricia curled back into her corner. I could feel her cat eyes watching me through the wisp of black.

"I've been dying to ask this question," Victoria said. "Do all women private eyes carry a walking stick?" She had turned as chatty as a girlfriend, and like most girlfriends she didn't wait for an answer. "I used to carry a walking stick. It's true!" she added as if we'd questioned her. "When I was twenty I was raped." She said this like I would say, When I was twenty I was an English major in college.

"Victoria . . . don't . . . " Patricia warned.

"Mother, as usual, turned a terrible situation into a situation of opportunity." The perfectly lined, painted, and glossed lips pressed together.

"Please . . . " Patricia begged.

The pink lips parted. "She decided that my rape would make great press. But she had to make my rape unique. I mean, what's another rape, right? Of course she had the good taste to tone it down a bit. Mother decided that the story should be that the man tried to attack me and all I had to defend myself with was a tatty old umbrella. But I was successful in beating off my attacker. Actually, the man succeeded again and again . . . well, that's another story. We had very little money, but she

146

had a yellow suede outfit made up with a yellow suede walking stick to match. Then she wrangled an interview with this syndicated columnist. Four martinis at lunch and he'd print anything you told him. We told him that I always carried a walking stick because I was so distraught by this man's attempted rape. You know — if a man tried it again, I'd hit him over the head with my cane." Victoria laughed. Patricia cringed. I didn't blame her.

"Mother told him I had a polka-dot walking stick to match my polka-dot bikini. Do you believe it? A walking stick to match every outfit! The guy bought it — though I think we paid for five martinis. I was in every newspaper from here to some little town in Maine. Me and my walking stick, fighting off men because I was so sexy. So beautiful."

"It worked!" Patricia blurted. *"You've* worked. You've never stopped. You're a star."

"Television star," Victoria corrected.

"The only kind left," Patricia snapped.

I couldn't believe what I was hearing. And Claire was sitting there listening and nodding her head as if she were attending a lecture on nuclear fission. Why didn't she ask about Bobby Alt?

"That's really interesting," I said. "But do you know a man — "

"Actually, I carry a walking stick because I've had my female parts excised," Claire said, interrupting me.

That put a damper on the conversation. Patricia curled away from Claire. Victoria stared out the blackened window. I stared out mine. I used to think that they darkened the windows in limos so the public couldn't see into the car. But now I decided it was to keep the people in the limo from seeing too much of the outside. The people who rode around in these cars needed reality tinted.

"I wish I didn't bleed," Victoria said to no one in particular.

"By the way, how long have you known Brian Waingrove?" Claire asked.

"Mother went to one of his symposiums. He now manages our money."

"Does he manage the Kenilworths' money?"

"When he found out I was the daughter of Ellis Kenilworth, he tried to ingratiate himself with Father. I told him it wouldn't work."

"Judith thinks she's in love with him," I said.

Victoria's glossy pink lips formed a smile. "If one road is closed to Brian, he always tries another. It's what makes him so good with money. You can imagine how awful he felt when he discovered that the Kenilworths didn't have any."

"They once owned the hotel where I reside," Claire said. "I'd think their profits from that sale would have left them quite well off."

Patricia smiled. "They sold that monstrosity in the fifties. Nobody in the family ever worked. They had no concept of how to handle money. They made bad investments. Thirty-some years go by and you have no money left. Victoria and I are wealthier than the Kenilworths. Of course, we work for our money, and we never make bad investments." She licked her lips as if she could taste the money.

"So the coin collection is all they have left?" Claire asked.

"The house . . . some jewelry . . . but according to Maggie they don't even own the collection. She says Ellis willed it to you."

"Do you think Waingrove knew the collection was worth four million?" Claire tapped the top of her walking stick.

"I'm sure. Why else would he bother with Judith?" Victoria asked.

"I got the impression, listening to you and Waingrove in the church, that he's more than just your business manager," I said.

"I allow him into my bed."

"And you don't care if he plays around with Judith?"

"That's just business to him," Victoria said.

"Very romantic." I smiled.

"I hope he breaks what's left of her shriveled little heart," Patricia said.

"What do you think Ellis wanted me to discover for my four million?" Claire looked at both women.

Patricia turned away and again stared out the window.

"You're the detective, not me. Pull over here," Victoria commanded the driver.

"Would you mind if your chauffeur helped me out? I'm still not quite up to snuff," Claire said.

"Of course. Mother gave Maggie our phone number, so you know where to reach us."

"We'll be getting in touch."

Patricia turned from the window and faced Claire. "When?" Her hand reached out for Claire's wrist.

"Mother . . . " Victoria warned. Patricia recoiled.

The car door opened. The driver helped Claire out.

Patricia lifted the black veil and looked at me. "I wouldn't trust the Kenilworths if I were you. Any of them."

"Does that include you?"

"I'm not a Kenilworth." Patricia jerked the

veil back down over her face.

"Come along, Miss Hill." Claire's voice was firm.

Not having had my female parts excised, I crawled out of the car on my own.

We stood on the curb and watched the white limo pull away, the mother and daughter two shadows in the backseat. Boulton pulled up and got out of the car.

I turned on Claire. "What the hell was that all about? Why didn't you ask about Bobby Alt? We didn't learn one thing!"

"Bobby Alt is coming to see us after he drops Victoria and her mother off at the studio," she said, placidly looking up at a crazy-eyed chicken holding a deep-fried drumstick in its feathered hand. It smiled down at us maniacally from the top of a fast-food dump.

"Where are we, Boulton?" she asked.

"We just crossed from Pasadena into Arcadia."

"Arcadia." She repeated the name. "The city does have a pastoral flair," she laughed. But I didn't join in. I was trying to figure out how she knew the driver was Bobby Alt.

9

Claire settled into her corner of the Bentley. I sat silently in my corner.

"Drive to the Kenilworths', Boulton." She leaned toward me. "Miss Hill, I admit that the one quality I lack is a sense of humor."

"You lack a quality?"

"But even you must acknowledge that what I said back there was rather witty. It had irony, double entendre, and a certain je ne sais quoi. Of course, the joke does depend on one's standing in front of a large chicken and being in a city named Arcadia all at the same time. But then, great wit comes from seizing the moment and —"

"Nobody said anything."

"I didn't expect words, just a slight chuckle."

"I'm not talking about your joke. I'm talking about Patricia and Victoria. They didn't say anything. The driver didn't say anything. How did you know he was Bobby Alt?"

"It's not what they didn't say. It's what they didn't *do*. Patricia and Victoria didn't do this." She turned a handle, and a window rolled up between Boulton and us.

"He can't hear what we are saying, or at least our voices are muffled. In *their* new limousine, all they have to do is push a button. I have to crank," she sniffed.

"Since I only drive a Honda, I'm not up on the nuances of limo etiquette."

"Snobbery in any form dulls the senses, Miss Hill. You should try to watch it."

"Snob! I'm not a snob. You're the snob! Some poor middle-class jerk makes a comment about the wealthy and he's called a snob or he's labeled jealous instead of astute. That's how people are kept in their place in this country." The cheerleader in my high school was leaping toward the heavens, sneering down at me. I stopped.

Claire's dark eyes shined mischievously.

"Oh, hell, go on."

"Patricia is desperate for the suicide note which Ellis wrote on the back of a photograph. She doesn't know Ellis's last words. She thinks you do. She and her daughter have no idea what we are going to say. Our discussion could be very revealing, and yet neither one thinks it important to have the conversation in private. Why?"

"Because there's no reason for privacy if the chauffeur is the one who broke into my apartment."

"Exactly."

"But the limo could be rented. He could just be any hired driver."

"Before I got into the car I looked at the back fender. Limousine companies stencil numbers on the fenders of their cars to show they are commercially operated. There was no stenciled number. The car is privately owned — I assume by Victoria or her mother, or both. Therefore, the driver must be in their service."

"He's taller, bigger, blonder than his description."

"In this day and age, when the human body is considered architecture — not simply flesh and blood — a man or woman can change their façade rather easily. All those muscles only make him *appear* taller. He is still five foot seven. Being a tall woman has made me an excellent judge of height. When I was a young girl I could calculate to within an eighth of an inch just how much taller I was than each of my classmates. I am five and three-quarter inches taller than you, which would make you five foot six and a quarter."

I stared at her in amazement. I was five foot six and a quarter.

"When he helped me from the car, I slipped my card in his hand and told him he'd left a fingerprint in your apartment. If he didn't want to be arrested for breaking and entering, he should meet me at the cottage in about an hour and a half. His tan bleached before my very eyes." She all but smacked her refined lips.

"Why didn't you confront Bobby Alt in the car? Demand an explanation from Victoria and her mother?" I asked.

"Because we don't know the subject of the photograph or the content of the suicide note. They think *you* do. I'm hoping, away from their presence, Bobby will describe for us exactly what he was looking for in your apartment."

"You mean, tell us who is in the photograph? Then that means Patricia and Victoria would have to know who was in the photo."

"Yes. How else would Bobby know what he was looking for? God knows we're all photograph-silly in this country. If he didn't have an idea of the subject matter, he might come back to them with a picture of you and your ex-husband. And you might've written on the back of the photo 'till death do us part.' You see?"

"You're right. You don't have a sense of humor."

"But what those two women do not know is the content of the suicide note. And they obviously would go to any length to discover it."

"And you think that information will eventually lead us to who took the codicil?"

155

"In our first step is also our last step, Miss Hill."

I leaned back and looked out the window. Okay, I was impressed. She wasn't just an eccentric. She was good. I saw a dry-cleaning shop, a gas station, an old man in a snappy straw hat sitting on a bus bench, a realty company, a woman guiding her three little ones in front of her like a mother swan guiding her cygnets down a river. I saw a block of ordinary life pass by me. I imagined a gangly young Claire desperately calculating her schoolmates' heights. A tall young girl could never be ordinary.

"Can't you just call me Maggie?" I asked her, still looking out the window.

"I'm uncomfortable with the familiar," she sighed.

There were a lot of Cadillacs, Lincolns, and Chryslers parked in front of the Kenilworth house. There was also Waingrove's silver Mercedes.

Boulton stopped the Bentley opposite the house.

"When you worked for the Kenilworths, where did you park your car?" Claire asked.

I pointed to a big, shaggy oak. "Usually under that tree, for shade."

"Anybody leaving the house would see your car?"

"Yes. Why?"

She didn't answer. "I'm interested in finding out how that retarded young man . . . what's his name?"

"Jerry."

" . . . Jerry got into the garden unattended."

She tapped her stick on the back of the front seat. "Boulton, while we are paying the grieving family our last respects, drive around to the back of the house. See if you can find some sort of access. Check out the neighboring houses. Maybe you can find out where Jerry lives."

"Yes, madam," Boulton said, looking in the rearview mirror. He was talking to her, but his brown eyes were on me.

As we made our way up the slope of lawn to the house, Boulton turned the Bentley down a side street toward the back of the Kenilworth house. I knocked on the big mahogany door. It was Waingrove who opened it. "The family is not expecting you," he said imperiously.

"The last time I saw you you were taking over Kenilworth's office. Now you're taking over Aiko's duties. Is there anything you don't do?" We stared at one another, no love lost.

"Miss Hill, please. I'm Claire Conrad," she announced.

He looked at her as if an imaginary person had suddenly come alive.

"Brian Waingrove." He shook her hand, then quickly brushed his palm down the side of his trousers as if he were sweeping off lint. But I had the feeling he was really brushing off the lingering sensation of the female touch — a touch he didn't like. "The Kenilworths' lawyer is here. He wants to talk to you," he said.

"I want to talk to him," Claire said.

We followed him into the library. The room was filled with somber people frantically eating and drinking, trying to prove they were still alive. The French doors stood open. Guests spilled out onto the veranda. Waingrove moved through the group of people, nodding his head and smiling like a politician. He led us onto the veranda. Judith and Sutton leaned against the balustrade, listening intently to a large, barrel-chested man talk. Behind them the bushy green seal clapped. The fish jumped. The cat curled in sleep. Pegasus flew.

Judith tugged at Sutton's coat sleeve. He peered in our direction and smiled. "Maggie, so glad you could come," he said warmly. "Ellis would have wanted it."

"Thank you."

"This is Claire Conrad," Waingrove said quickly.

Judith stiffened. Sutton continued smiling.

"How nice to meet you," he said. "I'm Sutton Kenilworth, and this is my sister, Judith."

"How do you do?" Claire asked. Her gaze moved from the brother and sister to the garden.

"I think this is in very bad taste," Judith hissed at me.

The barrel-chested man cleared his throat.

"And this is David Proctor," Sutton said. "Our lawyer." Proctor wore a tan suede vest dotted with food stains under a rumpled tweed jacket.

Gray-blue eyes scrutinized Claire. "I have made inquiries on behalf of the Kenilworth family. Found out you're a private investigator. Well respected."

"If not well liked," she said, still surveying the garden. "This is very whimsical topiary. Almost child-like."

"I preferred the old rose garden," Sutton said sadly. "The topiary was Ellis's idea."

"From what Miss Hill has told me, your brother doesn't sound like a man of whimsy."

"Why don't you just tell her what the reality is," Waingrove snapped at Proctor.

"Reality?" The lawyer's eyes turned cagey. "I'll tell Miss Conrad what *our* reality is. She may have a different one." He threw his head back and laughed. Fleshy chin shook. Nearby guests turned and stared.

"David, please," Judith said. Waingrove sniffed.

Proctor stopped laughing. "Sorry, Judith. Why don't we all take a little stroll in the garden?" Like a fatherly shepherd, he herded us toward the steps. "I sometimes think if my roots weren't so firmly planted in old Pasadena, Judith, you'd fire me."

"Mother makes those decisions," she said.

"Fire me for somebody a little slicker." He slapped an arm around Waingrove. "Like this fellow."

"I'm not a lawyer." Waingrove sidestepped the bear-like embrace and adjusted his jacket and tie.

"Thank God, thank God. Too many lawyers around."

We started down the steps, but Claire continued down the veranda.

"This way, Miss Conrad," Proctor yelled after her.

Claire didn't respond. She stopped in front of the large arched window, then opened the door and went into Ellis's office. We waited at the bottom of the steps.

"What is she doing?" Sutton asked.

"She's an ill-mannered woman," Judith whined.

"She's looking out the window," Proctor said.

The sun bore down on us. My beige dress was beginning to cling to my body as if it had a life of its own. Waingrove moved next to me. He spoke in a low voice. "What is she up to?"

"I'm not sure. Maybe she's trying to get lucky, like Valcovich." I smiled.

He edged closer. His breath smelled drugstore sweet. "Give it up, Maggie, before people stop being polite." He moved quickly away and stood by Judith. Sweat trickled down my back. It felt cold.

Claire came out of the office and strode down the steps. "You were saying?" she asked Proctor.

"I wasn't, but I will. I checked with Roger Valcovich, and he said as far as he knew there never was a codicil," Proctor said.

"Yes, yes, I know," she sighed. "He came to the house on behalf of Miss Hill."

"Exactly."

"Excuse me." Claire walked at a fast pace down a graveled path between phalanxes of bushy green animals. We trailed after her.

Claire stopped and looked back up the path toward the office window. Shadowed by a seal and a giraffe, she began poking her stick at a section of the hedge that ran along the back of the garden.

"This is the only part of the hedge I could

see from the window," she explained. "Right between the giraffe and the monkey."

"It's a seal," Sutton corrected.

"With ears?"

"Fins."

"Is there a gap or an opening along here?" She poked at the hedge.

"Yes, there is a gap somewhere." Sutton's face was blotchy in the bright sun. "But I don't see what that has to do —"

"Why don't we get back to the subject at hand," Waingrove said. A single line of perspiration ran from his temple down into his shirt collar. Judith dabbed at it with her handkerchief. He jerked away from her.

"Here is the access." Claire disappeared through the hedge, then reappeared. "So this is how Jerry gets into the garden," she said.

Sutton stared at Claire.

"I don't see what Jerry has to do with any of the outrageous accusations made by Maggie," Judith said.

"I think, Proctor, we should get back to the reality of the situation," Waingrove persisted.

Claire turned on him. "But Jerry is a reality. The day of the suicide Miss Hill left her purse on the veranda. Now, this unfortunate young man might have wandered in through the opening. Or maybe he never left the garden. Without understanding the importance of his actions, he might have looked in Miss Hill's purse and taken the codicil. Have you asked his parents?" She stared at Judith and Sutton.

"That seems very farfetched," Sutton said.

"Especially since the piece of paper you're talking about does not exist," Waingrove said.

"And if I can prove it does?" Claire asked the lawyer.

Proctor wagged his head sadly. "A man who sits down and gives a four-million-dollar collection to a woman he doesn't know and then goes upstairs and kills himself, couldn't be in his right mind. I hope that makes our position clear."

"I would guess Ellis was in an angry state of mind. Some angry men kill their families first and then kill themselves." Claire looked at Sutton and Judith. "You're very lucky he only took a coin collection away from you. I hope that makes my position clear."

Sutton stepped back from her. Judith's face turned a sickly white.

"Get off my property!" yelled a voice from the other side of the hedge. There were scuffling sounds. The hedge shook violently. A man, hammer clutched in his hand, flew backwards through the opening into the garden. He sprawled onto the ground. Judith let out a small scream. Boulton plunged through the hedge. Jerry scampered after him, followed by a woman with mad ice-blue eyes and straggly brown hair. An old man, toothless and drooling, appeared last. He wore one shoe and carried the other.

The man with the hammer scrambled to his feet, sandy red hair glistening in the sun, eyes blinking with uncertainty and fear. He faced Boulton. They circled one another. The man bounced the hammer in his hand, feeling the weight of it. Boulton's eyes were deadly impersonal — the eyes of a trained killer. Some of the guests, still balancing sandwiches and drinks, had moved down from the veranda and stared in fascinated horror at the two men and their surrealistic entourage.

"Drop the hammer, you little sod!" Boulton said. His English accent was as out of place as everything else.

For a moment the man looked like he was going to. Then he shook his head. And I knew an age-old ritual had begun between Boulton and this man — and both were going to see it through to its bloody conclusion. The man lunged. The clawed end of the hammer glinted in the sunlight as he swung. Boulton raised his left forearm, blocking the blow of the hammer. He smashed his right fist into the man's face. Legs crumpled. The man went down and didn't move. The woman with the mad blue eyes began to laugh and clap like an insane fan at a wrestling match. The old man pounded his shoe on his head. Jerry swayed. The guests moved uneasily, like nervous cattle bumping into one another.

"Get them out of here! Make them go away!" It was Eleanor Kenilworth's voice.

We all turned and looked toward the house. Upstairs in the glassed-in rotunda a window had been thrown open. Eleanor leaned out, face contorted with rage, screaming, "Make them leave! Make them leave!" Rage turned to deep, violent sobbing. Aiko and Maria rushed to her and gently pulled her away. Aiko shut the window.

"Do something," Judith pleaded to her brother, then turned to Waingrove. "Please."

"You and Proctor take the guests back into the house," Waingrove commanded her.

Proctor took Judith's hand. "Come, come — the show is over, ladies and gentlemen." He guided the milling, questioning group toward the veranda.

Sutton approached Boulton, who was pulling the man to his feet. "Release Mr. Erwin. I demand to know who you are," he asked awkwardly. Authority didn't come easily to him.

"He's my butler and chauffeur," Claire said

simply. She was leaning on her walking stick in the best Ascot tradition.

"This is inexcusable," Waingrove said.

A Chicano woman moved cautiously through the gap in the hedge. Her dark eyes shone with fear. She put an arm around Jerry and took the hand of the mad-eyed woman. She looked at Erwin. A big, ugly lump was forming under his left eye.

"Take the poor souls home," he mumbled to her.

She guided them back through the hedge.

"The younger one's Jerry," I said to Claire. My mouth was dry and I sounded out of breath.

Erwin started talking. "This man was snooping around my house. I'm fixing the fence so the poor souls can't get out and he won't leave me alone. Keeps asking questions." He never raised his head high enough to look anybody in the eye.

"We're very sorry about this, Mr. Erwin," Sutton said. He turned and looked at me as if I had betrayed him. "I'm sorry, but I'm going to have to ask you and your friends to leave."

"I think we should take advantage of this situation and get a few things straightened out," Waingrove said officiously. "Mr. Erwin, I'm Brian Waingrove, a friend of the Kenilworth family. There have been some accusations made about Jerry."

Erwin quickly looked up, then back at the grass. "Jerry's never done anything wrong. Doesn't know how."

Waingrove looked at me with the same officiousness. "What time did you leave your purse in the garden?"

"From about one o'clock to about two," I answered.

Waingrove studied Erwin. "Could Jerry have come into the garden, the day before yesterday, and taken a piece of paper from her purse?"

Erwin shifted his weight. "All the poor souls go to special school from eleven to three each day."

Waingrove glowed with triumph. He turned on Claire. "Now, you may leave."

Claire smiled. "You've been very helpful. I'd like to ask Mr. Erwin a few more questions, if you don't mind."

"I do mind. And so does Sutton," he added quickly.

"Miss Conrad wishes to ask some questions," Boulton said.

"I don't give a damn what Miss Conrad wishes," Waingrove said. Boulton moved toward him. Waingrove stepped back. "You don't intimidate me." Waingrove's eyes never left Boulton.

"Yes I do," Boulton said matter-of-factly.

"I don't see, Brian, how a few more questions would matter at this point," Sutton offered nervously.

"Are you Jerry's father?" Claire asked Erwin.

"I could breed better than that." He looked quickly at the men, his eyes seeking masculine approval before they looked back down. "They're wards of the state. I'm paid to care for them in my house. And I do a good job," he added defensively.

"I think I can explain," Sutton offered. "About three, four . . . maybe even five years ago . . . time goes so fast . . . somebody in Sacramento decided that certain mental patients . . . the ones who are not dangerous . . . could be spread throughout southern California. The people who live here were not pleased at the time — Mother and I among them. But the neighborhood was already changing." He shrugged his shoulders helplessly. "Mother . . . well, they still upset her. But, I must say, the poor souls, as Mr. Erwin calls them, haven't caused any problems."

"What state hospital do they come from?" Claire asked.

Erwin rubbed at his chin. "I don't know. Different ones."

"You know that Ellis Kenilworth is dead?"

"Yes."

"Who told you to fix your fence?"

"Nobody." Again the eyes darted toward Sutton.

"I did," Sutton said. "Ellis was the only one who enjoyed Jerry's company."

Claire studied him. "Why did he enjoy his company?"

"We are a family that doesn't express our emotions easily. Ellis especially. I think that's why he liked Jerry. He was fascinated by his simplicity." A tone of superiority crept into Sutton's voice. "His primitiveness."

"His innocence?"

"Yes, you could put it that way." He looked at Erwin. "Your eye is swelling. Would you like to see our doctor?"

"I'd like to go."

"You may leave," Claire said.

Erwin picked up his hammer and without looking back slipped through the hedge.

"By the way," Claire said to Sutton, "it must be exciting to have such a famous niece."

"Niece?"

"Victoria Moor."

"I don't think of her as family. But yes, I guess she is my niece. We rarely see one another."

Claire reached in her pocket. "My card. In case you need to get in touch with me. I live quite close to you."

"Oh . . . the hotel . . . things do change . . . we never should've sold it. Life would be so different. Have you heard what they plan to do with the hotel?"

"I think they've sold it to the Japanese, who will tear it down and rebuild, of course."

"Of course. Times change," he said sadly. "Well, good afternoon." He turned and looked at me as if I were somewhere far away from him. "Goodbye, Maggie." He and Waingrove walked back to the house.

"Where is the car, Boulton?" Claire asked.

He sauntered to the hedge. "This way, madam."

"Oh, God. Come along, Miss Hill."

I followed her through the privets into an alley lined with garbage cans. The alley was a block long. The Kenilworth property ran about three-quarters of the block. Opposite us was a small house. A wood fence surrounded the backyard. The house was flanked by apartments on the right and two larger houses in need of paint on the left.

"Is that where Jerry lives?" Claire asked Boulton.

"Yes. The house faces Beech Street. I got the address. Testy bloke."

"More nervous than testy, Boulton."

We walked down the alley to the Bentley. The damp, bitter smell of garbage mixed with the sweet, fresh smell of fruit trees. Flies circled like miniature vultures. We got into the car.

I stared at Boulton. "You've got blood on the side of your face. "

He peered at himself in the mirror. "So I do. He must've nicked me with the hammer."

I leaned back in my corner and watched him wipe at the side of his face. I remembered a fight Neil had been in. We were in a bar where policemen hang out, and he and this other cop got into it. Over what . . . it doesn't matter. They punched each other silly. Blood poured down their faces. Exhausted, they collapsed into each other's arms, holding one another, crying. As a woman I'd never felt so isolated.

Boulton turned around, his big brown eyes taking me in.

The blood was gone.

"Better, Maggie?"

10

We drove back to the cottage. The white limo was there. Bobby Alt leaned against the front fender, head tilted back toward the sun, reflective glasses pushed on top of his orangy-blond hair, eyes shut, white shirt open to the top of his tarnished brass belt buckle. A black chauffeur's jacket was folded neatly on the spread of white hood. Boulton let us out. He took the car around to the garage in the back of the house.

Alt opened his eyes, blinked, and stretched his muscular, tanned arms, puffing his broad chest. "I can almost feel myself growing under the sun." His voice was thick with self-satisfaction. "Your maid wouldn't let me in." Self-satisfaction turned to hurt.

"Gerta's instructed not to let visitors in while I'm gone. Button your shirt," Claire said flatly.

His head tilted to one side. His mouth curved open, revealing a flash of teeth as white as the limo he drove. "My sex appeal bother you?"

"Wasted effort bothers me." She walked down the stairs and pushed the doorbell with the tip of her walking stick. Gerta peered out and let her in.

Unperturbed, Alt transferred his efforts to me. Eyes playing with mine, he slowly moved his hands up his chest, buttoning his shirt. He had spent a lot of time looking into the mirror getting that flagrantly sexy pose just right.

"Do I bother you?" He dropped his arm to his side. His hand brushed his crotch.

"Only if you're the jerk who ransacked my apartment and destroyed my belongings."

His eyes widened, making him look like a surprised little boy. Giggling, he grabbed his jacket and bounced down the stairs. There was something disturbing about Bobby Alt. And it wasn't his sex appeal.

I dragged behind him, watching his broad shoulders, narrow waist, tight little ass. I needed a bath. I needed to lie down. I needed to get out of this ugly beige dress. I was tired. I was tired of men. Tired of their big arms around me. Tired of their big brown eyes on me. Tired of their manly rituals. Tired of their overt poses. Tired of their neediness. Tired of their seductions, rejections, and betrayals. Tired of their tight little asses — especially asses that looked better than mine.

Claire imperiously graced her Queen Anne

chair. The crown would never be too heavy for her. Bobby sat among the wine-colored pillows, stroking his right thigh. The guy couldn't leave himself alone. I sat on the sofa across from him. Boulton leaned against the big round table in back of him.

Claire fixed her eyes on Bobby. "You dislike classical music with a passion."

He paused in the feeling of his thigh. "Huh?"

"Is it true that you dislike classical music?"

"It gives me stress. You can't get a hold of music like that. It keeps moving away from you. I need music my body can feel. You brought me here to discuss music?" Another flash of thick white teeth.

"Miss Hill had classical music playing in her apartment."

"Good for her."

He continued stroking his thigh and let his eyes play coy with mine. It was his eyes that disturbed me. They didn't fit his overt sexuality. He had the eyes of an eager, untroubled child. Relentlessly innocent eyes. Virgin eyes.

"She had classical music on when you broke into her apartment," Claire said.

The innocent eyes blinked at her. "My being here doesn't mean I did anything. I just came to hear what you have to say. That's all." He leaned back on the sofa pillows and

174

stretched his arms, pleased with himself.

"The classical music put undue stress on you, so you changed to a station that played music your body could feel. Suddenly there was a banging on the door. The landlady was screaming at you, demanding you change the station or else she'd come in with a pass key. You rushed to the radio and changed the station back."

Lines formed around his mouth and showed across his forehead. He raised his guiltless eyes to Claire.

"A landlady hears music she doesn't like — what does that have to do with me? Are you saying she saw me in the room?"

"No."

"Then I don't think there's anything more to talk about."

He stood up. Boulton put his hands on Bobby's shoulders and shoved him back down onto the sofa.

"Hey! What's going on here?!"

"Sometime before the landlady started pounding on the door, you took off your gloves. I can only assume you were warm or they were causing you undue stress. In your haste to change the station you forgot to put on your gloves."

The lines tugged at the corners of his mouth, drawing it down. "I don't get it."

"As I told you, you left your fingerprints on the radio. We had a policeman friend of Miss Hill's check the fingerprints and up popped your name."

"You told the police?" He looked shocked and betrayed.

"As of this moment, Miss Hill hasn't pressed charges. But if she doesn't like the way you answer my questions she will."

"And if she does like my answers?"

"I'll think about it," I said.

"That's no kind of deal!" He started to stand, remembered Boulton and thought better of it.

"Who told you to go to Miss Hill's apartment? Patricia Kenilworth?" Claire crossed her long legs and gave him a sideways glance.

"Not exactly."

"Terrible answer," I said.

"Victoria wanted me to go. Patricia didn't think it was a good idea."

"What were you looking for?" Claire asked.

"A photograph with some writing on the back of it."

"Not good enough," I said.

"It's the truth! Look, Victoria showed me a photograph — said you had a duplicate, and that it was hers and she wanted it back."

"Describe the photograph," Claire said.

He giggled, and his lips spread into a depraved smile. The eyes remained naive. "She and some guy were going at it — not exactly *doing* it, but pretty hot." He went at his thigh again.

"And who was this man?" Claire asked.

"I don't know."

"Stupid answer." I decided to sound bored.

"It's not a stupid answer. She didn't tell me his name."

"Very stupid answer," I yawned.

"You got yesterday's paper? *L.A. Times?* I saw his picture in there. Now, that's a good answer." He stretched triumphantly.

Claire went to the big table and took a newspaper from under other papers and handed it to him. Slowly, he went through the paper page by page. He lovingly licked his index finger before turning each page. I had the feeling he was getting off on it. Since I hadn't read the paper yesterday, I had no idea what famous person was in there. I wondered if Brian Waingrove was famous enough. The famous, the rich, the poor, and the crazy are the only people ever written about in the newspapers.

"This is him!"

Claire took the paper. "Are you positive?"

"Yeah."

Claire handed it to me. I stared at a picture of Ellis Kenilworth smiling happily from his two-column obituary. I slammed the paper down on the coffee table.

"I don't believe it! It can't be." I looked at Bobby, his eyes wide and blameless. "I don't like your answer. You better come up with a better one."

"That's the only answer there is."

"Kenilworth would not . . . not with his own . . . do you know Victoria Moor is his daughter?!"

"Hey, I just drive her. I don't know . . . *daughter?*"

He thought about that for moment. The corners of his mouth turned up, and the lines disappeared. Revelation made Bobby Alt look younger. "You mean *insex?*" he asked breathlessly.

"Yeah, I mean *insex*. And I think you're lying through your caps."

"These are my real teeth!"

"I'm calling the police!"

"I'm not lying! I'm not!" He turned to Claire and pleaded, "Victoria showed me the photograph so I'd know what to look for. I swear on my mother's grave that's the man in the photograph."

I leaped up. "We talked to your mother this morning. Unless you buried her between then and now you're a liar."

"All right! I only said that 'cause you think

178

I'm lying and I'm not. I'm not!"

"Where's the phone?" I demanded wildly. Anger mixed with some sort of deep hurt I couldn't get hold of, and I knew I was losing control. "Where's the goddamn phone?"

"On the table," Claire said quietly.

Bobby scooted along the edge of the sofa closer to Claire and babbled, "Don't let her call them. I'm telling the truth. I swear to God! Ask Victoria. Ask her!"

I pushed past Boulton and grabbed the phone. "You're lying. I know Ellis Kenilworth!"

"Do you, Miss Hill?" Claire asked.

I stared into her calm, inquisitive eyes. *Did I know Ellis Kenilworth?*

"Oh, hell." I slammed the phone down and glared at Boulton just for the thrill of it. He had on his discreet butler face. I went back to the sofa and glared at Bobby.

"What kind of photograph is it?" Claire asked.

"I told you. It was a picture of Victoria and . . . her . . . her . . . daddy," he giggled.

"I mean, was it in color? Was it taken with one of those instant cameras?"

"That was weird. The photograph was black and white. Like an old snapshot."

"Did they appear younger in the photograph?"

179

"No. It was just an old black-and-white photograph."

"Excuse me a moment." Claire went into her bedroom.

"If you're lying, you're going to jail," I reminded him.

"What are you so excited about? He wasn't your old man."

Claire came back into the room with a box of photographs and put it in front of Bobby. "Pick out a photograph that resembles the shape and size of the one Victoria showed you."

I got up and looked over Alt's shoulder. He searched through the box as if it contained chocolates and he was looking for the best one. Everything this guy did had a specialness to it. I wondered if that was how he looked when he was ransacking my apartment. A picture flipped over and a young tall girl in jodhpurs stared up at me. Her face was somber. Her eyes squinted in the direction of the camera as if she were studying it. Another picture showed a tall, handsome man and a stylish woman of the forties standing by a Bentley. The gangly young girl stood next to them holding a small bouquet of wildflowers.

He plucked a black-and-white snapshot from the box. "Like this one."

Claire took the photo. "This was taken in

the fifties, I believe." She handed it to me. "Is this similar in size to what you saw?"

I looked at a picture of two women wearing funny white caps and long aprons over their dresses. Servants. I studied the shape of the photograph. "I think so."

"I gotta get back to the studio. They'll wonder where I am."

"Which woman is your *new* mother?" Claire asked, sitting back down.

Bobby looked at her. "I don't know what you mean."

"Yes you do." She leaned her head back and closed her eyes. "Who is she?"

"You really did talk to my mother." He realized Claire had her eyes shut, so he turned it all on me. "I hurt her when I told her that. I was angry. I didn't mean mother in the real sense . . . just that she takes care of me . . . loves me."

He stroked his arms lovingly.

"You're irritating me, Mr. Alt. Who loves you?"

He sucked at his lower lip. "Patricia."

"How did you meet her?"

"I was delivering flowers at the time. She had some guy sending them to her practically every day. We got to talking. She was going to buy a limo. I told her I had a chauffeur's license. One thing led to another. Let's face it, she likes my body."

He took a deep breath and expanded his chest. He exhaled, but the chest remained puffed. He looked coyly at Claire. She still wasn't looking, so it was back to me.

"You won't tell them, will you? I mean, that I was here? That, you know, I have a record? They don't have to know that you know I was in your apartment."

"Why shouldn't I tell them?" I demanded.

" 'Cause Victoria will fire me. She doesn't like people who make mistakes. Come on, I didn't take anything! I just messed the place up a little bit, like she told me to."

"Why did she want you to do that?" Claire asked.

"Scare her." Virtuous eyes peeked at me.

"You're a real prick," I said.

"I don't care what you think of me. Just because I forgot to put my gloves back on doesn't mean I should get kicked out. Hey, this is my chance to be a part of the center."

"The center?" I asked.

"Yeah. Where everything happens."

Claire reluctantly opened her eyes. "Just remember, Mr. Alt, Miss Hill has the power to put you in jail. Another place where everything happens. You'll be hearing from us."

"What do you mean, I'll be hearing from you?"

"You may go."

"Wait a minute. I cooperated. Don't you understand? Victoria won't like it if she finds out I talked to you."

For the first time his baby-pure eyes darkened with fear. "I don't have anything else to give you."

"We'll be the judge of that. Show him out, Boulton. And tell Gerta to bring in tea and sandwiches. I'm starving."

"A guy makes one mistake and everybody makes him pay!"

"Who else is making you pay?" Claire asked quickly.

"The world!" He tossed his jacket over his shoulder and swaggered after Boulton.

A short time later Gerta brought in a tray of dainty, crustless sandwiches filled with watercress, and cucumber sliced as thin as a pale-green chiffon scarf. Before she returned to her kitchen she put her hand under my chin and gave me a motherly squeeze. I gave her a daughterly smile and glumly ate three of her sandwiches.

After my second cup of tea I decided to make an announcement.

"I just want to find the codicil. I don't want to find or know anything else."

"I have to see that photograph." Claire touched a linen napkin to the corner of her lips.

"You go right ahead."

"Do you still have that number Patricia gave you?"

I nodded.

"Call and tell her we have important information and we would like to see them tomorrow."

I dialed the number, got an answering service, and left the message.

"What information?" I asked. "That we know what's in the photograph, but we don't *have* the photograph?"

"They think we do. I want them to think we are ready to sell it to them."

"We don't have anything to sell!"

"Miss Hill, genius doesn't always have to be logical. But it must be creative." She looked at her watch. "I'm going to my room and rest. We should leave at five forty-five if we're going to make our six-thirty appointment with Roger Valcovich."

At exactly six thirty Boulton parked the car in front of Valcovich's building. He opened the glove compartment and took out a gun.

"Valcovich is greedy and crooked, but I don't think he's dangerous," I said.

Boulton put the gun between his belt and the small of his back.

They followed me through the tiled lobby

and up the back stairs. Rock music still clashed with Muzak. The world peace movement was working overtime.

Outside Valcovich's door Claire said, "I'll go in first. Wait about four minutes, then come in."

"I don't like it," Boulton said.

"He'll recognize Miss Hill, and your presence will make him suspicious." She opened the door and went in.

I leaned against the wall. Boulton stayed by the door. The rock music stopped. Two peace marchers came out of the office. "See ya later, man," a bearded kid yelled and hurried down the hall to the stairs. The other kid, all pink and red-haired, gave me a wink as he locked the office door. I winked back. It was all in the name of peace.

"Men like you, Maggie," Boulton said.

"I'm the only female in the hall. Winks and wolf whistles aren't compliments — just instinct. The male sexual howl."

"We men are just automatons to you? We have no discernment?"

"You looked pretty mechanical when you were beating up Erwin."

"I could have killed him. But there was no need to. What does that have to do with an attractive woman?"

"I don't know. But I have a feeling there's a

185

connection there somewhere, and I'm not sure I like it."

He smiled. It was a full, spontaneous smile, not secretive and insinuating like Neil's. I imagined pressing my lips against his.

He looked at his watch. "Shall we go in, Maggie?"

"Sure," I said, wishing I hadn't imagined kissing Boulton. The last thing I needed in my life was another macho man, even if he did speak as if he belonged on PBS. But, let's face it, the last thing a New Woman needs is a New Man. Oh, hell.

The reception room was empty. A lamp, surrounded by a messy pile of magazines, glowed on a small Formica table. There was the smell of cold cigarette butts. The filing cabinets were open. Manila folders and papers littered the floor.

Boulton took out his gun. "Where's the office?"

I pointed down the hallway. He made his way quickly, quietly toward Valcovich's door. I was behind him. He kicked the door. It slammed against the wall, making a dull slapping sound.

Claire sat in a chair, across from Valcovich, observing him as if he were a priceless oil painting. Valcovich was in his white leather chair. His head sagged awkwardly to one side.

Mouth gaped open. Tongue, crusted with blood, rested in the corner of his bluish-white lips. A jagged, fleshy red hole was where the knot of his tie should've been. Blood had spilled down his vest into a puddle on his lap. Red pools had formed on his desk and veined out, covering two eight-by-ten glossies of Valcovich smiling for all he was worth.

"Now, the case begins," Claire said.

I walked around the side of his desk.

"Don't touch anything," she warned.

Careful not to touch, I leaned over Valcovich's wastepaper basket and puked up Gerta's dainty, crustless sandwiches.

"I haven't checked that for evidence yet," Claire said peevishly.

Boulton moved toward me. "Feeling a bit faint?"

"No!" Yellow dots, lined in black, danced in front of my eyes once again. I swallowed my own bitter saliva. "I'm just not used to seeing two dead men in two days."

"She's going to faint," Claire said.

Boulton's arm curved around me, and he guided me toward the white Naugahyde sofa.

"Put your head down."

"I'm all right."

The room swayed.

He put his hand on the back of my damp neck and pushed my head down toward my knees. "Stay that way." He went and stood by Claire.

I shut my eyes. Their voices came to me through waves of nausea and dizziness. I could hear the evening traffic outside — people going home from work. The air brakes of a bus made a whooshing sound. Some German number honked, sounding like a lovesick mallard.

"This is the best time of a murder," Claire said. "Right after the violence and just before the police bureaucracy takes over. Rarely do I get such a chance."

"Shot in the throat," Boulton said.

"The trachea is a very small target."

"The killer was either an excellent marksman or a very lucky shot."

"Lucky shot. The first bullet missed. It's embedded in the wall above his head."

"It appears nobody heard the shots."

"I'm sure it got lost in the cacophony of music in the hallway."

"How long do you think he's been dead?"

"Hard to tell. If the bullet hit the carotid, it would only take several heartbeats to empty. If it didn't hit the carotid, it took him about ten minutes to bleed to death. I'd say a half-hour at the most. In his desk diary he circled six o'clock. No name next to it. Then he wrote 'Edith Wharton' at six thirty. All his other appointment times have names next to them — except the six o'clock."

"Did you see the filing cabinets?" he asked.

"Yes. Did you notice the secretary's desk?"

"No."

"It's been cleaned of everything personal. Are you still with us, Miss Hill?" Claire asked.

"I am." I slowly raised my head. Just a few dots remained.

"What was the secretary's name?"

"The Smoker? Do you think she shot him?"

"I have no idea. But she did clean out her desk. Her name?"

"I don't know. Wait a minute . . . I stood outside that private door listening. I think he called her Helen . . . no, Ellen. It was Ellen."

"Last name?"

"I don't know."

Claire got up and stood by Valcovich. She leaned across him. His chin rested on her arm as she deftly slid her gloved hand under his jacket. Her hand slipped out, holding a shiny address book.

A siren screamed down Pico. Boulton peered out the window. "Ambulance. No police cars."

"We'd better be going," I said.

Claire sat down and began to go page by page through the address book.

Voices came from outside the private door.

189

Boulton and I stared at one another. Claire read. He moved quietly to the door and listened.

"Cleaning crew," he whispered.

"They'll have a master key," I warned.

Still studying the address book, Claire casually ran her gloved finger along the top of a table next to her. She held up her finger — dust clung to the tip of it.

"He doesn't have a cleaning crew."

So Valcovich was greedy *and* cheap.

"The Kenilworth number is in here."

"Ellis probably gave it to him," I said.

"Probably. This may be it. Ellen Renicke. Sound familiar?"

"She'll always be The Smoker to me."

"Write this down. She lives at 6986 Howard Place."

I got out my Filofax. "I think that's near here."

"Brian Waingrove's number is listed."

She carefully slipped the book back into Valcovich's breast pocket. "Shall we go?"

I forced myself to take a last look at Valcovich. Death had taken all the greed out of his eyes. He looked almost as innocent as Bobby Alt.

We made our way toward the waiting room. Boulton opened the door and peered out into the hallway. He motioned to us. We walked quickly down the hall to the back stairs, through the tiled lobby, and out into the safe night air.

We had driven for about five blocks when Claire told Boulton to pull into the lot of a closed gas station. He parked near the one phone booth.

"You know what to say," she said. "Make it anonymous. Do not use 911. And just give the police the address."

Boulton nodded and went to make the phone call.

"Why don't you use the car phone?" I asked.

"I don't want the call listed on my bill."

"I can't believe this has led to murder," I said, leaning my forehead against the cool window glass.

"It usually does."

"Valcovich thought he got lucky."

"Maybe now he agrees with the Egyptians. They believe life is unlucky. And death is lucky."

"They say you never get used to it."

"Used to what?"

"Death."

"They are wrong."

I turned and looked at her. A small yellow light from the car ceiling illuminated her long, pale hands and glowed on her somber, elegant face.

"You're used to death?" I asked.

"All but my own."

"What about your parents' death?"

She looked at me sharply. "I've accepted their death. I haven't accepted the reason given for it. What's taking Boulton so long?"

"They probably have him on hold."

"Try to do a good deed and what does it get you."

Boulton got back into the car. "Had me on bloody hold. Try to do a good deed and what does it get you!" he said.

They looked at each other in righteous indignation while I tried to figure out just what the good deed was.

Ellen Renicke lived about ten minutes from Valcovich's office in a residential area off of Fairfax. The houses looked as if they'd been designed by Munchkins — tiny castles with dwarfed turrets, shrunken down for the middle class and their little slice of the property pie. The Smoker's house had a sloped roof shaped like the top of a mushroom.

We pulled up into the driveway. The Bentley's lights shone down the length of the drive, revealing an empty carport. Boulton took a flashlight, and we got out of the car. The house was dark. Claire knocked on the front door. Silence. She tried it. Locked. We went down the driveway to the back of the house. The back door was ajar. Claire took the flashlight. Boulton took out his gun.

We filed into a dark kitchen. The refrigerator sighed and the wall clock ticked. We moved through a door into a small dining room. The flashlight swept over a glass bowl filled with fresh flowers; it illuminated gold-flocked velvet wallpaper and heavy velvet chairs. We followed our small circle of light down a hallway. In a tiled bathroom the light swept over neatly folded green towels. We continued down the hall toward the circle of light into a bedroom. I prayed to God that we wouldn't find The Smoker dead. I prayed to God to let her die of natural causes, like lung cancer.

Claire moved the light over an open suitcase on the bed. Clothes hung over the sides of dresser drawers. The flashlight settled on an open closet door. One coat and a sad-looking evening gown were left. They looked as if they were still waiting to be taken to the dance. The light went back to the suitcase. Like moths, we moved toward it and peered into the case. Valcovich framed by sterling silver grinned up at us. It was one of his eight-by-ten glossies.

"If I'd just killed a man I don't think I'd want to take his picture with me," I said.

"This woman left in a hurry, as if she were

afraid for her life," Claire said.

"Maybe she knows who shot Valcovich," Boulton said.

"So why doesn't she just tell the police?" I asked.

"Ellen Renicke knows something." Claire tapped the flashlight in the palm of her hand. "Where did you say Waingrove was holding his symposium?"

"The City Hotel." I stared down at the silver-framed photo. "She must've loved Valcovich. That's a very expensive frame."

11

Valcovich was a son of a bitch. And, contrary to popular opinion, sons of bitches usually get theirs. It was *how* he got his and *why* that left me with a chill that wouldn't go away.

"What if somebody thought I was a daughter of a bitch and decided it was time for me to get mine?" I blurted.

Claire turned away from the car window and peered at me. "I beg your pardon?"

"Am I in danger of being murdered?"

"Probably. The more troubling question is who the murderer might be." She looked back out into the night.

"Oh, hell."

Century City, located between Beverly Hills and Westwood, is a little island of officious-looking high rises angled and positioned like giant glass soldiers on a tiny battlefield. Boulton turned the Bentley onto the Avenue of the Stars. The battlefield was once the back lot of Twentieth Century–Fox. I guess that's why they named the street Avenue of the Stars —

even though there aren't any stars, only corporations.

The City Hotel is a sleek modern temple to the businessman's fantasy. Fountains lit by colored lights gushed envy-green. Women in puffy evening gowns, looking vaguely disappointed, curled their arms around themselves against the night air. Tuxedoed men searched their wallets for money and parking tickets so the red-jacketed valets would retrieve their cars and put an end to the evening.

A valet took the Bentley and we made our way into the lobby. Chandeliers the size of my ex-apartment dangled balls of crystal from the ceiling. Marble floors and zaftig columns were the color of flesh. Big, deep, leather chairs curved out their arms, almost begging for people to sit in them.

We took the escalator down to the foyer of the International Ballroom. A portable bar had been set up among potted palms. Red-faced men with easy grins laughed and coughed over their drinks. A long table, draped in green, displayed books, pamphlets, records, and video cassettes. Waingrove's face was plastered over every one of them. He managed to look debonair while clutching thousand-dollar bills in each hand. Three young women stood behind the table. They wore tight money-green T-shirts over short leather skirts. Spread across their large breasts was the word "Profit."

"We're looking for Brian Waingrove," Claire announced to them.

A bleached blonde, with dark roots defiantly on show, stopped picking at her crusty elbow and said, "Thirty dollars per person unless you're taking the special classes — then it's fifteen." Her purple lipstick was smeared around the edges of her mouth as if she'd just been interrupted in the middle of a big, wet kiss. I was still struggling with liberation, and suddenly there were all these young, sexy reactionaries undulating around looking like they'd just got off a hot, sweaty man.

"We would just like to talk with him," Claire said.

The blond Profit shrugged. "He's supposed to be on stage, but he's late. Oscar's warming up the audience. All I know is I leave at ten o'clock no matter what." She turned to Boulton, breasts first, rest of body following. "How'd you get such big muscles?"

"I polish tea sets," he said, looking at me.

"Sure." She gave a false laugh.

"I need warmth," I said and walked over to the bar and ordered a double martini. I downed half of it and stared through the potted palms at a door marked MEN and another door marked EXIT. I finished my drink. My chill was almost gone. The exit door opened and Waingrove came in. He went into the men's room. Before the exit door could close it was pushed open again. Mr. Erwin, still nursing a bruised eye, also had to use the john. I motioned for Claire and Boulton to join me.

"Erwin and Waingrove had to use the john at the same time," I said.

"Erwin?" Claire peered through the palms. I ate my olive. I ate another olive. I ordered a single martini.

"Miss Hill, we have work to do." She tapped the finger burdened with the rock on top of her walking stick.

"It's this chill I have."

"I could think of a better way to warm you up," Boulton said softly under his breath.

Erwin came out of the men's room and went right back out the door marked EXIT.

"Stay with him," Claire said to Boulton. He moved quickly and gracefully, I thought, toward the door.

"Come along, Miss Hill."

I finished my single, paid for my drinks, and followed Claire toward the ballroom. She opened one of the doors, and we were greeted by about three hundred people chanting, *"Profit! Profit! Profit!"*

"You can't go in there without paying," the blond Profit whined.

"We won't stay long," Claire said.

We went in and stood against the back wall. The chanting, shirt-sleeved crowd's attention was focused on a bald-headed man, who I assumed was Oscar. He paced back and forth on the stage, waving his short, hairy arms in the air like a berserk accountant. Every now and then he'd stop and shake his fat ass. The crowd roared its approval. The lights dimmed. Oscar held one arm in the air. The crowd fell silent. A red spotlight darted around the room.

"Here's who we've been waiting for, folks. Are you ready?" Oscar asked.

The crowd screamed, "Yes!"

"I didn't hear that," Oscar chided.

"*Yes!*" the crowd roared louder.

Oscar held his hand up for silence. The crowd obeyed.

"*Brian Waingrove!*" Oscar screamed.

The red light swooped around the room. The audience turned in their chairs trying to follow it. The door next to me opened. Waingrove slipped in, holding a cordless mike in his hand. Makeup gathered in the creases of his eyes. Breathing hard, he contrived a winning smile. The red light found him. The crowd screamed and applauded wildly. He ran down the aisle, holding the mike in the air as if it were the Olympic torch. He leaped onto the stage, pin-striped jacket flaring to reveal a bright red lining. He held up his arm, quieting the crowd. He raised the mike to his lips.

"Money. Money is *not* the root of all evil." His voice was low and filled with sexy reverence. "Money is not an entity unto itself like the devil. A little pile of money sitting all by its lonesome doesn't have any power to cause evil. But the devil sitting all by his lonesome can get into a hell of a lot of mischief."

He cocked an eyebrow and twitched his nose. The audience clapped and hooted. Brian Waingrove could get real folksy.

"Money doesn't have to lead you to evil. Money, if manipulated honestly, can lead you to a state of grace! There are people here tonight who are in a state of grace. Would the rest of you like to join them?"

"Yes! Yes!" the crowd confessed and then applauded itself.

The red light darted around the room, momentarily capturing Judith Kenilworth. She didn't applaud. I guess she didn't have to. She was already graced.

"Judith Kenilworth is here," I informed Claire.

"I see her."

"Now, I know some of you are thinking that the people who have made money started with money," Waingrove cooed. "That's not true! They did what you are going to do. You are going to reach that state of grace by making money with other people's money. Legally. A state of grace must be a legal state."

Waingrove's lips brushed the mike, almost caressing it. For a moment I thought he was going to commit fellatio with it. Judith got up and left. I didn't blame her.

"Let's go," Claire said, sweeping past me.

The coughers and laughers were gone. The bartender yawned. Oscar chatted with two bored Profits while he groped the ass of the third. She squealed and smiled for him, then turned and rolled her eyes at her co-Profits. Judith was halfway up the escalator. We got on, and the escalator dumped us into the main lobby. Judith marched through the lobby toward the gold-leaf door of the Regency Room and went in. We gave her a few moments, then entered the restaurant.

The decorator had captured the purple-blue of twilight and dyed the velvet walls and chairs to match. I hate twilight almost as much as I hate dawn. They're times of transition, and I hate transition. The room brought my chill back.

Judith sat alone on a banquette against the

far wall. Even candlelight couldn't soften her strict face.

A tuxedoed maitre d' swooped up next to us like a giant crow. "May I help you?"

"We're guests of Judith Kenilworth. I see her. Thank you." Claire imperiously dismissed him.

He tilted forward as if he were going to peck a worm from the purple-blue carpet, then backed away from us.

"Hi, Judith," I said.

Judith had her head down, secretively checking her reflection in a small round mirror. The table was set for two. A bottle of red breathed. She looked up.

"Maggie? What are you doing here?"

"You remember Claire Conrad."

"If you'll excuse me, I'm expecting someone."

She slipped the mirror into a little velvet bag and carefully put it in her purse, as if it still contained her reflection. Without being invited Claire sat in the little spindly chair across from her. A bus boy rushed another spindly chair to the table for me.

"I told you this is a private dinner. You've talked to our lawyer. I don't know what else I can do for you."

"Roger Valcovich is dead. Shot in the throat." Claire stared into Judith's eyes.

"It took him about ten, fifteen minutes to bleed to death," I said. It felt good to say that out loud. I bit into a bread stick to show how tough I was. Judith wasn't so tough. She blanched. I poured her some of the red.

"Brian always tastes it first," she snapped.

"Good for him. But you look as if you need it. Valcovich's death seems to have bothered you more than when you heard about your brother's," I observed, pouring myself some wine.

"It's the way you described it, that's all. I've only met the man once. When he was in the office doing some work for you because you'd been in a — "

"Come off it, Judith. You and I both know that's not true."

I downed the wine and started to pour some more. The waiter took the bottle out of my hand and poured it for me. "Would you like to order?" he asked.

"No!" Judith hissed at him.

The waiter retreated.

"Please leave. I have nothing to say to either one of you."

"Judith," I said. "You don't seem to understand. Valcovich has been murdered. This is no longer a game of who's got the codicil."

"I was under the impression that Erwin and Waingrove just met for the first time this afternoon," Claire said.

"Erwin?" The severe lips barely moved.

"We saw Waingrove talking to him before he went on stage." I poured myself more wine.

"He's probably taking the lecture series. A person could do that without personally knowing Brian." Her strict eyes looked away from us as she talked.

"You're a terrible liar, Judith." I took a long swallow.

"My family and I just want to be left alone. We haven't done anything."

"It really hurts you to lie." I was feeling perceptive. "I can see it in your face."

Her severe eyes softened. She wasn't looking at me.

I looked in the gold-leaf mirror above Judith's head and saw Waingrove standing behind Claire and me. I caught his reflection just before he adjusted his public state-of-grace smile. In that fleeting moment he stared at the three of us with total disregard, and I knew that Waingrove was one of those heterosexual men who don't like women. They don't like our femaleness: breasts, thighs, hips, vagina. They don't like the way we laugh at ourselves or at men. They don't like our smell. And they especially don't like us when they think we are in their way. I had the

204

feeling that if we were three small animals in a road, Waingrove would aim his car at us. My chill returned. I downed the last of my wine.

"Brian!" Relief filled Judith's voice.

He squeezed onto the banquette next to her. Even in that close space he managed to keep his body from touching hers. She smiled at him. Her eyes glowed. Waingrove did for Judith what candlelight couldn't. Being in love with this jerk made her prettier. Oh, hell.

Ignoring Judith, he asked, "How are you, Maggie?" The clever eyes darted to Claire. "Miss Conrad?"

He took the wine bottle and poured. A few ruby drops and sediment gathered in the bottom of his glass. He looked disdainfully at Judith.

"*She* drank it!" Judith was reduced to a tattle-telling child.

"Don't worry, Judith. We'll order another." His voice was rational and authoritative. "And to what do we owe this pleasure, Miss Conrad?"

"Roger Valcovich was murdered."

His only reaction was to gesture for the waiter.

"He was shot in the throat," I elaborated.

"Odd place to shoot somebody," he said as the waiter appeared. He ordered another bottle.

"We found your name in his address book," Claire said.

"That's probably because I gave it to him."

"When?" she asked.

"Yesterday. I was talking to him on the phone. Maggie can verify it. She was standing right there. If she hadn't walked out in the middle of the conversation, she would have heard me give him my name and number in case he had further information."

"God, you could sell anything!" I leaned back in my chair.

"This afternoon was the first time you'd met Mr. Erwin?" Claire asked.

"That's right."

"Then why did he drive all the way from Pasadena to Century City just to talk to you in the men's room?" I demanded.

"Sutton was very upset about how you treated Erwin. He was afraid the man might bring legal action. I found out where he lived and gave him a complimentary ticket. To-night, we happened to run into each other in the parking lot. He was still very agitated. I like to wear a little makeup for my performance — my lecture — so I had him come into the bathroom. We talked while I applied my makeup. He has quite a little business go-ing. I hope he enjoyed the lecture."

Judith looked like she was going to get

down on the floor and kiss the hem of his pin-stripes.

"After he talked to you he left the hotel," Claire said.

"I did all I could for him. He is a strange man."

"I can't believe you can sit there and lie like that!" I said.

The waiter arrived with the wine. We fell silent while he went through the ritual of opening the bottle. After sniffing and tasting Brian said, "We'll let it breathe." The waiter left. I grabbed the bottle and filled my glass.

Waingrove's nose twitched.

"The day your brother killed himself, you left to come here to the symposium, didn't you?" Claire asked Judith.

"Yes. Brian was having afternoon work-shops."

"Did you and Sutton go in the same car?"

"Yes."

"When you pulled out of the driveway, you had to see Miss Hill's car, I assume."

"She parked it there. Every day. Right in front of the house." Her voice filled with re-sentment.

"And you would certainly notice if Miss Hill's car was all smashed in, wouldn't you?"

"I . . . don't . . . know . . . " she faltered.

"Just before you left, you were told she was

in an accident. I think it would be only natural to take a look at her car. Especially since it was parked where you could see it."

"That's right," I said. "My car doesn't have any dents. You saw that and you became suspicious of Valcovich — began to wonder what he was really doing in your brother's office."

"Judith only knows what Maggie told her. And I only know what Valcovich told me," Waingrove said.

"It's convenient that he's dead," I said.

"What are you implying?" He rubbed his nose.

My spoon got in the way of my hand and fell on the floor. "I'm implying that Valcovich knew the codicil existed. I'm implying that Judith looks a lot better to you with a four-million-dollar coin collection than without a four-million-dollar — "

"We're in love!" Judith blurted.

"Did you hear that, Waingrove?" I leered. "Say the word, Waingrove. I want to hear the word 'love' fall from your lips. Say it!"

Silence. I had him now.

"This man is not in love with you, Judith. He would turn to salt if he whispered the word 'love.' He doesn't love women. He doesn't even like women. Let me tell you something — "

Waingrove leaned toward Claire. "Maggie's

obviously had too much to drink. I'll be glad to help you . . . "

"You're a very helpful guy, aren't you? Why? Have you ever asked yourself that, Judith? He wants something from you — and it isn't love. He wants that old state of grace. Yours."

"Keep your voice down. People are looking," Waingrove commanded.

"You don't love her. You don't want passion."

I had important thoughts and the vision and the guts to say them. If I could just keep them from rushing into my head all at once.

"Vir . . . gin . . . ity wouldn't have to make a comeback if all the men in the world were like you, Waingrove. Because it never would have left."

"What is she talking about?" Waingrove demanded.

"But you've turned it all rotten . . . rotten virginity . . . " I still hadn't quite made my point. It was right on the tip of my —

"Tell her to stop," Judith cried to Claire.

"Sick . . . sick . . . isn't it, Judith?" I asked. "What is sick?"

"Sick . . . virginity . . . sick . . . "

It was so clear to me. I had to make them see. I looked at Claire. She leaned back in her chair, hand resting on her walking stick, eyes closed. Closed? I turned on Judith.

"I know what you need." I leaned over the table to get closer to her. Something spilled. "You need a little more fuck you in you."

"That does it!" Waingrove slapped his napkin onto the table.

"Then you could tell the bastard to go fuck himself. He doesn't even want to touch you . . . don't you know that? You don't want that kind of virginity . . . that kind of . . . kind of . . . " The one word that would say it all was floating somewhere . . . "Death! That's it. Like Valcovich. Death . . . "

Death? Blood? Flesh? No, no, the word . . . the idea . . . was . . . just off . . . the . . . tip . . .

12

Dark. Head throb. Wanted heartthrob. Blink. Eyes work. Scratch. Skin sore. Noise. Door open. Light!

"Good morning, Maggie!" Boulton banged the breakfast tray down. My limbs shook. I clutched at the comforter covering me.

"You made Gerta very angry last night." He went on in an excruciatingly loud voice. "In retaliation all you get this morning is coffee and this."

He came toward me holding a glass of juice as thick as jellied blood.

"No, no, no."

"A bit of the hair . . . "

"No, no, no. Why is Gerta angry?" And why did my lips feel numb?

"You told her last night, while holding on to me as if I were a lamppost, that she was not your mother and that you were tired of her superior but needy glances. I think that was the phrase. You went on to explain that you could not possibly fulfill whatever it was that was

211

lacking in her life."

"No, no, no . . ."

"Yes, yes, yes. You then began to surmise just what was lacking in her life. You observed that you were not responsible for the fact that she wasn't married, that she had never had a child, and that she was a lonely woman who must work for others."

"No, no, no!"

"Yes, yes, yes."

I peered out from under the comforter. "You're enjoying this, aren't you?"

"Yes. Yes. Yes." He grinned.

"I detest women who get drunk." Claire's voice pierced my skull.

All in white, she stalked my bed like an avenging angel and glared down at me with the same look of disgust she had had for my landlady.

"You mean you detest *people* who get drunk. Otherwise that's a sexist remark," I mumbled.

"I mean exactly what I say. The words we select are one of the few forms of independent choice we have left. I do not take that choice lightly."

She moved in agitation around the room, picking up a few of my remaining possessions, staring at them, then banging them back down. The ivory walking stick tapped.

"Draw her a bath," she commanded Boulton.

I groaned. "You've got to be kidding. I know, I know, you're not. Every word . . ."

"There are few pleasures in life, Miss Hill. I like to accumulate as many as I can. One that I particularly enjoy is a good breakfast — served properly! Do you know what I had this morning? Eggs that looked like Gerta had stepped in them. And my toast was the color of my onyx walking stick. I do not consider myself a picky person. I don't mind the obligatory seed floating in my orange juice to assure me of its freshness. But I will not be choked to death on them!"

"Don't talk about food . . ."

"Miss Hill, you have destroyed one of my simple pleasures."

"I'll apologize to her."

"You will do more than that. You will grovel!" She rapped the cane on the floor. My eyes rolled in their sockets.

"I think you could be a little more sympathetic. I'm in a vulnerable state."

"You are an immature woman with a hangover."

"Immature?" I raised up but immediately fell back. I glared at her over the folded edge of the blankets. "I've had to be the strong, the mature person my whole life!"

"You sound resentful. It is a problem peculiar to the female species that while they are resentful of having to be strong and mature they cry out for more opportunities to display their strength and maturity."

"Please, please . . ."

"Your body, your heart, your soul may be female, but your brain is sexless. It is no more female or male than an IBM computer. I wish you would use it accordingly."

"My brain is shaped by my past."

"The past. What excuse would we have without it? Is your brain clear enough of that relentless past of yours to take in some facts?"

"Yes . . . if you just wouldn't talk so loud."

"I am talking at my normal level."

She reclined in one of the chairs, stretching out her long legs. The idea of discussing facts had turned her look of disgust into an excited glow — the glow that most women get when they think they're in love.

"Boulton followed Erwin to Ellen Renicke's house last night."

"Erwin knows The Smoker?"

"Think, Miss Hill. We know that Waingrove and Erwin talked. Immediately after that conversation Erwin goes to Renicke's house. I can only assume that Brian Waingrove told him to go there."

"Waingrove knows The Smoker?"

"Maybe he just knows where she lives."

"Did Erwin go into the house?"

"A police car was parked in the driveway. Two policemen were standing at the front door. The house was dark. Erwin obviously didn't stop. Boulton followed him to Pasadena, then turned around and came back to the hotel just in time to carry you out of the Regency Room. I'm afraid you didn't make a very good impression on Waingrove or the other guests."

"Brian Waingrove is a misogynist." My head was pounding, and facts weren't clearing it up. "I don't understand. Why would he send Erwin to The Smoker's house?"

"What are we looking for, Miss Hill?"

Carefully, I raised my head from the pillow. "The codicil."

She smiled.

"The Smoker has the codicil?!" Slowly, I let my head fall back on the pillow and shut my eyes. "I don't understand. You mean she killed Valcovich and took the codicil?"

"I don't think she killed him. I think she was in love with him, as you observed last night."

"With my sexless brain."

"I think she took the codicil after he was murdered, or he had given it to her for safe-keeping before he was murdered. The Smoker

215

might be trying to make some money out of her tragedy. Waingrove might've sent Erwin there to either pay The Smoker off, or to kill her, or simply to set up a deal to be consummated at a later date. The Smoker is playing a very dangerous game. That's why she's on the run. I hope she's a clever woman. Otherwise, I'm afraid we'll find her in the same condition as Valcovich."

"How does Waingrove know Erwin?"

"More importantly, why did they pretend not to know one another? We have a lot of interesting problems."

"Wonderful. I'm glad we've got a lot of interesting problems," I groaned.

"So am I," Claire said, delighted. "By the way, while you were sleeping, Victoria Moor called. She and her meretricious mother would like to see us as soon as possible."

I thought of Ellis Kenilworth, and for the first time my memory didn't conjure him up in bloody pieces but as the elegant, wistful gentleman I had once worked for, I had once admired, respected. I thought of Bobby Alt's description of the photograph. I decided I wanted to keep Kenilworth elegant and wistful and a gentleman. Even if it wasn't true.

"I don't want to see those two women. I'm not interested in the photograph. Just the codicil."

Claire stared at the ceiling and said, "The key to all of this is Ellis's suicide. If we find out why he killed himself, I think everything else will fall into place. You will find, Miss Hill, that when the wealthy steal and murder, it may be under the guise of money, but there are usually complicated familial motivations behind their need for money."

"What about the poor?"

"They're different. They have no money."

My head was beginning to clear. "Wait a minute. If Waingrove sent Erwin to The Smoker's house, then that means he had to know that Valcovich was dead."

"So it would seem."

I sat up. We stared at one another.

"Waingrove murdered Valcovich?" My voice sounded hollow.

"Knowing someone is dead does not necessarily mean you killed them. But it could mean that he knows who did. It could even mean that the murderer asked him for his help. Waingrove seems to enjoy helping the Kenilworths."

"Judith? Sutton? No, I can't believe it."

"They had the most to lose if the codicil were made public. Of course, Waingrove could've helped them by killing Valcovich himself."

"Oh, God, I'm so confused."

Boulton appeared and announced with a perfectly straight face, "Your bath is ready."

Groaning, I got out of bed and gasped. I was naked! No, I still had on my beige dress. It was twisted and crumpled like old skin.

"You put me to bed with my clothes on?"

"Miss Hill, count yourself lucky. I was all for dumping you on the side of the Pasadena Freeway. Boulton thought it unwise."

I looked at Boulton. "Thank you."

He bowed. The perfect butler.

Claire stood up and stretched. "I feel out of sorts. I always do when I haven't had a proper breakfast. You will remember to grovel, Miss Hill."

She strode out the door with Boulton following her.

I staggered into the warm, steamy bathroom. Leaning against the sink, I took a swipe at the misty mirror. There I was. Not a pretty sight. The eye liner, shadow, and mascara I had put on yesterday were smeared in an abstract replica below each eye. My bright-red lipstick was smudged beneath my pale lips as if I had somehow miraculously kissed myself on my chin. A woman should never go to sleep with her makeup on. A woman should never go to bed with her ex-husband who is going to marry another woman. A woman should never get involved in murder. A woman should never have a female brain . . . Oh, hell.

I stood in Gerta's kitchen trying to hold my head straight so it wouldn't tip to one side, spilling out my female brain on her spotless black-and-white tiled floor.

She stood with her back to me, facing a huge stainless steel stove. Small flames flickered like eternal lights under heavy cast iron pots. The smell of cooking cabbage mixed with the sight of freshly chopped lamb on a blood-smeared cutting board made my stomach turn.

"I'm sorry." My words hung in the air.

She shrugged her heavy shoulders.

"I don't know exactly . . . I mean . . . I don't remember . . . I said something about you not being my mother . . . which is the truth . . . but . . . well . . . I really wouldn't want to hurt you . . . so I'm sorry . . . if I hurt you." Oh, God.

She turned and stared at me, a big wooden spoon in her red hand. Standing there in her black dress, dark stockings and black sensible shoes, Gerta looked as solid as one of her iron pots. And suddenly, I wanted to put my arms around her and bury my head in her motherly breasts.

"Maggie . . . " She paused, touching the

curved back of the large spoon to her lips as if she were kissing a child's forehead. The gray eyes glistened. "I had a husband and a child. I lost them."

"I'm sorry."

"I'm not. Too many women, they are afraid of losing nowadays, so they never try."

"It's just that we have so many options . . . "

"Options! Excuses. That's all you have. I hope you'll be very happy with them."

"Yes. Well . . . I just wanted to apologize."

"I accept."

She beamed her motherly expression. I smiled my good-daughter smile.

"You want something to eat?"

I knew this was a dangerous question, because it involved the giving and receiving of food. I knew that if I said yes that meant I was truly sorry — which I was. I also knew that if I said no, Gerta was not going to accept my apology. I knew that if Gerta were my real mother I'd be fat.

"I'd love to eat. But Claire wants us to leave now. We have to see Victoria Moor."

"The hunt always comes first with her."

"The hunt?"

"The search. She is always searching."

"For what?"

"The murderer. In Hungary I know who murdered my family. The KGB. She doesn't know who murdered hers."

"You mean her parents' deaths weren't an accident?"

"You go. She doesn't like to be kept waiting."

Gerta turned back to the stove and began to lift large pale-green leaves out of the pot and into a colander.

In the Bentley, I stared at the small bunches of wildflowers placed in the little crystal vases. Clusters of blue, yellow, and white.

"Where do you get the flowers?" I asked.

"A florist delivers them every morning," Claire answered, putting a black-and-white snapshot in an envelope.

"They look like a child's bouquet — the kind a young girl might pick to give to her parents before they drove away in their Bentley."

Claire looked up sharply. Penetrating eyes studied me. "Very astute, Miss Hill."

"I saw the photograph of you holding a similar bouquet. Why didn't you tell me your parents were murdered?"

"I can't prove it. And it's best to keep your mind on one case at a time."

"All right. Victoria and her mother are going to want to see the photograph I supposedly stole. And you're going to show them a picture of your indentured servants from the fifties. This is not going to fool them."

"The photograph was chosen for its shape and size, not its content. Trust me, Miss Hill, I have a plan. All I will need is a diversion."

My head still pounded. I leaned back in my corner and wondered why I didn't trust her.

Boulton maneuvered the Bentley up a long black ribbon of a driveway. Victoria lived in a nouveau castle high in the mountains looking down on Beverly Hills. The house had more turrets than a castle in a Grimms' fairy tale. Every gray stone, every oak-framed and beveled window oozed money, and yet the whole structure looked as unstable as a drunken woman teetering on expensive high heels.

Wrought iron gates stood open. Boulton pulled the car in and parked next to a truck filled with camera equipment. Two men dressed in Levi's, T-shirts, and work boots sat on the open gate of the truck, playing backgammon on a portable board.

"What's going on?" I asked them, getting out of the car.

"I just drive," one man said, rhythmically shaking the dice in a leather container as if it were a maraca.

"Public-service announcement with Victoria Moor. Don't trip over the cables," the other warned, gesturing toward the house.

Cables, like entrails, gushed out of the open front door.

Claire pointed to one of the turrets. Above us a little blond-haired girl somberly watched our arrival. She was about eight or nine. I waved. She didn't.

"Don't ingratiate yourself to children. They don't like it," Claire said.

"I'm just trying to be pleasant. It's not such a terrible thing to be pleasant."

"You just can't see yourself as the intruder, can you? Victoria didn't mention she has a child."

"Maybe it's not hers."

"They have the same eyes. Depleted."

I looked back up at the turret. The window was empty.

"Wait here," Claire commanded Boulton. "Come along, Miss Hill."

We walked into the house, careful not to trip over the cables taped to the hallway floor.

"I suppose if we follow them, we'll find her," Claire observed.

"Like Dorothy," I said.

"Dorothy who?"

"Dorothy following the yellow brick road in *The Wizard of Oz*."

"A subversive story."

"Subversive?"

"It shows a young girl how terrifying her imagination is. Imagination has the power to take her away from home — the implication being that she can only be happy in Kansas, preferably in her own backyard without a thought in her head."

"I never looked at it that way."

The cables veered right. We followed them down a long galleria. Large contemporary paintings, depicting ugly men and ugly women doing strange things to one another around geometrically shaped swimming pools, lined the stark white walls.

"Freud wins," Claire sighed.

An archway, breaking the line of paintings, disclosed a vast living room draped in cabbage-rose chintz. The synthetic smell of the new and unused wafted out at us. An oil painting of Victoria Moor, looking like Winged Victory in a cocktail dress, hung over the fireplace.

The cables continued past the living room and veered left into a group of people, lights, and a camera stuffed into a small, cozy den. As we approached, two people turned and held their fingers to their mouths, warning us to be quiet. We stopped in silence by the door of the den.

"Ready, Victoria?" a man standing next to the camera asked solicitously.

She sat on a green tufted leather sofa, wearing simple slacks and a girl-next-door plaid shirt. A ribbon held back her long blond hair. She looked young and fresh and sincere.

"We're going to pick it up from the children of poverty. Here we go. Everybody ready?" The man leaned close to the camera.

Holding a clap board, a younger man, in flowered Bermuda shorts and a polo shirt, stepped in front of Victoria and said, "Poor children, take three." He snapped the board and ducked away from the eye of the camera.

"And . . . action."

"Yes. There are children starving in America." Victoria spoke earnestly to the eye of the camera. "The children of the homeless. Of the poor. Children from abusive families. Runaway children. Children of single parents."

She paused. Eyelids dropped. Slowly she raised them. Victoria was no longer just sincere; she had transformed herself into a woman of unimpaired morality. The moist, perfect lips were firm with integrity. I had seen that look before. She used it on "Family Rites" when she was going to lie to her wealthy stepfather.

Her voice was strong with principle. "You can adopt a starving child in America for just seventy-three cents a week. That's all. Seventy-three cents. Less than you would spend for a diet cola. Please . . . save a child. And here's how you do it."

"Cut. Perfect. Perfect. Just one more."

Victoria stood up and saw us.

"Was there anything technically wrong with that last take?" she asked the director.

"I just thought when you lowered your eyes — "

"Use it. I told you I only had an hour to give to this. Thanks, everybody." She moved toward us. "Follow me."

We followed her back down the galleria, past the unused living room, through the hallway, to a room that looked like an English pub. Claire stopped and studied the dark wood paneling.

"It's real," Victoria said, pausing by a row of French doors. "I had the whole inside of the pub brought over piece by piece. Cost a fortune."

"I hope the pub owner was going out of business," I said.

"The owner came out all right. Samuel Johnson's initials are carved in the top of the bar."

Claire ran her fingers over the *S* and the *J* and the date 1759. "The year his mother died," she said softly.

"What about Boswell's initials?" I asked.

226

"Who?" Victoria leaned against the bar.

I looked at Claire. "They're not all equally famous."

"I don't read books anymore," Victoria said. "I'm beyond revelation. Take you, Maggie — I wasn't surprised you had the photograph. I won't be surprised at the huge amount of money you'll want me to pay for that picture. And I also won't be surprised when you settle for less."

She stared directly into my eyes as if I were a camera. The woman of unimpaired morals was gone. Claire was right. Her green eyes were depleted.

"Let's go outside. Mother's by the pool."

She opened one of the many French doors, and we stepped out into Shangri-la. A vast, rolling garden was decorated with pink roses, pink bougainvillea, pink orchids, and pink camellias. There were other pink flowers, but they looked so rare and so expensive I was sure their names were unlisted. Three waterfalls intersected over a stone wall and cascaded into a rock-formed swimming pool. Weepy-looking trees gently brushed their melancholy branches against the lawn. A Japanese footbridge arched, as gracefully as a dolphin, over a stream to a small island. A white filigree gazebo, which looked as if it belonged on top of a giant wedding cake, was plopped in the middle of the island. I guess it was no longer enough to just have a pool and a tennis court. The rich and the famous needed to turn their backyards into theme parks.

Patricia, covered in a pink caftan and big pink hat, leaned over the edge of the pool, giggling and dripping water onto Bobby Alt's perfectly flat stomach. He floated on a pink candy-striped raft. A thin piece of white fabric cupped his genitals. In preliberation times Patricia, or Victoria, would've been floating on that raft with a man dripping water on her perfectly flat stomach. So this is equality — we trade our sex object for your sex object.

"Mother!" Victoria snapped.

Patricia and Bobby looked toward us and stopped laughing.

"We have guests. Go away, Bobby."

"You don't have to talk to him that way," Patricia said meekly.

"That's okay." Bobby's innocent eyes avoided us. He slipped off the raft and swam even breast strokes underwater toward the stairs. I knew he was wondering what we were doing here, if we were going to take away his grab for the center. He came up out of the baby blue and walked up the stairs, pushing back his wet hair. Only when Victoria turned away to pick up a towel did he sneak a searching look at us. Claire's face was impassive. I gave him a big smile. He shifted his eyes away.

Victoria tossed him the towel. "After you put some clothes on, see that the crew gets out of the house without stealing or breaking anything."

"And Bobby dear, don't walk through the pub with wet feet. Chlorine stains the floor." Patricia cooed like a seductive mother.

"Sure." He winked an innocent eye and sauntered off.

"You have it!" Patricia turned on me. "I want it. Now!"

I quickly stepped back from her, remembering her sharp nails.

"Mother, please. Blackmail has a certain ritual, a tradition that must be carried out. It's not polite to say 'Give it to me.'" Victoria had a cruel smile on her face.

"I detest the sun. May we sit in the shade and discuss this?" Claire asked.

Patricia gathered the skirt of her caftan around her and led us across the little footbridge to the gazebo.

Pink fish sluggishly undulated in the stream beneath us. One floated belly up.

"Your fish is dead," I said, stopping to take a look.

"They didn't engineer the stream properly — not enough air or something. So they keep

229

dying on us. The gardener will scoop him out tomorrow," Patricia said, continuing her march to the gazebo. The pink caftan billowed around her.

"I didn't expect to see death in Shangri-la," I observed.

"Shangri-la? I don't understand what you mean. It's just a dead fish," Patricia said from the gazebo.

Claire peered down into the little stream and whispered to me, "You see how complicated the wealthy make things?"

"Maggie's making fun of our garden, Mother." Victoria leaned against the filigree railing, scrutinizing Claire and me as we entered the shade of the big white structure.

"But it's just a dead fish. I don't understand what the problem is." She settled herself on a white wicker lounge filled with sherbet-colored pillows.

"I agree," Claire said. "We live in a society that is more concerned with the death of minor species than the death of the human species. Roger Valcovich was murdered last night."

"Who?" Patricia looked at me. "Oh. Isn't that the man you were asking about at the Kenilworths'?"

I nodded.

"Well, we don't know him. Ask the Kenilworths. They're capable of most anything."

"I think our attitudes about death are shaped in childhood," Victoria said. "When I was five I won a goldfish at a school fair. It looked like a minute lady's fan floating in the water — as if some beautiful woman had accidentally dropped it. When I woke up the next morning, the fish was dead. I remember staring at it for a very long time, thinking, This is death. I should cry. So I did. That's when I first learned I could cry on cue. I knew, way down deep, I just wanted to get rid of it. And I did. Flushed it down the toilet. Mother was proud of me."

"Screw the damn goldfish! I want that photograph. Where is it?!" Patricia snapped.

"We know that you have a copy of the same photograph. We would like to see it," Claire said, leaning against a carved white post.

"How do you know?" Victoria asked sharply.

"Because I think you're being blackmailed. And I imagine the blackmailer wrote something on the back of it."

Patricia's hand went to her mouth. Victoria stared at us with a calculating coldness. I looked at Claire. How did she know all this? Or was she just guessing? Or was this her plan?

"What makes you think we're being blackmailed?" Victoria asked.

"Ellis . . ." Patricia said. "He told? In the suicide note?"

"Yes," Claire lied. She held up the envelope with the picture of her servants in it.

My head and heart began to pound, and I knew my body wasn't just reacting to an overdose of booze.

"What did he say?" Patricia asked timidly.

"Mother!" Victoria faced Claire. "I'm not easily frightened. I will pay you five thousand dollars. And that's all I will do."

"No, no. Wait!" Patricia pleaded to Victoria. "They've already seen the photograph. What can it matter if you show them the copy?"

"Be quiet, Mother. That's my offer."

"Let's go, Miss Hill." We moved toward the stairs.

"Wait!" Patricia screamed. She turned to her daughter. "Victoria, please, please! Show them. We've worked so hard."

Victoria stared at the envelope in Claire's hand. "Show me what's in the envelope first."

"I've already explained my terms."

"Please, Victoria, I must know what he said." Patricia stroked her daughter's hand.

"They may not have the photograph, Mother. Something's wrong. I don't trust them."

"Maggie's already seen it." Patricia looked

at me. "When you found Ellis. You saw it then, didn't you?"

"Yes," I lied.

Patricia turned back to Victoria. "You see? She already knows."

"Who was in the photograph?" Victoria asked me.

I looked at Claire. Claire nodded. I reminded myself to thank her later for that shake of the head. What in the hell did she want me to do? Tell them what Bobby Alt told us? Make up another story? What? I decided, as usual, to play it down the middle.

"It was a picture of Ellis and a woman."

"Who did the woman look like?" Victoria asked, as calm as a district attorney.

"She looked a whole lot like you."

"And what did . . . Father . . . write on the back of the photograph?"

I was trapped.

"That's what you're paying us for," Claire said flatly.

"Please . . . please . . . I want it to be over. I want you to be safe." Patricia was sobbing and stumbling toward the stairs.

"Mother! Don't!"

"I'll get it. I'll be right back." She hurried over the footbridge.

"Mother!"

A blue jay screamed and flew out of one of

the weepy trees with a small egg in its beak. Blue jays didn't belong in Shangri-la, either.

I sat down on a chair. The wicker creaked under my weight. Claire remained standing.

Victoria stared at us. "Now my personal life is as cheap as my television show."

I felt a little cheap myself and a little uneasy. I wanted to know how we were going to get out of Shangri-la without letting them know we didn't have the photograph.

The little girl appeared on the footbridge. She stood just at the top of it, staring across at us. Victoria moved across the gazebo and leaned out toward her.

"Mommy loves you, darling," she called across to the child.

The child rose up on half-point and curved her arms over her head and twirled. She ended by curling herself into a curtsy. Thick blond curls bounced.

"That's very good!" Victoria applauded enthusiastically.

The child smiled, but her eyes remained emotionless. Victoria blew her a kiss. The child leaped up into the air and caught it. Her hand tightly closed around her mother's imaginary kiss. She ran back up the garden and into the house.

"You have a lovely daughter," Claire said. "I didn't know you were married."

"I've never been married. Like me, my daughter, Rebecca, has never had a real father. Of course, when you make the kind of money I make, I'm not sure she really needs one. I'm not so sure she needs any man. I'm not so sure Rebecca isn't better off . . ." Tears filled her eyes. Her cheeks flushed. "I sometimes think if I hadn't pursued my father, none of this would have happened."

"What do you mean, you 'pursued' him?" Claire asked.

Victoria sat on the wicker lounge. Two sherbet-colored pillows fell to the floor.

"I was only eighteen. All I wanted was him to acknowledge me. No, more than that — love me. Like a father should love his daughter. But he wasn't capable of that kind of love. He desired me. And I was so needy. You don't look well, Maggie. Blackmail make you feel a little queasy?"

"It's hard for me to think of Ellis Kenilworth . . ."

"Seducing his daughter?"

"You've been seeing your father since you were eighteen?" Claire asked.

"After our first couple of encounters . . . I stopped seeing him. I loathed myself. He never tried to get in contact. All those years of him not seeing me. All those years of letting Mother and me scrounge while they stayed safe and rich. As I told you in the limo, Mother had a way of turning disaster into opportunity. Of course, she was smart enough not to tell the papers that it was my father who raped me. That might turn the public off. Make the sex object less desirable — even pathetic. But it was the beginning. We were on our way to being safe and rich."

"Why did you start seeing him again?" Claire asked.

I looked out at the garden. Victoria Moor had always been unreal to me. I couldn't handle the very real, tortured look on her face.

"Three years ago, when I turned thirty, I decided that I was famous enough and wealthy enough to go back and seduce him. Eleanor didn't think Mother was good enough for her son. Well . . . I was. Would you like to hear the intimate details? I think you should get your money's worth."

"That's all right," I mumbled.

"Maggie's not as good at this as you are." The depleted eyes stared at Claire.

"It's a matter of experience," Claire said.

"Isn't it always? Do you know what I experienced? Power. Power over my father. Finally."

I watched Patricia emerge from the house, waving a white envelope in her hand like a flag of surrender. She hurried around the pool

236

and down the rolling lawn. As she reached the top of the footbridge a gust of wind blew her hat off. It floated in the air. Patricia grabbed wildly at it.

"Mother," Victoria whispered sadly.

The hat sailed slowly down into the stream. She watched it for a moment, then hurried into the shade of the gazebo.

"My beautiful hat!" Patricia gasped as she sat next to her daughter on the lounge.

"Tomorrow the gardener can scoop it out with the dead fish," Victoria offered.

"You've been crying. What have they said to you?"

"Nothing, Mother."

She grabbed her daughter's wrist. "What have you told them?"

"The truth."

All the tightening, all the lifting, couldn't keep Patricia from suddenly looking very old.

"Only as you see it. He did it to *you*. He's responsible. Not you." She turned on us. "He did it to her!"

"I wasn't a child."

"But with him you were." She stroked her daughter's cheek. "Don't you understand? You still are. You are. You're mine." She turned to Claire. "Here, look at it! Damn you!"

She threw the envelope at her. It fluttered

to Claire's feet. Claire picked it up and took out the photo and studied it. Patricia and Victoria sat on the lounge holding on to each other. I sat on the little wicker chair, feeling like shit and wondering if Victoria Moor was the ultimate good daughter. I took a deep breath, stood up, and peered over Claire's shoulder at the photograph.

Ellis Kenilworth faced the camera, pressing Victoria Moor to his body, his mouth wide with pleasure, eyes half-closed with satisfaction. Victoria's arms embraced him. Her head tilted back and to the side; a profusion of blond hair cascaded down, framing her chiseled nose, turned-up chin, and opened lips. A white blouse draped off one shoulder, revealing a curve of breast. Ellis's hand cupped her ass. His other hand was under her skirt, pushing her bare leg up around his waist. Dark clouds formed an abstract pattern over their heads. A disturbing, overwhelming passion emanated from this grainy black-and-white snapshot. Claire turned it over. Words cut out from a newspaper were pasted to the back. They read: THERE ARE MORE.

Patricia whimpered.

Victoria said, "I look as if I'm enjoying it, don't I? Maybe I was."

"Stop talking like that," Patricia said.

"Can't you just see it by the cashier's stand

238

in your supermarket?" Victoria's mouth curved down into a deprecating smile.

"Where was this picture taken?" Claire asked.

"I think at Zuma Beach. We sometimes went up there."

"Do you know who took the photograph?"

"No. All I can think of is that somebody either followed us or just happened to be there who knew who I was and . . . found out Ellis was my father. May we see your photograph?"

"When did you receive this in the mail?"

"About six months ago."

"Could you tell where the picture was mailed from?"

"I don't want to talk about it."

"Was Ellis being blackmailed at the same time?"

"Yes."

"And you have no idea who is blackmailing you?"

"That's my business."

"How do you pay?"

"I repeat, that's my business."

"Why have you never gone to the police?"

"I'm not interested in justice. I'm interested in keeping my life private."

"In other words, you're going to go on paying your blackmailers." Claire dropped her walking stick. "Would you pick that up for me, Miss Hill?"

I leaned over and retrieved the walking stick.

"As I said, that's my business. Give me your photo." Victoria held out her hand.

"Tell her, Miss Hill," Claire said as I handed the stick back to her.

"Tell her what?"

"Tell her the truth."

"*The* truth?"

"Yes."

"What's going on?" Patricia moved toward me.

"We . . . ah . . . don't have . . . the photograph. . . . We . . . just wanted to see what it was that you were looking — "

"You bitch!" Patricia was on me, her nails digging into my arms.

"Mother! Stop it! Stop it!" Victoria screamed.

I shoved Patricia as hard as I could. She staggered backwards across the gazebo, falling on the lounge. More sherbet-colored pillows spilled.

Claire handed the photograph in the envelope back to Patricia. "Thank you for your time."

Breathing hard, she snatched it from Claire's hands. "Get out! Get out of here!" She clutched the envelope to her breast and sobbed. Victoria leaned over her mother, stroking her shoulders.

We made our way over the footbridge. I could smell the dead rotting fish. Hell, everything and everyone was rotten. Kenilworth's body was rotting, and so was my image of him. I was rotten for tricking two desperate women. Only Claire, striding boldly in front of me, was determinedly above the rottenness. But then she could stay in bed and not get her clothes wrinkled.

"Hurry, before they open that envelope," Claire said, holding one of the French doors for me.

"You didn't give them their photo back?" I exclaimed, entering the cool darkness of the English pub.

"I exchanged theirs for mine."

"When?"

"While you were picking up my walking stick. Being a detective is a little like being a magician. When you're doing something devious with your left hand, make sure the audience is looking at your right hand. In this case you were my right hand. Of course, Patricia's attack on you gave me a little extra time."

We hurried by the bar. My arms began to throb and burn. I stopped to look. Patricia had left me with something to remember her by. Long welts swelled red from the inside of my elbows to my wrists.

"Now, that's really rotten!" I moaned.

A hand reached out and grabbed me. I whirled around.

"Did you tell them I talked to you?" Bobby Alt asked desperately.

"No. But remember, Bobby, I can send you to jail," I said viciously.

"But you can't. You can't," he whined after me.

Why shouldn't he feel rotten too?

We were out the front door. I looked up at the turret. The little girl with jaded eyes stared down at us. I wondered if she would grow up to be a good daughter.

Boulton aimed the Bentley down the drive. We pulled out onto the street. A silver Mercedes sped by us up the driveway. I recognized Brian Waingrove's car.

13

We were back at Conrad Cottage. Claire sat with her long legs dangling over the arm of the Queen Anne. She peered through a magnifying glass at the photograph. I sat at the big table. The welts on my arms throbbed.

"My arms were the only part of my body that didn't hurt. Now all of me hurts. I wish you would've let me in on the fact that I was going to be the diversion."

"A serendipitous moment, I assure you. Boulton's bringing you some sort of miracle medicine for cuts, scratches, et cetera. There's something wrong with this photograph."

"There's nothing wrong with the photo, just the people in it."

"Not the content. The angle. The camera is tilted upward. Do you know anything about photography?"

"Say cheese."

"Neither do I."

"You mean there is something you don't know about?"

"I know my limitations, which frees me to surround myself with people who have abilities I do not possess." She gave me a long, thorough look, then turned her attention back to the photograph. The telephone rang. I answered it.

"Conrad Cottage. Maggie Hill speaking."

"Maggie, this is Sutton Kenilworth. Mother would like to meet with Claire Conrad around eight o'clock this evening, if that's convenient."

"Hold on." I put my hand over the receiver. "Eleanor Kenilworth wants to see you tonight at eight if it's convenient."

She looked up from the photo. "Eight o'clock is a very civilized hour."

"A very civilized hour," I said into the phone.

"Judith told me about that poor Valcovich. Awful business. The police were here. A Detective Neil Brock found our name in Valcovich's address book. He seemed to know that you had worked for Ellis."

I'd forgotten Valcovich's office was in Neil's division. It wasn't exactly the first thought that came to mind when I saw Valcovich's corpse.

"I suppose you told the police the truth about the codicil."

"Eight o'clock, then. Goodbye, Maggie."

He hung up the phone.

"Oh, hell. Neil's the detective in charge of Valcovich's murder."

"Is he any good?" Claire asked.

"That's not the point." I stared at the welts on my arms. "I feel like Mrs. Henderson."

"Who is Mrs. Henderson?"

"I saw her on the 'Today' show. She was a victim for twenty-two years."

"I don't think this case will last that long."

Boulton came in with a silver tray covered with white linen and lined with little bottles of medicine.

"Here we are." He set the tray on the table. "Hold out your arms."

I did. He knelt down before me. I liked that. He poured some dreadful-looking liquid onto some cotton.

"Right." He dabbed at my wounds, face somber with concentration.

"That stings."

"Yes. Well, we don't know where Patricia has been. I thought it best to use the strong stuff."

"Very thoughtful of you."

The soft brown eyes looked up at me and I felt my brain turn even more female.

"I want you to take a look at this photograph, Boulton," Claire said.

He took the magnifying glass and studied the picture.

245

"There's too much sky and clouds," Claire said.

"Yes," he said. "There's something haphazard about the composition. Almost as if the photograph were taken by accident. It could've been taken by somebody lying down, who didn't have control over the camera — or it could've been taken by a child."

"A child!" Claire began to pace.

"I would say that the camera which took this picture was probably an old point-and-shoot model. An inexpensive camera, like a Kodak Instamatic," Boulton said.

"How can you tell all that?" I asked, impressed.

He peered at me through the magnifying glass. "I'm fascinated by American gadgetry." I smiled. "Photography is a hobby of mine."

Claire stopped pacing. "Yes, a child."

"You don't think some kid was walking along the beach and accidentally took a picture?" I asked. "Then her parents have it developed and see Victoria and blackmail them?"

"We don't need some mystery child to walk by conveniently and take a picture. There *is* a child. Victoria Moor's child."

"But . . . I don't want to be silly about this . . . but that means that strange little girl is blackmailing her mother and grandfather?"

"Hardly. But that doesn't mean she didn't take this picture. And it does mean Victoria and Patricia could have been blackmailing Ellis. Incest is still a major sin in our society."

"But not for the gods and goddesses of television land. I would think if this photograph were made public, Victoria could go on all the major talk shows, like Mrs. Henderson. Be the victim. Confess."

"But there is no such venue for Ellis Kenilworth."

"So he kills himself," I said, resting my arms on the globe. "I thought it a little strange they were so quick, so willing, to pay us and to keep on paying their so-called blackmailer. It makes sense."

"Miss Hill, you've somehow managed to drape yourself all over my globe."

"It feels good. I'm leaning on the world."

Claire slumped in her chair. "Before the world leans on you. It doesn't make sense. Something's wrong. Terribly wrong." She closed her eyes.

"But it does make sense! She hated her father. Patricia hates the Kenilworths. The ultimate revenge." I looked at Boulton. "What do you think?"

"I think this solution does not answer the question as to why Ellis Kenilworth does not want his mother, brother, and sister to profit from his coin collection."

Claire slowly opened her eyes and smiled at him. I gave the world a spin. The doorbell rang.

"Excuse me." Boulton retreated from the room to answer the door.

I watched the continents whirl by in a blur of greens, yellows, browns, and a lot of blue.

Boulton returned and announced to Claire, "Detective Neil Brock would like to see you."

Claire slipped the photo into her pocket. "Send him in."

Before I could stop, my hand went to my hair.

He came in with his hands in his pockets, his tie pulled loose. The dark eyes took me in, then worked on Claire. He was smiling. He took one hand out of his pocket. A badge was in it. He gave her a look at it, then had the audacity to give me a look at it. "Just to let you know I'm here on business," he said.

"How can I help you?" Claire asked.

"I've got this dead lawyer on my hands. Name is Roger Valcovich. I can't figure out why he's dead — other than the fact that somebody named Edith Wharton blew his throat away and then puked in the wastebasket. At least that's what some of the guys on this case think. You forget what division I'm in, Maggie?"

"Aren't you a little out of your division now?" I asked.

"Out of my division. Out of my league. Out of my class. But hell, that's never stopped me before. See, this young peace marcher gave me a description of this man and woman standing in the hallway outside this dead lawyer's office. It was last night around six thirty."

He took out a pad and began leafing through it. "Ah, here it is. The man was described as being in his late thirties. About six three. Brown hair. Brown eyes. Had on a funny dark suit and white shirt. Looked to this kid like this man was a bouncer."

Boulton's eyebrow arched.

Neil smiled. "What do peace marchers know from butlers? He said the woman was in her late thirties."

My eyebrows arched.

"Dark, shortish hair. Nice mouth. She was kinda sexy, so this young kid says. She even winked at him. He said they both looked like they were just waiting around for something to happen. It was hard to know if the kid meant they were waiting around for something to happen between the two of them or in this Valcovich's office." He looked at me. "Valcovich . . . I'm not too good with these long foreign names. Am I pronouncing it right, Maggie?"

249

It was a good try.

He slipped the pad back in his pocket and continued. "I have to admit I didn't make any connection. Why should I? But then Charlie, our token faggot, is looking at Valcovich's appointment book, and he almost loses it — his voice gets real high and his wrist bends and he squeals, 'Edith Wharton!' Later he tells me the only Edith Wharton he ever heard of was a writer."

"What's your purpose, Detective Brock?" Claire asked.

Neil's smile went back to being secretive. The eyes turned hard. "My purpose? To tell you I don't like me or the guys being fucked around."

Boulton took a step toward him. Claire put her hand up and he stopped.

Neil smiled at him. "She's got you well trained. Hand commands."

Boulton was back to being the discreet butler. Not a muscle twitched.

"Where was I? Oh, yeah. We have this basket of puke tested and what do you think forensic finds? Watercress. Some of us didn't even know what that was. And bread. No crust. And a hint of cucumbers. Charlie said it sounded like high tea."

"What would you do without your faggot to give you a little sense of civilization and literature?" I said.

We looked at one another and all the old battles and all the old passions were there connecting us.

"You still don't look very good, Maggie." He took my hands. "Cat scratch your arms?"

I tried to pull away. His grip tightened.

"Charlie got me thinking about a fight you and I had once. Over your books. Remember?"

"Like a good fascist you tried to destroy them."

The smile stopped. Anger flushed his cheeks. He released his grip, and slowly the lips curled back into their smug place.

"I just threw them on the floor. I didn't really understand why you had to pay so much attention to them and not to . . . well, that's another story."

"If this is going to turn into a domestic catharsis, I'm leaving the room," Claire announced.

The bastard turned to Claire. "No. This concerns you . . . *Miss* Conrad. You see, I felt bad about this argument Maggie and I had. I decided it would be nice of me if I put her books back. I got to looking at them, reading the titles, and the authors' names. I came across this woman writer called Edith Wharton. She wrote this book called *Eddie Frome*."

"*Ethan*," I corrected.

"You sure?"

"Yes."

"I thought I might try to read it. Get on Maggie's good side. Couldn't you just see me sitting down to high tea with her, and discussing Edith Wharton? But I never got around to it. Funny that Charlie should make me remember all this."

"I'm sorry your attempt at the classics was so halfhearted. Is that all you have to say?"

"I don't like being fucked around, lady. I don't like the thought of a bunch of hard-working guys out there looking for some woman named Edith Wharton, who they think spilled her high tea in the basket after she blew Valcovich away. They're also looking for his secretary. They think the two women might be connected." He turned on me. "And I don't like to think that this was some clever literary joke to be played out on what you think are a bunch of assholes in uniform."

"I never thought that!" I scrambled to my feet.

"You've always thought it. You think it of me!"

Claire rapped her walking stick on the floor. "Please! Both of you sit down!"

I sat. Neil started, then thought better of it.

He put his hands in his pockets and looked casual.

"Detective Brock, I assume before you came here you checked me out."

"I did."

"And?"

"The guys in the three-piece suits tolerate you."

"I'll take that as a compliment."

"It's easy when you don't have to play within the rules."

"I always play within the rules. I suggest you do the same. Ask your questions directly, and if I can, I will answer them."

"Besides maybe murdering Valcovich, what were you doing at his office?"

"We had an appointment to see him. I discovered him dead. Just exactly as you found him. We were the ones who phoned the police."

"After you thoroughly went through everything. What did you want with a guy like Valcovich?"

"That involves client privilege."

"Who's the client?"

"Miss Hill."

"Client privilege is bullshit. I found Valcovich's address book. It had Ellis Kenilworth's number in it. Didn't you work for him, Maggie?"

"Yes."

"Yeah. He blew his head off. Made you very upset." The dark, assessing eyes took me in. "Remember?"

"I remember."

"Detective Brock, we know you've talked to the Kenilworth family. Why do you persist in making this more difficult than it has to be?" Claire sighed.

"They say they met Valcovich once. He was in their brother's office having a meeting with Maggie. Did you tell them it was about a car accident?"

"Yes. But . . ."

He turned away from me and looked at Claire. "The next thing the Kenilworths know is that you're with Maggie and accusing them of stealing an amendment to their brother's will. Something about a four-million-dollar coin collection. They say it doesn't exist, and they make a very good case for their point of view."

"So they do. But I choose to believe Miss Hill."

"Where does Bobby Alt fit into all this?"

"I don't know if he fits anywhere. He may just be a young man who enjoys being used."

"Where is he now?"

"We took advantage of your resources. I suggest you do the same."

The smile turned cruel. "We're on this. I

can't stop you from interfering. But I want you to stay out of my way." He faced Boulton. "What kind of gun do you carry?"

"It depends on the occasion and my attire."

"Last night. What were you carrying?"

"Forty-five."

"Let's see your license."

"You have no search warrant!" Claire rapped her walking stick against the floor. "But if you wish, Boulton, you may show it to him," she added politely.

Boulton took out his wallet and flipped it open. Neil didn't bother to look.

"Valcovich was shot with a Derringer. I bet you have a couple of those sweet little babies for your vest pockets."

"Show him out, Boulton," Claire snapped.

"I want Maggie to show me out."

"That's up to her."

I stood and walked toward the hallway.

"Edith Wharton died fifty years ago," Claire called after him.

"Nineteen thirty-seven. I looked it up. She died in August in France. Supposed to be real hot then in France."

He turned and followed me to the front door. In silence we walked up the steps to the street and stood by his car. As usual, if the conversation was going to be personal, I had to start it.

"Why didn't you tell me you were getting married?"

"That's what the champagne was for. I thought you'd get a big joke out of it. Celebrating my marriage. Getting rid of me."

"Why didn't you tell me? Is this the same girl you had the affair with when we were married?"

"Yeah."

"Why let me go to bed with you?"

"I thought you needed me . . . or at least needed the kind of sex we have — *had* — together. Hell, I'd go to bed with you any time you asked, Maggie."

"Wonderful. What about her?!"

"This Friday. Ten o'clock. Little Brown Church. Coldwater Canyon. Wanna come?"

"You son of a bitch!"

"That's right, Maggie. And what are you? Why didn't you tell me to get the fuck out the other night? You've done it before — why didn't you do it then?!"

"I needed . . . I needed . . . "

"What? *What?* I hope you know what you need now, Maggie, 'cause you're in trouble all the way up to the top of your ears."

We looked at each other. The dark eyes were no longer assessing, just tired and sad. He got in his car and drove away.

14

It was the civilized hour. Claire and I stood outside the Kenilworths' house waiting for someone to open the door. My stomach was doing battle with Gerta's stuffed cabbage. The rest of me was doing battle with a bout of melancholy. So I had on my pink-and-black with the big shoulders for protection.

Sutton let us in. His hand trembled when he smoothed his blond hair.

A brass chandelier spilled pools of light onto the marble floor. A silk-shaded lamp in the library spread golden shadows on the damask sofa. I expected to see Ellis Kenilworth appear at any moment and gesture, in his mannerly way, for me to enter his office.

Sutton took my hand. "Remember how I used to escort you to the office, Maggie?"

"Yes."

"A meaningless gesture, but I miss it. Mother is waiting. Do you mind coming up to her sitting room?"

"Not at all," Claire replied as we moved

toward the stairs.

"Mother will do the talking," Sutton said stiffly. "I'm afraid the police being here has . . . well, she will do the talking."

He led us down the hallway and tapped gently on Eleanor's door.

"Mother?" He opened the door.

The room still had the heavy, sweet smell of a wealthy old woman's expensive debris. Four crystal-based lamps, wearing pale green shades, shimmered light. The fire licked and leaped behind the hearth screen. Eleanor was on her chaise lounge. A pale green bed jacket and a matching throw covered her. The aquamarine eyes glistened alertly from her skeletal-white face.

"Sit down." She gestured toward two chairs, covered in tapestry, which had been pulled close to her for the occasion. Sutton moved behind his mother and rested his hand on her shoulder. She stroked his hand. The circle of diamonds twisted and twinkled. The eyes focused on Claire.

"I want to make something clear. You are only in my house because a man has been murdered and I must protect my children, who, as usual, have acted stupidly. But their stupidity does not make them murderers. Judith will talk first. I must have your word that what she says will not go beyond this room."

"As you know, the police are already involved," Claire said.

"There are ways of answering their questions."

"True. But I can't make you any guarantees before hearing what Judith has to say."

Eleanor studied Claire for a moment, then turned to Sutton. "Go and get her."

Sutton left the room. Eleanor leaned toward the fire and held her hands up to its flames.

"Ugly, aren't they? Knotted with arthritis. Shriveling with osteoporosis. Yet when I look at them, I see my great-grandmother's hands. Pioneer hands. It was her land my husband built the hotel on. I inherited it. My late husband made it work. And my pitiful sons lost it. One silly mistake after another. Slowly bleeding the family dry. It's one thing to be a leech on somebody else. It's another to be a leech on yourself. You should never *have* to sell land. All that pioneer strength. That good lineage. Shrinking. What happens to families?" The aquamarine eyes glowed with spite.

There was a soft tap on the door.

"Enter."

The door opened. Judith, clutching her gray cardigan to her shoulders, quietly crossed the room and stood at the foot of her mother's chaise lounge. Her eyes were swollen from crying. Her mouth remained a thin, strict line. Sutton took his position behind Eleanor.

"Tell them," she commanded her daughter.

Judith pressed her lips together as if to keep her words from spilling out. Slowly, the lips moved. "I took the codicil from your purse, Maggie."

Truth. Just like that. So easy. I adjusted my shoulder pads. Not looking at Judith, Claire pushed back her chair, stretched out her legs, and stared into the fire.

"How? When?" I asked.

"Start from the beginning," Eleanor hissed.

Sutton stroked his mother's hair. Judith kept her head down.

"I believed you at first, Maggie. That Valcovich was really your lawyer. But Miss Conrad was right. When I left that morning I looked at your car. There was no sign of an accident, and I began to wonder. Sutton and I drove all the way to Century City trying to figure out why you would lie. Wondering who this lawyer really was. I sat through one of Brian's symposiums remembering how terribly Ellis had treated me that morning, thinking that Ellis hadn't been himself lately. He had been threatening to sell the coin collection. If he did . . . we'd have no way of paying . . . " She looked quickly at her mother.

"Anyway, he'd been talking strangely. I told Sutton how I felt, and we left the conference and drove back to the house. We didn't know what we were going to do. Confront Ellis. Tell Mother about the strange lawyer. Talk to you, Maggie. We didn't know. We slipped in through the hedge."

"And Valcovich was looking out the window and saw you. He thought you'd made him a very lucky man," Claire said.

Judith's pale cheeks turned crimson. "We ran through the garden and up the servants' stairs," she continued.

"Weren't you afraid of being seen by the help?" Claire tapped her stick on the white marble hearth. Judith looked flustered.

"At that time, Aiko and Maria are usually in the kitchen preparing lunch," Sutton said. "The stairs cannot be seen from the kitchen."

"We waited in Sutton's room till we heard the clock in the hallway chime and knew it was time for lunch. Aiko always serves Maggie on the patio, unless, of course, it's raining. And Ellis had told us over breakfast that he was going out for lunch. We waited a few moments; then Sutton went to search Ellis's bedroom. I ran back down the servants' stairs through the back hall to the foyer and into the office. I began looking around. I saw ashes in the wastepaper basket. I looked in Maggie's

261

desk, and Ellis's, for anything that might tell me why the lawyer was there. And then . . ."

"You heard a gunshot," Claire said.

"Yes. I watched Maggie through the window. She leaped up and started running toward the office. I ducked down behind her desk. She ran right past me into the foyer without knowing I was there."

"Why?" For the first time Claire looked at Judith.

"What?"

"Why did you hide behind the desk?"

"I was afraid. I wasn't supposed to be in the office."

"But weren't you the least bit concerned, if not curious, about the gunshot? You knew Sutton was upstairs. You didn't know your brother was going to kill himself."

"Of course not."

"Your mother might have been endangered. Weren't you worried about her?"

"Yes . . . but . . . I wasn't supposed to be there . . . in the office . . . in the house. . . . I was confused and frightened. . . . I . . . I'm not going to continue if she keeps asking me questions," Judith whined at her mother.

"Go on." Claire leaned back in the chair and continued staring into the fire.

"After Maggie ran into the foyer, I just stood there not knowing what to do. Then I saw it — her purse on the patio. I never remembered her carrying her purse onto the patio before. I used to watch her from upstairs. Aiko serving her. An employee being served by our Aiko."

"They're not interested in your pettiness, Judith," her mother said sharply.

"I'm sorry."

The apology was by rote. She had said the phrase so many times in her life that it no longer had any meaning.

"I went through your purse, Maggie." Her voice was a whisper.

"Speak up!" Eleanor demanded.

"Your purse! I went through it!" She spat out the words with disdain. "I found the envelope and opened it. There was the codicil. I kept it. And put the envelope back. I ran down into the garden, out through the hedge and into the alley. He was standing there. That awful lawyer."

Claire looked back into the fire. "Go on, Judith."

"I tried to go around him. He moved in front of me, blocking me . . . smiling. He pulled the codicil from my hand, looked at it, and said, 'I hope you didn't have to kill anybody for this. I'll be in touch.' He walked down the alley to his car and drove away. I ran down to the side street where we had parked

the car and waited for Sutton. I was so frightened. So confused." Tears rolled down her
tense face.

Claire looked at Sutton.

"Go on, tell her," Eleanor prompted.

"I searched Ellis's room." Sutton lovingly
curled a strand of his mother's hair around his
index finger as he talked.

"What did you find?" Claire asked.

"Nothing. Except his shotgun was out of its
case and there was a box of shells on his desk.
I heard someone come down the hallway, so I
hid in his closet. Ellis came into the room.
He sat at his desk and began writing. When
he had finished, he picked up the gun, loaded
the shells, and went into the bathroom. I
stepped out of the closet. I could see him
through the half-open door. He was undress-
ing. And I knew he was going to kill himself . . . " His voice faltered.

Judith sobbed. Eleanor stroked her son's
hand. "Go on," she said gently.

"He was sitting naked in the shower. His
legs drawn up. Knees shaking. He placed the
butt of the gun in the corner of the shower and
the end of the barrel under his chin. He stayed
that way for a few moments until his knees
stopped shaking. Then he pulled the trigger."

"You didn't try to stop him?" I demanded.

"No," he said simply. "It must be difficult

for you to understand, Maggie, but he'd caused the family, and especially Mother, a great deal of pain."

"I assume you heard Miss Hill come down the hallway?" Claire asked.

"Yes. I shut the connecting door. I could hear her in the bathroom, and then I heard her talking to Mother in the hall, taking her to her bedroom." He looked at me. "I'm grateful for that, Maggie."

"And then you opened the connecting door and took the suicide note," Claire said.

"The suicide note is none of your business," Eleanor said. "Our only common interest is the codicil."

"All right. When did Valcovich contact you?" Claire asked Judith.

"Early the next morning. He wanted five hundred thousand dollars."

"And that was when we told Mother," Sutton said.

Claire tapped her fingers on the walking stick; the lapis shimmered in the glow of the fire. "And what did the three of you decide to do?"

"Actually, four of us." Sutton cleared his throat.

"Stupid girl had to tell that evangelistic economist." Eleanor glared at Judith.

"He's the only one who cares about me," Judith pouted.

"He doesn't care about you!"

"We decided," Sutton cut in, "that Judith should go to Valcovich and try to reason with him."

"You were in the office! The first time I was there!" I said.

"I went out the private door when you came in. I was so afraid you saw me. There was no reasoning with him. Last night, Brian and I took him a check for a hundred thousand. We hoped it would keep him quiet for a while. And . . . there was blood everywhere . . . he was dead!" Her thin body swayed.

Claire stood, but Judith was closer to me: I grabbed her and helped her sit down in my chair. Sutton and Eleanor stared at her. Compassion wasn't one of this family's strong points.

"I'm all right." Judith's body stiffened under my attention.

"What time did you go to Valcovich's office?" Claire asked.

"A little after six. We left immediately."

Claire stood up and moved slowly around the room, staring at the silver-framed photographs and the delicate porcelain. Judith's fingers kneaded her skirt. Sutton and Eleanor watched Claire. The fire cracked and popped.

Claire faced Eleanor. "Instead of distancing herself from Valcovich's murder, your daughter's story puts her right in the middle of it."

"I didn't want to tell you. They made me tell you!" Judith cried.

"Shut up!" Eleanor leaned forward, slapping her hand on the side of the lounge, then turned on Claire.

"Don't you think I realize the implications of her story! I know my daughter is not capable of murder! Nor is my son!"

"He let his brother kill himself."

"He will have to live with that. But it was not murder."

"What do you want?" Claire asked her.

"To protect my daughter and son. And to retrieve the codicil."

"I don't need your protection!" Judith stood. "Brian will protect me. He'll say I was with him. I don't need — "

"Brian Waingrove will think of himself first," Eleanor hissed. "Then he will think of Victoria Moor. I doubt you will even enter his mind!"

"Victoria? What do you know?"

"Leave the room."

"Mother, please, tell me! What do you know?"

"Leave!"

"It's not true. It's not true!" Judith sobbed quietly.

"I said, leave!"

Judith stood and, like a scolded child, quietly left, shutting the door behind her.

Eleanor smoothed the sleeves of her bed jacket and said to Claire, "I have a proposition for you. I believe whoever killed this dreadful Valcovich also has the codicil. You find his murderer and I will split the revenues of Ellis's coin collection with you eighty-twenty. I will have to rely on your discretion."

"I can't believe this!" I blurted. "That coin collection belongs to her one hundred percent. She doesn't have to split with you or anybody."

"Miss Hill, please," Claire warned.

"None of this makes sense. You're not seriously considering — "

"Consider this," Eleanor interrupted. "If the codicil turns up — and that's a big 'if,' because paper is so easily destroyed — we will contest it, and we will win. My son *did* kill himself, and nobody in his right mind kills himself."

"It always comes back to Ellis, doesn't it, Mrs. Kenilworth?" I said.

"I'm not talking to you, Miss Hill. You were just a pawn used by my sick son."

Claire took the photograph from her pocket and handed it to Eleanor. "Is this an example of your son's sickness? Would you use it in court against us?"

Eleanor's gnarled hands shook as she studied the photo. Her lips drew back, and a mournful sob escaped.

"Where did you get this?"

"Victoria and her mother gave it to me. Inadvertently."

"She's a slut. A slut!"

"Mother, Mother . . ." Sutton spoke soothingly.

She grabbed for his hand and rubbed her cheek against it.

Claire moved closer to Eleanor. "I will consider your proposition if you will be honest with me. Are you being blackmailed?"

Eleanor's hand tightened around the photo and she began to crush it. Claire placed her hand on Eleanor's and carefully removed the picture.

"Your son was a sick man who could not face his desires for his own daughter. My guess is that he was being blackmailed because of those desires. And so he killed himself. But why did he will the collection to me and not to you, his family?"

"How many times do I have to say it? He was not in his right mind! There *was* no reason!"

"Maybe he was trying to reach out of his sickness. Maybe he thought I could find the answers for him."

"What more of an answer do you need than this!" She clawed at the photo, but Claire held it out of reach.

"Let Sutton tell me what your son's last words were."

"Show them out, Sutton. I've been a very foolish woman to expect your help, Claire Conrad."

"You don't strike me as a foolish woman, Mrs. Kenilworth. Where are your son's last words?" Claire looked into the fireplace. "In here?"

"Show them out!"

In the hallway Sutton turned toward the stairs. Claire headed toward the glassed-in rotunda. I hurried after her.

"What are you doing?"

"Servants' stairs, Miss Hill."

"What?"

"Just a minute," Sutton said, coming after us. "I was told to show you out."

Claire peered down a dark stairwell where the hallway connected to the rotunda — stairs I'd never noticed.

"Are there lights?" Claire asked.

"Of course." Sutton ran his hand along the wall of the stairs and found the switch. A dim light displayed simple wooden steps covered by a rubber matting.

"When I was a child I used to play with

270

dolls on our back stairs," Claire said.

"It's hard to imagine you playing with dolls," I said.

"Childhood and old age are great equalizers." Claire walked down a couple of steps. "It's only in between we have the chance to define ourselves."

She disappeared around the curve of wall.

I started to follow; Sutton stopped me. "Maggie, I want you to understand. If I had stopped Ellis, he would have killed himself eventually. It seemed easier just to let him do it. Can you understand?"

"I've never taken the easy way out."

"No. You wouldn't." He smiled sadly. Youthful beauty glimmered in the dim stairwell, then disappeared. "He caused Mother so much pain. I think I let him die to save her."

He walked down a few steps and peered around the wall. I followed him. "Where is Claire Conrad? How dare she." A cold, superior tone edged his voice.

He hurried down the stairs. I was right after him. The stairs ended in a small, narrow hall. I could hear the sound of a television from behind a closed door. I followed Sutton down the hall. He moved quickly toward an open back door. I followed him outside to a small brick patio and down another flight of stairs to the sculpture garden. I stopped. At night the animal sculptures looked black and ominous in the glare of the garden lights. I saw a white form. I stepped onto the grass. It was Claire. She lay awkwardly on her back among the topiary, as if she'd been carelessly tossed there.

"Good God," Sutton groaned.

I ran, kicking off my shoes so I could move faster. I sank down on my knees next to her. Her eyes stared.

"Good evening, Miss Hill. Lovely view from here." She smiled.

"Damn you!" I gasped.

"I beg your pardon?"

"I thought you were dead!"

"Is she all right? She's not . . . " Sutton came up behind us, breathing hard.

"Of course I'm all right." Claire rose to her feet. "I hope you're not disappointed," she said to Sutton. "Just took a tumble. Come along, Miss Hill. Don't forget your shoes."

The Bentley rolled toward the house. I rubbed my damp feet.

"Did you really fall?"

"Only far enough to see what I had to see."

"Which was?"

"I'll know better after we talk to Victoria Moor's daughter. When we get home, I want you to call Bobby Alt. Tell him we need to come to the house to see Rebecca, but only when Victoria and Patricia aren't there."

"He won't like it."

"That should please you."

15

"You will talk to the child, Miss Hill. I find communicating with children tedious at best and mind-numbing at worst."

It was eight thirty the next morning. We sat in the Bentley, waiting for Bobby Alt, at the bottom of Victoria's driveway.

"What should I ask her?"

"Ask her if she took this picture," Claire said, handing me the photograph. "The detective business is usually quite straightforward."

She was all in black today. I was beginning to figure it out: one day she wore white, next day black, then white, then black.

"Do you ever get confused and wear white when you're supposed to wear black?" I asked her.

"Never."

"Which color did you start with first?"

"White, of course. And I'll probably end up in black. We all do in one way or another."

The white limo pulled up alongside.

"He's here. Let me make sure he's alone," Boulton said, getting out of the Bentley.

He checked the limo, then motioned for us to get into it. We settled in the backseat. Boulton got in front, next to Bobby. Bobby squirmed around and started babbling to Claire.

"What is it you want? I can't let you take anything. Wouldn't be right."

"Are Victoria and her mother gone?" I asked.

"I told you last night — Victoria had an eight o'clock call at the studio. I just dropped them off."

"The little girl is still at home?"

"Yeah." Innocent eyes blinked nervously. "And someone else. If he sees you . . . "

"Who?" Claire asked.

"His name's Brian Waingrove. He sometimes spends the night. I saw his car in the garage when I took Victoria and Patricia to the studio. He thinks he's hot shit. But you should see him in a bathing suit. Hair everywhere. I mean *gorilla*."

"Poor Judith," I said to myself.

"Where do you usually park the car?" Claire asked.

"In the garage."

"Do so."

We drove in silence up the long curve of asphalt. I looked out the window at the profusion of ferns lining the edge of the drive. They were as feathery and as provocative as a fan dancer's fans, but they couldn't hide the sharp, steep hillside and its dry, bumpy terrain. I bet when the Santa Ana blew, tumbleweeds rolled across Shangri-la. I turned away from the window and saw Bobby's virgin eyes in the rearview mirror, watching me. His wide-eyed innocence belonged to the young — the very young.

He looked away and pushed the buttons on some gadget. The wrought iron gates slid open, as did the garage doors. He guided the car in and the doors gently closed behind us. The garage was the size of a house. Snuggled in it were a cute, creamy Mercedes convertible, a hunter-green Jaguar, and Waingrove's silver Mercedes.

"Where are your quarters?" Claire asked.

"Over the garage. If you'd just tell me what it is you want . . . "

"We'll talk in your room."

He led us out a side door and up some stairs.

No expense or detail had been spared on the chauffeur's quarters: beamed ceiling, wooden floor, built-in refrigerator, and a built-in entertainment center with all the equipment for one's visual and audio needs.

"Fantastic, isn't it?" He swaggered around the room.

"I think I'll take up limo driving," I said.

"You gotta get with the right people, though," he said earnestly.

Claire moved quickly around the room, looking out the windows and into the bathroom. Boulton leaned against the front door.

"What time does Waingrove usually leave?" she asked casually, looking through a pile of papers on his built-in desk.

"He usually takes a swim, then he gets dressed and leaves about now," he said, eyes intent on the papers in her hands. "Sometimes he sits around the pool and talks real loud on the phone. That's my private stuff."

"Where's the child's room located?" Claire opened an envelope.

"What do you want her for?"

"Where is her room?"

"South side of the house. Victoria and Patricia's rooms are in the north wing." He liked saying "the north wing."

"Is there a nanny?"

"Her room is right across from Becky's. She'll be getting dressed to take her to school."

"And the child?"

"Getting dressed."

"You've got a very large phone bill. It must be all these toll calls to Pasadena."

"Who are you calling in Pasadena?" I asked.

"A friend. Is it so unusual to have a friend in Pasadena? I mean, it's not like I'm calling some extravagant place like . . . like . . . Paris, France."

"What's your friend's name?" I asked.

"Just a friend. What are you so hot and bothered about Pasadena for?"

"Bobby, if I don't like your answers, you'll be blinking your big, innocent eyes from behind bars — remember?"

He bolted. His hands were on the doorknob before Boulton could grab him by his right arm and swing him back onto the bed.

"Don't hit me! Don't hit me!"

He pulled his knees to his chest and covered his face with his arms.

"I'm not going to hit you, you little sod." Boulton moved back to the door.

I sat down next to Bobby on the bed. He pulled himself up to a sitting position and leaned against the wall.

"Come on, Bobby, who's your friend in Pasadena?"

"Why can't you just leave me alone? I never done anything to you. I mean *really* anything."

"Is his last name Erwin, Bobby?" I asked.

The virgin eyes widened. "Yeah, that's him."

I looked at Claire; she shook her head.

"I think his friend is his new mother," she said.

Bobby's eyes focused on the door, but he didn't try for it. "Patricia's my new mother. I told you that. Why don't you just get what you came for and leave?"

Claire handed me his phone bill. "Is that the Kenilworth telephone number?"

"Yes."

"I wondered how Eleanor knew Victoria was having an affair with Waingrove. How much does she pay you to spy for her?" Claire asked.

"None of your business."

"I don't like your answer, Bobby," I said.

"None of your business!"

Boulton walked over and slapped him hard.

I leaped off the bed. "Wait a minute! You didn't have to do that."

"Miss Hill, please," Claire said softly.

Bobby was holding a blanket to his face, the eyes wide with betrayal. "You said you weren't going to hit me."

"Boulton has a tendency to fabricate," Claire said, pulling the blanket away from his face. "What kind of information do you give Eleanor?"

"Just everyday stuff."

"An example, please."

"If Patricia has a crying jag, or she's drinking too much. Waingrove sleeping with Victoria. If I overhear what Victoria is planning to say in interviews. I don't know . . . just stuff."

"What else?"

"Just regular stuff."

Claire got up and looked out the window, down at the front of the house. "It doesn't look as if Waingrove is leaving early. You'd better go and talk to the child, Miss Hill."

"What if I run into Waingrove or the nanny?"

"You're a very resourceful woman, Miss Hill. You'll think of something."

"Thanks. How do I get into the house from here?" I asked Bobby.

"The back door is under the stairs. It's unlocked in the morning." His eyes blinked purity. "Oh, I forgot to tell you. There're two maids — one upstairs, one downstairs."

"Wonderful."

Claire pulled a black leather chair up to the bed and sat down. "Eleanor arranged for you to deliver the flowers to Patricia, didn't she? You were supposed to seduce her. Was that the plan?"

Bobby tugged at the blanket.

"Are you going to tell Eleanor about us being here?" she asked.

Bobby looked at me. I smiled. "It's either the police or him," I said, patting Boulton's shoulder. "Or you could answer her questions."

"It was so easy. I mean, Patricia was so ready." He grinned and stretched, puffing his chest.

I was almost glad to leave the room. I made my way down the stairs. Near the back door was a locked wrought iron gate. I peered over it and was able to glimpse a piece of Shangri-la. Waingrove was in the pool doing laps. I moved to the back door and listened. I heard the sounds of a washer and dryer performing their functions. I opened the door and breathed in the sharp smells of bleach and detergent. My adrenaline was pumping. I kept telling myself to stay calm. I made my way around a pile of dirty clothes on the terracotta floor and into a big kitchen with a brick fireplace and an eating area. Everything was blue and white, down to the plates hanging on the walls. The dishwasher purred on the dry cycle. This was the kind of kitchen dreams and commercials were made of.

I stood by the fireplace and peered around the corner of an open door into the dining room and the dark eyes of the downstairs maid — unless it was the upstairs maid, who had come downstairs.

"Yes?" she said, eyes narrowing with suspicion.

"I'm Mr. Waingrove's secretary," I blurted.

"He's swimming."

"Yes, I know. He wants me to get him his briefcase. Upstairs."

"Yes?"

"Yes."

We stared at one another for a moment. Smiling and nodding my head inanely, I slowly moved past her through the dining room. I didn't hear her running or screaming, so I kept going and ended up in the English pub. From the French doors I could see Waingrove spread-eagled on the candy-striped raft bobbing in the pool. Two men, their backs to me, stared into the stream. One held Patricia's limp pink hat in his hand; the other had the dead fish by its tail. The fish shimmered like a piece of jewelry in the morning sun. I made it through the pub and out into the main hallway. I turned toward the stairs and took them as fast as I could.

I saw her Maryjanes first and came to a dead halt. Rebecca stood on the landing, watching me.

"You were here yesterday," she said.

"I've come back to talk to you."

I could hear a woman humming down the hallway, and then the crisp sound of a sheet being snapped over a mattress.

"Did Mother send you?" The depleted eyes looked me up and down.

"Yes. Could we talk in your room?"

"I'm waiting for Anna to get out of the shower so she can button my dress."

"I'll button it."

"Are you a psychologist?"

"That's a big word."

She turned and walked down the hall away from the maid. I followed Rebecca into her bedroom.

Pink organdy puffed around the windows. Pink piqué cascaded from a dressing table. The rug was as soft as cotton candy. Dolls and stuffed animals were methodically lined up according to height around the room. The closet door was open. Maryjanes and expensive tennis shoes were placed neatly in a row. Dresses dangled from their hangers like a precision march of headless and limbless little girls.

Rebecca plopped herself down on her pink quilted bed and stared at me without interest. I sat down on the tufted stool in front of the dressing table.

"You have a lot of toys," I said. Oh, hell, it was a start.

I got a shrug for an answer.

"I bet you have a camera."

I got another shrug.

"I bet you like to take a lot of pictures."

"My mother is in pictures, so I don't need to take them."

"How old are you?"

"Nine and a half." Her voice was slow and bored.

"What gives you the right to be so condescending at nine?"

"And a half."

"Oh, hell, did you take this photograph?" I walked over and showed it to her.

"You're not a psychologist."

"Answer my question."

"Who are these people, anyway?" she asked, looking at the photo.

"Don't you know?"

"I think that's my grandfather. And it sort of looks like my mother. But I don't think it is."

"Why?"

Another shrug. If I ever have a kid, I'm going to put weights on its shoulders so it will never be able to shrug. She slipped off the bed, walked over to the dressing table, and opened a pink leather jewelry box. A tiny plastic ballerina in a wisp of tulle skirt tilted up and began to twirl stiffly to the tune of "Greensleeves." She took out a quartz watch and slammed the lid down.

"That's a pretty jewelry box."

"Grandfather sent it to me."

"Did you like your grandfather?"

"I don't know my grandfather. Why should I like him?"

"Good point. What about your father? Where's he?"

"I've never met him."

I looked away from her eyes. They made me as uneasy as Bobby Alt's. She was much too young to be so depleted of her innocence, and he was much too old to still have his. I noticed that when she got off the bed she had kicked the dust ruffle up. Hidden under the bed was a cardboard box. So she did have secrets, and they weren't all in her head.

"I bet you have a camera. I bet you took this picture," I said.

"I bet I didn't."

"Bet you did."

"I didn't."

"You did."

I was on my knees by the bed, pulling out the cardboard box. It was filled with bleached-blond Barbie dolls. Two of the dolls had their ripe, firm breasts pushed in. Another had been mutilated with scissors or a razor. Another Barbie had her missing pubic hair painted in in red ink. I looked at Rebecca. She was filled with sugar and spice and self-loathing, all the good things little girls are made of.

"My dollies," she said simply.

I placed them back in the cardboard box and shoved them under the bed with my foot. I hadn't discovered any camera; but I had discovered a pink nightmare, and I wanted out of it.

"If you didn't take this picture of your grandfather and your mother, do you know who did?"

"I told you that's not my mother."

"So you did. Do you know who it is?"

"No."

"This woman sure looks like your mother."

"Who are you? What are you doing in here?" A large, white-haired woman in a blue nylon uniform stood in the doorway.

"Hello . . . you must be Anna," I said, trying to keep my voice calm.

"I still don't know who you are."

"I'm Brian Waingrove's secretary."

She pinched her lips together at the sound of his name. She didn't like him, either.

"He's going to be staying here this afternoon and wanted me to come to the house and take some letters for him." I tried to keep my voice even.

"Oh. What are you doing in here?"

"I heard Becky calling for you and you were

in the shower so I came up to see if I could do anything for her. I was just going to button the back of her dress." I pulled Becky to me and began fumbling with the little buttons.

"Is this true, Rebecca? Remember, we always tell the truth," Anna commanded.

Rebecca shrugged. God, I loved that shrug.

"She's doing it wrong." Becky squirmed away from me and placed herself in front of Anna. "You button me!"

"Well, if there's nothing more that I can do . . . It was nice meeting you. I'll be around the pool, with Mr. Waingrove, if you need me."

I slipped past them and out into the hallway. Trying not to run, I made my way down the stairs, back through the main hall, and into the pub. There were milky-white footprints on the floor. Patricia was right — chlorine does stain wood floors.

A hand grabbed my shoulder. "If it isn't the ubiquitous Miss Hill," Waingrove said, keeping his hand firm on my shoulder.

I knew he didn't like women; but even before I could open my mouth, he had shoved me hard against the eighteenth-century paneling.

"What are you doing here?" he asked.

"Looking for the codicil."

"I was hoping you'd say that you came here to return the photograph you stole from Victoria."

"I don't know what you're talking about."

I moved sideways against the wall. He edged closer. His gray terry-cloth robe was open. He wore a wet black bikini. Water clung like tiny diamonds to the black hair on his chest and belly.

"Does Judith know you're screwing Victoria?" I asked.

I moved away from the wall, trying for the open French doors. He shoved me back again. His nose twitched, and he slammed his hand across my face. My cheek and chin burned as if they had been scalded. My eyes filled. I tried not to blink. I didn't want the bastard to see my tears. He came right at me, pressing the full weight of his body against mine.

"For a man who doesn't like women, this kind of closeness must bother you," I whispered in his ear.

He ran his hand down my right side and into my pocket. He found the photograph. We stared at each other for a moment. I raised my knee and jammed it into his groin. He sucked in air.

Something moved behind him. Boulton came into focus, slamming the butt of his gun into Waingrove's head. He crumpled to the floor, his gray terry cloth spreading out around him like a king's robe. Claire appeared in the open French doors. Bobby squeezed in around her and began moving frantically about the room.

"Is he dead? Oh, God, is he dead?"

"Just resting his eyes," Boulton said, picking up the photograph and handing it to me. "Miss Conrad was worried about you. I think you need some kind of weapon, Maggie."

"I handled him," I said.

"He wasn't very adept."

"I believe we've outstayed our welcome. Don't worry about us, Mr. Alt, we can walk down the drive," Claire said, as if she were leaving a tea party.

"What'll I do about him? What do I tell him?" Bobby gasped.

"Try not to be too clever, Mr. Alt. You might end up dead. Come along, Boulton . . . Miss Hill."

We followed Claire out the main hall and through the front door.

Bobby ran after us, screaming, "You've ruined everything! You bastards! Bastards!" He slammed the front door.

As we started down the drive, I turned and looked back at the house. Rebecca was in her turret, staring down at us.

"What did she have to say?" Claire asked.

"That the picture wasn't taken by her. And that it's not a picture of her mother."

Claire looked sharply at me. "Any reason?"

"No."

"Did she say who she thought it was?"

"No."

"What else?"

"She shrugs a lot."

"What did Waingrove say?"

"I think I get on his nerves. He wanted the photograph back."

We reached the large curve of the drive. Boulton stopped and cocked his head like an animal does when listening for its foes.

"Jump!" He yelled. "Jump!"

He lunged for Claire, clutching her to his body. He grabbed for my hand. It slipped from his as he took her over the edge of the drive. Numb with amazement, I watched them roll down the hillside.

And all the time he yelled, "Maggie! Maggie!"

I heard the limo and whirled around. Its chrome grille pointed right at me. I felt the heat of the engine. The screeching front tire pulled at the hem of my skirt. Bobby Alt's virgin eyes drove right into me. I jumped. Dirt filled my eyes as I hit and careened down the hill. My head, elbows, knees banged into rocks. I grabbed at ivy, roots, air. I kept falling, rolling. Dry bark scraped at my skin. I slammed into a tree. Dusty leaves rattled. I opened my eyes. The sky was a blue canopy over me.

Boulton's face blocked out the blue. "Did he hit you?"

"No."

"Damn it, Maggie! When I say jump, jump!"

He gently lifted me to my feet. I was missing a shoe, and both my hands clutched hunks of ivy and geraniums in a death grip. I looked up toward the drive. Claire stood about halfway up the hill, leaning precariously on her walking stick. Her black suit was covered with dust and ivy; leaves and twigs clung to her hair.

"That is a disgusting young man!" she observed.

"Right," Boulton sighed.

16

"Children make mistakes," I said, following Claire into the cottage. "Or maybe she just didn't want to believe it was her mother. This is a pretty shocking photograph."

"That child may be only nine, but she does not look as if she is easily shocked." She collapsed into the Queen Anne chair. Little puffs of dust billowed around her.

"I think she's permanently shocked. She'll probably grow up to be a private detective."

"Experiencing horror when one is young is an excellent prerequisite." She picked more flora off her jacket.

"All right, if this isn't Victoria Moor in this photograph, who is it?" I slumped on the sofa.

She leaned back and stared at me without answering.

"And why would Victoria Moor make up a story about incest to protect whoever is in this picture?"

She shut her eyes.

"And why would she and her mother be so

interested in the photograph if it's not her? It has to be her."

"Her daughter doesn't agree."

"A nine-year-old child."

"Whom Victoria did not tell."

"Didn't tell what?"

She opened her eyes. They shone with the excitement of thought. "She didn't tell Rebecca that the woman in this photograph was supposed to be her. Children are so easily overlooked."

"Explain, please." I crossed my legs and watched another run squirm down my knee to my ankle.

"A picture is not worth a thousand words. Before we even saw this photograph, it had already been interpreted for us by Bobby Alt. When we finally see the photograph, with our very own eyes, Victoria and her mother are right there with us, performing the equivalent of instant analysis by describing its content and context for us."

"Yes?"

"I just wonder how we would've interpreted this photo if we had not been told who was in it and what they were doing."

I took the photo out of my pocket and studied it. "The exact same way. This is Ellis and Victoria. Even Eleanor Kenilworth agrees that it's Victoria and her son."

Slowly, Claire pulled herself out of the chair. She rubbed her backside, then took the photo from my hand. "I wonder what it is they don't want us to see in this picture. . . . I'm going to change. You should do the same." She started toward her bedroom.

"There's one thing they can't hide in that picture," I said.

"And what is that?"

"The passion."

She studied me for a moment, then her face brightened. "*Passion!* Very good, Miss Hill." She disappeared into her room.

Wondering what was so very good about passion — it had brought me only pain — I made my way down the hall to my room. Boulton, all brushed and clean, was in the dining room, laying out the silverware for lunch.

"You make us jump off hills and now you're setting the table."

"But I saved your life." He carefully folded a napkin. "And now you can enjoy that life at a properly set table."

"I'm going to wash the dust off me."

"After you do, I'd like to give you something. It's in my room."

"I'd like to see your room."

"Why is that?"

"Might tell me something about you."

"It's a Spartan's room, Maggie." He picked

294

up another napkin, snapped it efficiently in the air, and smiled at me.

I went to my room and showered.

Applying makeup is a ritual done by rote. A woman can put on her makeup without taking a really good look at her face. But now and then, without any warning, you are suddenly aware of your bare face in the mirror. Sometimes you greet it as an old friend; sometimes you back away from it, hoping distance will improve what you see. I had one eye done before I realized how mournful my eyes looked and how determinedly my mouth was set. The combination gave me a peculiarly wise look. But it was a wisdom I didn't feel or understand. What I did understand was that my life was never going to be the same again, and that tomorrow I was going to Neil's wedding. Why my life was never going to be the same again, I didn't know. Why I was going to Neil's wedding, I didn't know. I *did* know that I wasn't as wise as I looked.

I quickly finished, grabbed my pink-and-black number, and was on my way to Boulton's room.

His door was open. He sat on a straight-backed chair, facing a desk that looked more like a workbench, lined with books and various tools. His jacket hung on the back of the chair. A gray blanket was pulled tightly over his bed. A set of tortoiseshell brushes was arranged on a linen towel on his dresser. There was a locked gun case on the wall.

Seeing me in the doorway, he stood. His shirt sleeves were rolled up. "Come in, Maggie. You see, very Spartan."

"I see."

"I do have a few possessions that I carry around with me." He looked at the brushes. "These were my great-great-grandfather's. They survived the Zulus. He didn't. Even a Spartan bloke like me has to carry something around from the past. Otherwise I wouldn't be a true Englishman. We have a hard time shedding our history."

"I have a hard time remembering mine. Like a true American."

He opened a dresser drawer and took out a burl box. "I want you to have this."

"It's a beautiful box . . . but I couldn't. We don't know each other. . . . "

"Open it."

I turned a little brass key and unlocked the box. Nestled in green velvet was a small pearl-handled gun.

"A gun? You're giving me a gun?"

"It was my mother's."

"That's very sweet . . . I think. But I don't want a gun."

"She killed two Germans with it."

"Nazis?"

"No. Just two Germans."

"Wonderful. Thank you. But I don't believe in guns."

"You don't believe in the existence of this gun in this box?"

"I don't believe in the *use* of guns."

"And you were married to a policeman." He took the gun out of the box and held it in his hand. "Navy Colt. Two-and-a-half-inch barrel. Nickel plated. Pearl handle. But don't let its delicate beauty fool you."

"I won't."

"You don't have to be as close to your target with this as you do with some of the other smaller guns."

"Target?"

He smiled. "All right, the person you intend to shoot."

"I don't intend to shoot anybody."

"Even with such a small gun there is a slight kick. So aim just below where you want the bullet to strike."

"I don't want a bullet to strike anywhere."

"Here is how you load it and unload it."

He emptied a small box of bullets on the dresser with the same care a woman might use to lay out her precious jewels. The bullets looked more frightening than the gun. He slipped them into the round chamber and snapped the gun together.

"All loaded. This is the safety catch. It's on."

"Boulton. I don't want it."

"Look, it slips right into the pocket of your pretty jacket." He put the gun into my pocket. "Trust me, Maggie."

I remembered Ellis Kenilworth slipping the codicil into my purse and asking me to trust him. I felt the weight of the gun in my pocket like Sisyphus must've felt the weight of his rock.

I started to remove the gun, but he grabbed my hand and held it gently. "I insist."

"I won't use it."

"Yes you will."

We were close. I could feel his warm breath. He smelled of soap and lemon and boot polish. His hand moved slowly up my arm, then stopped.

"I should be going upstairs. Gerta likes her food served promptly. And Miss Conrad likes to eat promptly."

He took his jacket from the back of the chair and gave it a quick brush. Looking in the mirror, he slipped it on.

"I like to watch men get dressed," I said.

"Really?" He smiled.

"Men who aren't narcissistic about it."

"I like to watch women get dressed who *are* narcissistic about it."

I smiled. "I like to watch men get dressed. It reminds me of when I was a little girl watching my father get dressed. I loved watching him shave, pat on his terrible-smelling cologne, fasten his watch on his firm, flat wrist, scoop what little change he had off the dresser and put it in his trousers pocket . . . jingle it. He looked strong. Made me feel secure."

"I like to watch women get dressed who don't remind me of my mother."

We stared at each other in silence. There is always a solemn moment between a man and a woman before they're going to kiss for the first time, a sort of sexual, electrified formality which allows them to safely submit to one another. Boulton and I experienced such a moment.

He broke it by gesturing toward the door. "Shall we go?"

Damn the English! I started toward the door, Oh, hell. I turned and threw my arms around him and kissed him. His arms went quickly around me, his hand up the back of my neck. His lips pressed gently against mine, and our mouths opened. His lips pressed harder. His hand tightened on the back of my neck and he moved me against his bed.

"Wait a minute," I said. "Don't forget Gerta."

"Don't start what you can't finish, Maggie."

"What?"

He shoved me back onto the bed. His heavy body crushed down on mine. His kiss was all bone, teeth, and jaw. I tried to kick. He jammed his leg between my legs and pressed his hips down hard, dry-humping me. I wiggled one hand free from under his chest and went for his face. He leaned his right forearm across my throat. I raised my head. I choked, his arm a weight on my throat. I was helpless. I was as brittle as glass under him. His hand pushed up my skirt. I tried to talk; his arm pressed down. I couldn't swallow. I couldn't move. I thought of Kenilworth and Waingrove. I thought of Neil. I was tired of being shoved around by men. I wasn't going to let him do this to me. Don't start what you can't finish, Maggie. That's what he'd said, and he was right! I moved my hand slowly, carefully into my pocket. I felt the gun and pulled it out, driving it into his gut. We stared at one another again, sharing a new kind of solemnity.

He lifted his arm from my throat and said, "You see, Maggie, you used the gun. Only next time remove the safety catch."

He moved off me and sat on the edge of the bed.

"Let me show you. Do it in one motion. Finger on trigger, thumb — "

"Bastard!" I scrambled off the bed.

He stood, taking my hand, the one that still had the gun, and kissed it. "I just wanted to prove to you that you were capable of using — "

"Bastard!"

I swung from the heels and slammed my hand across his face and left the room.

Claire sat at the dining-room table, staring at her empty plate. As I sat down, she looked up at me. "Nobody is bringing me my food."

"I suppose you never considered getting up and getting it yourself," I snapped.

She leaned back and studied me. "You appear abnormally agitated for just taking a spill over a hillside."

"It's not the hillsides I'm having trouble with. It's the pitfalls."

Boulton came out of the kitchen carrying two plates of iced cracked crab. He set one down in front of Claire and the other in front of me.

As he retreated to the kitchen, she said, "That's an interesting red mark you have on your face, Boulton."

"Yes, madam."

"It looks to me as if you'd been slapped — by the intensity of the redness I'd say quite recently. You weren't criticizing Gerta's cooking, were you?"

"No, madam."

She studied him . . . and then took a good look at me. "I didn't think so. Poor men . . . poor women," she said, with a surprising amount of compassion.

"I quite agree, madam," he said.

"Must the effects of Miss Hill's presence always disturb my household around mealtime?"

"I'll see that it doesn't happen again," he said stiffly.

"*I* will see that it doesn't happen again!" I raved.

"Whatever is going to happen, or not happen, I would prefer it happen, or not, in the hours between my breakfast, my lunch, and my dinner. We have important matters to discuss. I would like you to join us, Boulton."

Boulton returned with a place setting for himself and his food. He sat between us. I did not look at him.

Claire picked up her silver tongs and expertly cracked a chunk of crab shell. With surgical efficiency she removed a small piece of white meat, dipped it in mustard sauce, and plopped it into her mouth.

I surveyed my plate with foreboding. I have never liked eating food that requires a lot of tools and dexterity.

"There was a reason you found me lying prone in the Kenilworth garden last night, Miss Hill," Claire said. "I was looking at the tops of the sculpted privets . . . trying to see them from a smaller person's — say, a child's — point of view. They look very similar to shadowy abstract clouds. In fact, in a grainy black-and-white photograph they might look exactly like dark clouds. There is another child involved in this case. A man-child."

I turned and sneered at Boulton. My fork slipped.

"Perhaps you would like me to show you how to use the utensils, Maggie," he said in his most British accent.

Claire let out a long sigh and continued. "Can Jerry communicate, Miss Hill?"

"He has Down's syndrome. I don't think so."

"Boulton, I want you to bring Erwin here. I don't care how you do it just as long as he is alone. Miss Hill, I want you to follow Boulton in your car to Erwin's house. You will remain there and search it thoroughly. He said his wards are in school from eleven to three, so you should not be bothered."

"What about the woman who takes care of them?"

"You'll think of something. You've han-

303

dled yourself very well so far."

"What am I searching for?"

"Photographs, an old camera, or any kind of writing that might imply blackmail."

"You think Erwin's the blackmailer?"

"I think I would like to discuss the possibility with him."

After lunch I went back to my room and got my purse. I took the gun out of my pocket and put it in the drawer of my nightstand. I headed out the door. Halfway down the hall I stopped. I went back to my room. I put the gun in my purse. Oh, hell, it was his mother's.

17

I strapped myself into my Honda and followed the Bentley through San Marino into Pasadena. Boulton turned down Erwin's street and parked the Bentley out of view of the house. I did the same. He got out of the car and waited for me. We walked in silence toward Erwin's house. He took the gun from the small of his back and held it in his pocket like a Hollywood thirties gangster. My life was becoming more and more unreal.

"Did you bring yours?" he asked.

"Yes," I said under my breath.

"Thank you," he said in a mock whisper.

"What would you have done if I hadn't pulled your dear mother's gun on you?"

"I would've told Miss Conrad that you were not capable of searching this house alone."

"That's not what I'm asking you and you know it."

"I wouldn't have hurt you, Maggie."

We reached Erwin's house. Boulton knocked on the door. It opened, and Erwin stood there looking as if he were expecting someone — and it wasn't us.

We shoved our way in. Erwin tried to duck past us and out the door.

Boulton pulled out his gun. "Don't." He smiled. Erwin stopped.

"Come slowly toward me with your hands in the air."

"What do you want?"

"Miss Conrad requests your company. And I want you to spread your legs and put your hands against the wall. Now, there's a good chap."

Boulton ran his hands up and down Erwin's body. The cloak-and-dagger game was carnal.

"Where's the lady who looks after your wards?"

"Out."

"How long will she be gone?"

"I don't know."

"The wards?"

"School."

"Who were you expecting?" I asked.

He shifted his weight. "Nobody."

Boulton looked at me. "Something wrong, Maggie?"

"No."

"Now, we are going to walk very slowly out of your house and down the street to the car." Boulton shoved the gun into his back.

"All right. All right."

"Don't be too long, Maggie," Boulton said, pushing Erwin out the door.

Erwin balked. "What are you assholes doing? She can't stay here! . . . What do you want?"

"Don't make a scene. We don't want the authorities called, do we?" Boulton's voice was smooth.

I watched them walk to the Bentley. Erwin kept making funny lurching movements and Boulton kept jerking at his arm. They looked like two drunks instead of one man holding a gun on another man. When they got to the car, Boulton had Erwin open the back door, then whirled him around and hammered his fist into his face. Erwin fell backwards into the car. Boulton slammed the door. I shut the door to the house and locked it.

Silence. Not even a clock ticked. To my right were the dining area and the kitchen. To my left was a hallway. I took the hallway. There were two doors on each side and one at the end, all of them closed. What the hell, I'd been peeking behind a lot of closed doors lately.

I opened the first door on my right. A pink carnation in a glass vase sat on a cheap, secondhand dresser. Over the bed was a framed poster of a Japanese woman. Her face was

307

powdered white; she was wrapped in a beautiful, intricate robe. Under her tiny feet were the words "Come to the Orient." As I moved around the room, I could feel her watching me over the edge of her painted fan.

I went through the dresser. The only thing I discovered was that Erwin shared the room with the woman. She was neat and he was a slob. I searched the closet . . . nothing. Under the bed . . . nothing. I even shoved my hands between the mattress and the box springs. Nothing.

I tried the next door. It opened into a large, beige-tiled bathroom. Paint was peeling on the ceiling, and the shower needed grouting. I looked through the medicine cabinet and under the sink. I found a lot of Ajax and toilet-bowl cleanser but that was all.

I moved across the hall and opened the first door. An earless toy monkey stared at me from one of the two twin beds; it had eyes just like Bobby Alt's. I went through a dresser. It rocked back and forth as I pulled open the drawers. I found a couple of pairs of well-worn jeans and threadbare undershorts. Jerry — Jerry Frant — had his name in some of the clothes. So did an Oliver Basscom; I guessed he was the old guy who drooled. Other than a collection of very ordinary rocks there was nothing else in the dresser. I went through the closet. Two windbreakers, two wrinkled shirts, and some tennis shoes with no treads left. I looked around the room. There was no camera. There was nothing. It was a sad, empty room for people who don't belong, for people we don't quite know what to do with. Depression spread through me. Oh, hell, I didn't have the time to allow myself the pleasure of depression.

I opened the next door upon a room that was exactly the same. I searched the cheap dresser. The name Penny Thomas was stamped in large, square-shaped panties. Penny Thomas had to be the woman with the mad blue eyes. I searched through a cotton slip, a lumpy cotton bra with bent hooks and eyes, and a collection of empty envelopes addressed to Occupant, Resident, and Affluent Buyer.

I looked under the twin beds and found little webs of dust. I felt under the pillows and mattresses. One bed was made; one wasn't. I opened the closet and stared at two big nylon dresses and a parka with matted fake fur around the hood. They hung from their hangers in sad desolation. The crazy-eyed woman didn't have much, either.

Closing the closet door, I noticed that the parka didn't hang evenly on its hanger; it dipped to one side as if something were weighing it down. I ran my hands over the jacket.

A heavy object was hidden in it. I took the parka off the hanger, sat on the bed, and unsnapped the old plaid lining. A pretty, pink-leather jewelry box fell to the floor. The lid flew open. The plastic ballerina turned stiffly to "Greensleeves." There was no quartz watch or pearls in this box, just more empty envelopes addressed to Occupant, Resident, and Affluent Buyer. I closed the lid and stared at my discovery. This was just like the jewelry box Rebecca Moor had in her room. Just like the jewelry box Ellis Kenilworth had given her. I wondered if the crazy-eyed woman took the box out at night and watched the ballerina go round and round. I wondered if she thought about all the good things little girls are made of. I wondered why she needed to hide the jewelry box. I snapped the lining back in place and hung the parka in the closet. Promising myself I would return it to her later, I slipped the jewelry box in my purse and left the room.

I stopped in the hall, deciding whether I should continue my search for the camera or get the hell out. I smelled smoke . . . cigarette smoke. I wasn't alone in the house. I stared at the closed door at the end of the hallway. Had I not had the gun in my purse, I think I would have run. But I was learning that a gun, like a couple of drinks, makes you bolder, though not necessarily smarter.

The door opened. She stood there staring at me with nervous eyes and a cigarette hanging out of her mouth. Her quivering hand pointed a gun at me. A gun in the purse is not worth a gun in the hand.

"Did they send you?" The Smoker asked. She didn't recognize me.

"Yes," I lied. "I didn't know which room you were in . . ."

"What happened to Erwin?"

"Don't need him around."

"Do you have the money?"

"Yes."

"Come in here. Slowly!"

As I walked toward her, she backed farther into the room till she was against the wall. Once I was in, she said, "Shut the door and sit on the bed."

I sat on the bed. It was a metal frame and a mattress. It was the only piece of furniture in the room.

"Where's the money?"

"Where's the codicil?"

She peered at me through a curl of smoke. Her eyes focused with thought. I knew I was in trouble. I could almost see her secretarial mind flipping through its cerebral Rolodex trying to place my face with my phone number and address.

"Hill, Maggie. Shit," she said.

"There are some skills a good secretary never loses."

"What do you want?" She coughed.

"Guess."

"Don't be cute. I've got the gun."

"True. But you should remove the safety catch."

She looked down at the barrel. I drove my hand into my purse, trying for my gun, but rammed it into the jewelry box. She fired. We stared at one another, eyes wide, mouths open. Her cigarette clung to her lower lip. It fell to the floor.

"The safety catch isn't on," she observed, crushing the cigarette with her foot. "Don't move."

She came toward me, jerked my purse from me, and threw it across the room. We both looked at my clasped hand. I held my grandmother's rosary.

"Gives me comfort in time of stress," I said, looking around at the wall in back of me.

The bullet hole was about two feet over my head. I wondered if that was an intended warning shot or if she just didn't know about guns kicking.

"What are you doing here?"

"I came for a pink jewelry box. Has a little ballerina that pops up and dances to 'Greensleeves.' Does that mean anything to you?"

"I think you and I are beyond pink boxes with dancing ballerinas," she sneered.

"True."

"So what the hell am I going to do with you?"

"You could give me the codicil and let me go."

"Shut up. I have to think. If you hadn't butted in on any of this, Roger would be alive. We'd have it made by now. I'll let *them* take care of you . . . that's what I'll do. We'll wait."

"Who are we waiting for?"

"Shut up!" She paced back and forth at the foot of the bed.

"Whoever it is, they'll probably take care of us both. Just like they did Valcovich," I said.

"But I've got what they want."

"But once you give it to them . . . "

"Shut up!" She jabbed the gun in my direction.

"Look, I was the one taken advantage of. The codicil was stolen from me by Judith Kenilworth. Did she tell you to come here?"

"I phoned her. Told her I just wanted a fair price. She said to call back in an hour. I did. A man told me to come here."

"Was it Erwin you talked to?"

"Different voice."

"Who killed Valcovich?"

"I don't know. Stop playing with that!"

I let the rosary fall into my lap. "How did you get the codicil?"

"I was getting ready to leave. Roger came out of his office and said he was going to strike a deal. But he wanted to play it safe, so he gave me the codicil. He thought as long as they didn't have it, they wouldn't hurt him." Tears filled her eyes. "He went back into his office. Whoever it was came in through the private door. It was only seconds and I heard the shot. And I knew." Tears rolled down into the deep lines of her dry, sunken face. "I hid in the closet. I heard the killer searching the files, my desk, and then he left."

"He? You saw a man?"

"The closet door was shut. I didn't see a thing. Man, woman — what does it matter now?"

"How can you do business with the people who killed the man you love?"

"I have a right to get something back for a change!" Her voice cracked. She coughed a couple of times. With her free hand she reached into her jacket pocket and pulled out a pack of cigarettes. "We were going to go away. Tahiti. You ever been?"

"No."

"I thought maybe you could tell me what it

was like. Doesn't matter. I'll go. Alone. I've always wanted to get away." Her shaking hand brought the pack to her mouth, and she nibbled a cigarette loose. "Anywhere. It doesn't matter. As long as I get away." The cigarette moved up and down when she spoke. She slipped the pack back into her pocket and came out with a lighter.

"Did you see the hole in his throat?" I asked.

The sagging skin on her cheekbones flushed.

"He didn't die right away," I said. "It takes a few minutes to bleed to death."

"I swear to God I'll fire this gun again if you don't shut up!"

She turned her head slightly and, sucking in, lit her cigarette. I lunged toward her, slashing the rosary across her face. She screamed. Beads and crucifix scattered across the room. The gun flew from her hand. It went off. We both threw ourselves to the floor. A bullet ricocheted. I got to my feet first. I went for the gun. She grabbed my ankle. Teeth punctured my flesh. Pain shot through my leg. I kicked her in the stomach with my free foot. She grabbed both my ankles. I went down hard on the bare floor. She crawled on her hands and knees toward the gun. She had it. I scrambled for her, throwing myself on top of her back. We rolled on the floor, our bodies pressing together. I could feel her breasts against mine, soft, vulnerable. Our hipbones banged sharply. Women's bodies aren't made for fighting. I ended up on top of her. She was breathing hard. Remembering Boulton, I jammed my leg between her legs. I laid my forearm across her throat. She raised her head and gagged. I jerked the gun out of her hand, took a deep breath, and drove it once against her head. Her eyes rolled back and closed. I pulled myself off her. Sore and dazed, I sat next to her. She looked too still. I leaned my ear close to her mouth. She was breathing.

I thought about getting in my car and driving out of Pasadena and never coming back. Oh, hell, I'd had that thought before. I crawled over to her purse and went through it. No codicil. I crawled back to her and felt the pockets and lining of her jacket . . . nothing. I ran my hands down her skirt . . . nothing. I yanked and pulled, trying to get her skirt over her hips. It wasn't easy; she was dead weight. I finally succeeded. She had on one of those girdles that comes down to the knees. Through little blue hearts embroidered on the stretchy front panel of the girdle, I saw the folded dove-gray paper pressed flat against her stomach. I shoved my hand between the girdle and her dry, loose flesh. Carefully, so it wouldn't tear, I pulled the codicil out. I leaned against the foot of the bed. I had the codicil in my hand. I had it!

I struggled to my feet and put it in my bag. I picked up my rosary beads. Forgive me, Blessed Mother. Forgive me, Grandmother. Forgive me, Mother. I looked at The Smoker. Forgive me, Smoker. I put the beads in the jewelry box. Then I shook her shoulders. "Wake up!" She groaned and was out again.

I couldn't leave her here. I opened the door and looked down the hall. The house was still. I decided that if I threw cold water on her, I could at least get her to her feet and maybe out to my car. Starting toward the bathroom, I heard keys jingling in the front door. I stopped. The front door opened. I hurried back to the room and shut the door. Looking around, I discovered an empty closet. I grabbed our purses and threw them into it.

"Erwin?" Waingrove's voice came from the living room.

Shit! I grabbed her by the legs and pulled her into the closet. Her head bumped noisily against the floor. I could hear him coming slowly down the hallway.

"Ellen Renicke?"

I shoved myself into the closet with her.

Closing the door, I saw the gun in the middle of the floor.

"Erwin?"

I rushed back out and picked up the gun. He was at the door.

"Ellen Renicke?"

I made it back to the closet. I pulled at the door; it wouldn't close — her feet pushed against it. Waingrove knocked on the bedroom door. I jerked the door as hard as I could. I held it by the handle. It remained open about an inch. I held the gun with my other hand.

"Ellen Renicke?"

I heard the bedroom door open. He came into the room. I held my breath. He came into view, standing at the foot of the bed. He had a gun in his hand. I gave The Smoker a quick look. Her eyes were wide open, watching me. She opened her mouth; I jammed the barrel of the gun into it. Her eyes bulged, but she didn't scream. Waingrove stood staring at the floor, then moved out of view. I heard him leave the room. I stayed, holding the door and keeping the gun in The Smoker's mouth till I was sure he'd had time to get out of the house.

I took the gun from her mouth and said, "Okay, you're coming with me. I want you to meet Claire Conrad."

She went into a coughing fit.

I had the gun in the small of her back. We walked down the sidewalk toward my car just as Boulton had walked with Erwin. Except for one difference. The Smoker stopped and said, "Shoot me."

"Get in the car," I said.

"Shoot me," she screamed, backing away from me. "Shoot me! I don't care how I get away. I just have to get away."

She was facing me, walking backwards down the sidewalk. I still had the gun pointed at her. Two children came out and stood on their porch, watching us. A man across the street leaned in his doorway, polishing off a beer. I couldn't believe I was standing on a sidewalk in the bright afternoon sun, in a cozy neighborhood, holding a gun on a woman who wanted me to shoot her while the neighbors watched.

"If you want what I have so badly . . . shoot me!" she demanded. "Go on! I don't care anymore. I just want to leave Los Angeles!"

Oh, hell. I put the gun in my pocket, got into the car, and drove away, leaving Ellen Renicke there on the sidewalk. I wasn't going to shoot her. I didn't have to. When she got home and looked in her girdle and found out she didn't have the codicil, she'd drop dead anyway.

18

I stood in front of the door I had once called conceited and waited to be let in. The crown slid sideways. I knew Boulton or Gerta was staring back at me. Gerta opened the door.

"Is Erwin still here?" I asked breathlessly.

"If you mean that frightened man they have in the living room, yes."

"Go in and tell Claire that I have to see her. It's urgent. I'll wait for her in my room."

"You're so disheveled —"

"Gerta, please!"

I hurried to my room. I took The Smoker's gun from my pocket, Boulton's gun from my purse, and along with the jewelry box and the codicil I laid them on the bed. I tried to organize my thoughts so that I could give Claire a clear picture of what had taken place. I stared at my strange bounty and realized that I was smiling. I had slammed a poor woman in the head with a gun, and I was feeling pretty good about myself. No, not just good — triumphant! Damn it, I had the codicil!

Claire knocked and opened my door all in the same motion. "You've discovered something, Miss Hill?"

I proudly handed her the codicil. She took it and read it. A slight smile flickered, then disappeared. "Inform me, please."

We sat on the chairs by the unlit fireplace and I told her everything that had happened, careful not to leave out the slightest detail, including the gun and The Smoker's head. She listened intently, tapping her finger on the handle of her stick. When I finished, she leaned forward. I anticipated her congratulations and had decided on a subdued but immodest acceptance.

"How in the world could you let her get away?"

"What?!" I leaped up. "That's all you have to say to me? I come back here with a document that awards you a four-million-dollar coin collection . . . and all you can say is — "

"Don't get huffy."

"Huffy? Huffy! What was I supposed to do — shoot her?"

"It's all illusion, Miss Hill. You don't have to shoot people. You just have to make them believe you *will* shoot them. You'll learn."

"I don't want to learn!"

"But you are. Let me see this jewelry box."

I took it from the bed and placed it on the

coffee table. Sulking in my chair, I watched her lift the lid. The music played and the ballerina twirled. She quickly closed the box.

"I have just come face to face with hell — doomed to pirouette for all eternity to 'Greensleeves.' What do you make of this odious pink box?"

"Rebecca has one just like it."

"She does?"

"Yes," I said smugly. "I saw it in her room. She told me her grandfather had given it to her."

"Ellis? How intriguing. Do you know if he befriended this woman with the mad blue eyes?"

"Not that I know of. I never saw her playing in the garden. Only Jerry. I would think if he was going to give a gift to anyone, it would be him. So why would he give her a gift?"

"I haven't the slightest idea."

"Don't you think it's odd that she had the jewelry box hidden in her parka?"

"Disturbed people often hide things. Their demons are very quick to give and very quick to take away. But they can also have an acute sense of guilt. They would hide things they know they are not supposed to have, just like normal people."

"But why shouldn't she have the jewelry box if it was given to her?"

"Maybe it wasn't given to her. Maybe it was given to someone else."

"Oh, God, I'm so confused. I thought if I found the codicil I would find the truth, and the only thing I've found is that I'm capable of knocking a woman senseless after I've struck her across the face with my grandmother's rosary."

"One does get a little dirty searching for the truth." Claire stood and walked slowly around the room, stopping at the bed. "You overheard something that was very important."

"I did?"

"Yes. You heard Waingrove let himself into the house with a key." She picked up Boulton's gun.

"Erwin could've given the key to him," I said.

"But why, if he was waiting there to let him in?"

"I don't know."

"A key implies ownership."

"Waingrove owns Erwin's house?"

"This gun has a slight kick."

"I know!" I snapped.

"I don't believe Boulton has ever given this gun to anyone before. It was his mother's."

"I know!"

"She killed two — "

"I know! I know! So Waingrove owns Erwin's house. I don't see the significance."

"Neither do I. We'll have to ask our Mr. Erwin."

She put the gun down and picked up The Smoker's gun.

"Valcovich was killed with a Derringer. This is a thirty-eight . . . and not well cared for. I don't understand why people have guns, pets, and children, and then don't care for them properly."

"Only you would lump guns, pets, and children together. Did you get anything from Erwin while I was gone?"

"I showed him the photograph, and he agrees that it's a picture of Ellis Kenilworth. He said the woman looked like a famous television actress. He couldn't remember her name because he doesn't watch television that much."

"So he sees the photograph like everyone else."

"Not everyone. Rebecca saw it differently."

"You're going to take that strange little girl's word — "

"I want you to call the Kenilworths and tell them we have the codicil. Tell them to come here immediately. I want to see what happens when they mingle with Erwin."

I went to the phone and dialed. Judith answered in a nervous, expectant voice.

"Judith, it's Maggie Hill."

"I can't talk now."

"I've got the codicil."

A very long pause.

"Miss Conrad would like you to come to the cottage as quickly as possible."

"But you can't have — "

"Trust me, Judith. I have it in my hand."

"I'll have to talk to Mother . . . Sutton . . . " Her voice quivered. She took a deep breath and said, "If you already have it, I don't see any purpose in my coming there. It's all over now."

"Hold on a second." I put my hand over the receiver and said to Claire, "Since you already have the codicil, she sees no reason for coming over here."

"Remind her that I do not want the codicil."

"You're kidding."

"As you know, a sense of humor is the only quality I lack."

I removed my hand from the mouthpiece. "Claire Conrad wants me to remind you that she has never wanted your four million bucks and she doesn't have a sense of humor." Silence. "Hello? . . . Hello?" Silence.

"It's Sutton, Maggie." His smooth, easy voice broke the stillness. "We'll be right

325

there." He hung up the phone.

"Sutton and Judith are on their way," I told Claire.

Picking up the jewelry box, she said, "Put this back in your purse and bring it with you to the living room. Take it out only when I ask. Hold out your hands." Grimacing, she opened the box and poured my rosary beads into my hands. She hurriedly snapped the lid shut.

"I know a woman who restrings beautifully."

"Rosaries?"

"Pearls."

Once a WASP, always a WASP.

She picked up the codicil and I followed her into the living room.

Erwin looked uncomfortable sitting on the sofa — maybe because Boulton was standing behind him. When Erwin saw me, he blinked nervously and took a swipe at his chin, as if he were brushing off something annoying.

Claire perched on her throne, and I took the sofa opposite Erwin.

"Would you like to tell us what Ellen Renicke was doing at your house with a gun in one hand and Ellis Kenilworth's codicil in the other?" Claire asked.

"I don't have to answer your questions."

Boulton rested his hands on Erwin's shoulders near his neck.

"You have no right to keep me here. I haven't done anything."

"Let's try another question. Why does Brian Waingrove have a key to your house?"

He took another swipe at his chin. "I gave it to him so he could get in."

"You're lying," I said. "Waingrove expected you to be there."

Claire extended her legs in front of her. She stared at the tips of her shoes. "Why does Waingrove have a key to your house?"

"I told you. I gave it to him."

She tapped the tip of her foot with her walking stick. "What hospital are your wards from?"

Erwin moved uneasily on the sofa. "The poor souls don't have anything to do with this. I swear to God. They're the one good thing in my life — my good deed, you know?"

"What is the name of the hospital?"

He fell silent.

"It will take me a day to find out by checking public records. I would prefer not to waste my energy and time."

"I told you they have nothing — "

"Boulton!" she commanded.

He jerked Erwin's head back, took out his gun, and pushed the barrel into Erwin's Adam's apple.

"Rose . . . wood," Erwin gagged.

"I'm sorry, I didn't hear you," Claire said politely.

"Rosewood State Hospital!"

"Release him." She turned to me. "Call Rosewood and tell them we are concerned about the living standards at 1345 Beech Street. We would like to know who owns the home and we would like an investigation."

I got up and crossed to the big table, dialed Information, and got the telephone number. I dialed Rosewood. Erwin squirmed around on the sofa and watched me. The stubble on his chin glistened like hot sand.

"Rosewood Hospital," a woman's voice answered.

"They're not going to give any information on the phone," Erwin said.

"I would like to find out who owns the home at 1345 Beech Street, Pasadena. It houses three of your patients," I told her.

"We're not allowed to give information over the phone. We will accept a query in letter form. Thank you." She hung up. Wonderful.

I decided to take a chance. "Yes, Beech Street." I spelled it out — I thought that was a nice touch. "I'll hold," I said to the buzzing sound.

"Wait a minute," Erwin said. "I run a good home."

328

"Yes?" I said into the phone. "Thank you for the information. And who do I talk to to make a complaint about this — "

"Hang up!" Erwin yelled. "Hang the phone up! I've never harmed one of those people. I do all the managing. He pays me. He owns a lot of houses. What does it matter to anybody if Waingrove owns the house?"

"I'm not certain that it does, Mr. Erwin." Claire walked over and stared down into his face. "I repeat the question. What was Ellen Renicke doing at your house?"

"Waingrove wanted to meet her. I just loaned him the use of the house, that's all. It was a favor. I don't even know who she is."

"She's the secretary of a man named Roger Valcovich. It was her house you drove to the night Valcovich was murdered."

"Murdered? I don't know anything about a murder."

"Boulton followed you to her house."

"Waingrove never said anything about a murder. He never said . . . "

Claire sat down next to him. "What were you supposed to do at her house?"

"Just talk to her. See if she had the codicil."

"Are you sure you weren't supposed to kill her, as you had killed Valcovich?"

"No! I didn't kill anybody! I swear! I was

just supposed to see if she'd sell it, that's all."

"Why you?"

He looked confused by the question. "Why me?"

"Why did Waingrove pick you to do his errands for him?"

"I'm not saying anything more."

"I'm sure the police would be interested to know what you were doing driving by Ellen Renicke's house. I'm sure they would want to know where you were at the time of the murder."

"Talk to Waingrove. I haven't done anything. I swear to God."

She took out the photograph. "Tell me about this."

"No, no. I can't. I could be killed."

"By whom?"

"Any of 'em could do it."

"Miss Hill, show us what else you discovered at the house."

I took out the jewelry box and opened it. Erwin's mouth went slack as he stared at the pink box. I closed the lid.

The eyes grew suspicious, and he shifted uneasily among the wine-colored pillows.

"You appear to be worried, Mr. Erwin. Why?" Claire asked. "It's just a pretty little jewelry box."

"It's Ginna's — the woman who helps me

care for the lost souls. It belongs to her."

"Then why did Miss Hill find it hidden in the parka of your female ward?"

"Poor soul steals. I gotta watch her all the time."

"That's a very good lie, but it's still a lie."

"Yeah. Well, I wanna live."

Claire pulled a tasseled cord by the fireplace. "We'll just have to wait, then."

She sat sideways in the chair, draping one long leg over the arm. Erwin said nothing. I watched sweat form on his upper lip. Gerta appeared.

"Yes, Miss Conrad?"

"Tea, please. Would you like some tea, Mr. Erwin?"

This question seemed to confuse him more than the others. "You gotta be kidding," he finally answered.

"Claire Conrad has no sense of humor," I told him.

"You'd better make it for six, Gerta," Claire said.

Gerta went off to the kitchen. Erwin silently moved his lips. He was looking at us and counting up to four.

"Who you expecting?" he asked, a little too casually.

"Put the jewelry box away, Miss Hill."

We waited in strained silence till the doorbell rang.

"I'll get it," I said, heading toward the hall.

"Be sure to see who it is first," Claire warned.

I did. Judith and Sutton peered at the door. Their faces had all the warmth of two death masks.

"Good to see you, Maggie," Sutton said as I let them in. Our eyes didn't flirt.

They followed me into the living room. I don't know what I expected to happen when the Kenilworths saw Erwin, but nothing did, except Sutton said the obvious. "Erwin? We didn't expect to see you here."

"Please sit down," Claire said.

Brother and sister sat on the sofa. Sutton did it with ease and elegance. Judith checked out the cushion first, as if it were a dirty park bench and she didn't want to get any pigeon shit on her.

Sutton smiled disarmingly at Claire. "I would prefer not to discuss anything with Erwin here. This is personal, family business."

Ignoring his remarks, Claire looked at me. "Show them the codicil."

I took it out of my purse and held it up for them to see. Judith stood and grabbed for it. I moved it quickly out of her reach.

"Sit down, Judith," Sutton commanded, sounding just like his mother.

Gerta came in with a tea tray and placed it

on a table next to Claire, then left.

"Who would like tea? Judith?" Claire asked.

"Please."

"Milk?"

"No, thank you." Judith had all her manners back.

Claire poured the tea as expertly as she had checked out the guns in my room. She handed the cup to Judith.

"I assume the Renicke woman contacted you," Claire said, looking at Sutton.

"Yes."

"Tea?" she asked him.

"Please."

"And you arranged a meeting with her?"

"Actually, Waingrove did."

"How much were you going to pay her?"

"Fifty thousand dollars."

"A woman with small dreams. Milk?"

"Please."

Erwin suddenly stood up and announced, "I don't want any fucking tea. I'm leaving. You can't keep me here."

Boulton pushed him back down. He slumped into silence.

"I really see no need to discuss this in front of Erwin," Sutton said. "It has nothing to do with him."

"One lump or two?" Claire asked him.

"Two."

"Waingrove arranged to have the meeting in Erwin's house." She handed Sutton his cup. "By the way, Erwin does not own his house. Brian Waingrove does. Tea, Maggie?"

"Two lumps."

Judith shot up from the sofa. Eyes wide with hurt, she stared at Claire, who was regally pouring my tea. "You're lying! You're lying!" she whined.

Sutton tugged at her hand.

"Ask Mr. Erwin." Claire handed me my tea and looked at Boulton. "Tea?"

"Please," he said, watching Judith intently.

"It's not true. You want us to think it's Brian. But it's not." Tears formed in her strict eyes. She looked at Erwin. "Is it true?"

"He owns a lot of houses. Mine is just one of them."

She sat back down. Her body was rigid as she tried to fight the hurt, the secret betrayal.

Claire handed Boulton his tea. Sutton sipped his thoughtfully. "So Brian owns Erwin's house. I don't see what that has to do with the amendment to my brother's will. We were willing to pay Renicke, so we will pay you for — "

Claire held up her hand. "Please. Aren't you the least bit intrigued by the fact that Waingrove never told you? And that he and Erwin pretended not to know one another the day of Ellis's funeral? Judith appears to be very disturbed by his deviousness."

"He's not being devious. He loves me. That's why he didn't tell me — he couldn't. He loves me. He does!" she rambled.

"I think we'd better go," Sutton said. "Our lawyer will be contacting you."

"You might be interested to know that Boulton, holding a teacup in one hand, can draw his gun and kill you without spilling a drop. He's English, you know." Claire sat down.

Sutton peered over the delicate china cup at Boulton. "Gun? We're not being held here . . . are we?"

Claire sipped her tea.

"You didn't answer me," Sutton said to her.

She studied him for a moment, then leaned back and closed her eyes.

It was Sutton's turn to stand. "Let's go, Judith."

Claire was right. Boulton had the gun in his hand and the teacup didn't even rattle. Sutton's face flushed. He quickly sat down. "This is ridiculous," he mumbled.

"Why don't I tell you what I think has happened here." Claire took the photograph from her pocket and tossed it on the coffee table. "I think Jerry accidentally took this picture.

Maybe Ellis gave him a camera as a gift." She turned to Erwin. "Or did you give it to him?" He didn't answer. "In any event, Erwin had the film developed and saw the picture of Ellis and a major TV star making love. A surprising photograph — but is it material for blackmail? Erwin is unsure. So he shows it to Waingrove."

"No . . . no." Judith twisted a handkerchief into knots.

"Waingrove talks to Victoria. Or maybe he gets Patricia drunk and through her finds out that there is reason for blackmail. Incest."

Judith took in a sharp breath, and her tight little mouth pressed white.

"But Victoria said this picture was taken on a beach," Sutton said carefully.

"I never lie on wet grass if I can help it. When you found me flat on my back in your garden, I was looking up at the privets. With the garden lights on them, they look like shadowy, abstract clouds against an evening sky — just like the clouds in this photograph."

"But why would Victoria lie?"

"I think she wanted to put some distance between this photograph and your garden. And Jerry. I think you all do. What I can't figure out is why. Even now, when you discover that Waingrove is your blackmailer, you do nothing. There's no outrage. There's no demand for calling the police. Why?"

"Maybe we don't believe you," Sutton said. "I don't think his owning that house is proof of anything."

"Then why did he keep it a secret?"

"He knew how Mother detested having *them* in the neighborhood." Judith thrust her chin toward Erwin in a mean little gesture. Nervous fingers kneaded the handkerchief. "She wouldn't let me see him if she found out he owned that house. He wanted to protect me . . . be with me."

"He wanted to protect himself. And you know that now, don't you?"

"No. I don't!"

Claire turned to Sutton. "Why didn't you tell Victoria and her mother that you destroyed the photograph Ellis left?"

"As you know, I wasn't supposed to be there. And I did let my brother kill himself. I didn't want Mother to know. Of course I had to tell her eventually, but at the time I thought if they knew it would somehow get back to Mother. She would find out."

"Through Bobby Alt?"

His face flushed again, and he fell silent. When he spoke, he sounded like a jealous child. "That was Mother's idea. I know she did it for me . . . for us . . . the family. She didn't feel she could trust Patricia and Victoria — especially Patricia. Mother was afraid they might do something rash, even more embarrassing to Ellis and the family."

Claire turned to me. "Would you show them what you found, please?"

I took out the pretty pink box and lifted the lid. "Greensleeves" tinkled and the ballerina twirled. Brother and sister watched without a twitch of recognition.

"Does this have any meaning to you?"

"No," they both said.

"It was found in Erwin's house. One of his wards had it hidden. Ellis gave a jewelry box just like this to Rebecca."

Judith looked quickly at Erwin, then back at her hands. Sutton sat silently.

"You may all leave," Claire said.

"But the codicil . . .what do you want for it?" Sutton asked.

She jabbed at the photograph with her walking stick. "I want you to tell me who the woman in this photograph really is."

"But . . . you already know," Sutton said. "Listen, you asked me what Ellis's last words were. I couldn't tell you in front of Mother, but I'll tell you now. He wrote: 'I loved her. I cannot forgive myself.' The woman in that photograph is Victoria Moor."

Claire waved her hand in the air. "Leave."

Judith stood with her head down, her handkerchief a tiny white ball in her hand.

Erwin stood and reached for the jewelry box. Claire slammed her walking stick across his hands. "That remains here."

"You stole that from my house. That's my property. And how am I supposed to get home?"

"I'm sure the Kenilworths will give you a lift. They seem quite willing to help you. Show them out, Miss Hill."

"No! I don't wanna go with them," Erwin balked.

"For God's sake, man! Come on." Sutton looked embarrassed.

I walked brother and sister to the hallway. Erwin reluctantly followed. I opened the door for them. Sutton and Erwin walked up the steps as if they were strangers. Judith turned to me. Her eyes were red and teary, her fists clenched against the world.

"You've caused all this. Why couldn't you just leave well enough alone?"

She ran halfway up the stairs, stopped, whirled around, and faced me.

"Fuck you, Maggie Hill!"

19

It hadn't been a particularly good day for sisterhood.

I shut the door and went back to the living room. Boulton placed the last of the teacups on the tray and carried it to the kitchen. Claire was still enthroned. I stared out the French doors. The setting sun spread a party-pink glow across the pitted, crumbling façade of the hotel. It looked like a bloated old lady wearing too much rouge.

"Loved," Claire whispered.

"I beg your pardon?"

"Sutton said that Ellis wrote, 'I loved her and I cannot forgive myself.' Not 'I *love* her' — '*loved*.' Past tense."

" 'Love' always becomes 'loved.' "

"A romantically jaded observation, Miss Hill, but not very helpful."

"If Waingrove is the blackmailer, do you think he killed Valcovich?"

"If what The Smoker says is true, the person who murdered Valcovich had to know about the private entrance to his office. Judith knew about it. She certainly could have told Waingrove about the private entrance. She also could have told Sutton."

"He did watch his brother commit suicide. You think he's capable of murder?"

"It does define his character — a man who is not afraid to let another man die. By the way, did Rosewood Hospital give you that information about Waingrove, or were you just bluffing?" she asked.

"Bluffing. They won't give information over the phone."

"Yes, you are definitely the person to chronicle my life."

"I don't want to write about you — follow you around like some little puppy dog!"

"There are worse things you could do with your life."

"Look, I am an independent woman!"

"Please, please, please! When you are in my presence, never put those two words together. You may use them separately, for they are useful words. But when 'independent' is used as an adjective to the noun 'woman,' all rational and independent thought stops."

"You are a sexist!"

"An example of what I have just said. Miss Hill, you are the one who just referred to herself as a puppy dog, not me. I see you as a snapping, aggressive, untrainable, full-grown Airedale!"

"Airedale?"

"I need silence. I need to think." She extended her legs, crossed her arms over her chest, and stared intently at the tips of her shoes.

I looked out the doors. Airedale! Airedales look like strutting old men! What's wrong with Lassie? Rin Tin Tin? Oh, hell. Get the codicil and get out of Pasadena. Wait a minute . . . I've *got* the codicil? I can leave!

I turned and looked at Claire. She was totally concentrated, as if she were in a trance. Oh, hell, I'll find out who killed Valcovich and *then* I'll leave.

"Why do you think Waingrove is the blackmailer?" I asked.

She raised her eyes from her shoes to my face. "You started me thinking when you called him a misogynist. This man who does not like women is involved with two very different kinds of woman. Victoria Moor I can understand — her fame puts him in the spotlight. But Judith Kenilworth can do little for Waingrove. And yet he is so very helpful to her and her family . . . so dedicated about finding the codicil and helping them make a deal with The Smoker. Why? These women have two things in common: they are being

342

blackmailed, and they are involved with Waingrove. I think he is protecting his investments. Did you notice how devastated Judith was when she learned that Waingrove owned Erwin's house? His ownership made it clear to her that he was the blackmailer. I'm sure of it."

The doorbell rang.

"But how? Where's the proof?"

She took her walking stick and pointed at the photograph on the table. "The proof is in here. We just have to decipher it."

Boulton appeared. "Patricia Kenilworth would like to see you."

"Just a minute." Claire took the jewelry box and put it back in my purse; then she slipped the photograph into her pocket. "Send her in."

We looked at one another as Boulton left and reappeared with Patricia. She rushed into the room. The diamond studs glared coldly against the glazed whiteness of her skin.

"I want it. Now!"

"*What* do you want now?" Claire asked.

"The photograph you stole from us."

"Sit down, please."

"No. I just want the picture."

"I have some information that will interest you."

Patricia licked her lips like an alcoholic

might at the offer of a drink. "What information?"

"Please sit down."

She sat on the sofa, and even in her nervous state she remembered to slowly cross her legs, displaying them to their best advantage.

"Will you need me?" Boulton asked Claire.

"I don't think so."

"What do you know?" Patricia's eyes shone with a mixture of curiosity and fear.

"How long have you known Brian Waingrove?"

"Three years, maybe. I told you I went to one of his lectures."

"How long has he been your daughter's lover?"

The cat eyes blinked; the lips pressed sideways, forming a smile. "My daughter will have many lovers, but only one mother. He means nothing to her."

"How long has he meant nothing to her?"

"On and off for the last year."

Claire reached into my purse and took out the jewelry box. Holding it on her lap, she opened the lid. Patricia stared at the ballerina.

"That's Rebecca's! How did you get it? Shut the damn thing off! I've always hated that song. Ellis loved it. Turn it off!"

Claire closed the box. "This doesn't belong to Rebecca. Miss Hill found it in the house

Brian Waingrove owns."

The cat eyes shifted from Claire to me and back. "I don't understand."

"The house in back of the Kenilworths'. The house Erwin manages for Waingrove. The house where the patients from Rosewood stay."

The glazed white skin turned pasty. "He owns . . ." Her voice trailed off and her hand went to her neck. "What do I care if he owns a house near the Kenilworths'?"

"I think you do. And so does Victoria. That's why she lied when she said the picture was taken at the beach. I think it was taken in the Kenilworths' garden. Why do you both care enough to lie?"

Patricia stood. "I shouldn't have come here." She reached into her purse and came out with a gun. "Just give me the photograph and I'll leave."

She was the fifth person today, including myself, who thought a gun might be necessary.

"Move over by Claire Conrad," she said to me.

"Do you want me to put my hands in the air?" I asked, moving carefully toward Claire, who was sitting very erect in her chair.

"I don't think we need to be theatrical."

"This is very foolish," Claire said. "My

man is in the house."

"I don't think you understand me. I would do anything to protect my daughter."

"Including paying blackmail for the rest of your life?"

"If necessary."

"How do you feel about your daughter making love to her blackmailer?" I asked.

"I'm not a sentimental woman. Neither is she. Give me the photograph."

Boulton appeared in the doorway. If I counted him twice, that would make six people with guns in their hands. He moved quietly toward Patricia. The floor creaked. She turned. Claire rose out of her chair, swinging her stick, knocking the gun from Patricia's hand. Boulton quickly picked it up. Patricia slumped onto the sofa, holding her wrist, crying.

"Why can't you leave us alone? . . . Why? We've done nothing to you. . . . Please, I'll pay you anything . . . just leave us alone."

Claire took the photo from her pocket and held it in front of Patricia. "Who is the woman in this picture?"

Patricia stared at it. She closed her eyes and began to rock back and forth, sobbing, "Victoria, Victoria, Victoria . . . my Victoria . . . "

Tears carved years into her face; she was a sad, terrified old woman. I had trouble looking at her. She had gone through so much to hide her age, I felt as if I were seeing something I shouldn't. I went to a small side table and poured some brandy from a crystal decanter and handed it to her.

"Where is Victoria?" Claire asked.

"At the studio. Working." She took the brandy and gulped it.

"We'll see her now. Did your chauffeur drive you?"

"I drove myself."

"We'll follow you to the studio."

She looked up at us. Ravaged green eyes turned coy. "Will you give me the photograph then?"

"After we talk to your daughter."

"Yes," she said softly. "Victoria will have the answers."

Boulton followed the hunter-green Jag through bumper-to-bumper traffic into Burbank — where Hollywood really exists. Patricia turned down a street lined with pepper trees and ranch-style homes. At the end of the street was the gate to the Valley City Studios. I guess for the people in these houses it was like living next to the mill.

Patricia stopped the Jag and talked to a security guard standing in a little wooden booth. She drove on. He waved us by. We followed her through a maze of narrow streets and giant cement sound stages that looked as if they were built to house nuclear weapons. We parked and headed for one of these austere buildings. Boulton waited by the car.

Just as the heavy, vault-like door closed behind us, a kind of whistle sounded. A man yelled "Quiet!" in an angry, tired voice. Next to me a red light began to spin. Patricia motioned for us to stay where we were.

All human life, in this dank warehouse of television images, froze in mid-action, like Keats's lovers on their urn. A hairdresser, brush in hand, stopped inches from the lush, dark hair of an actress. Unmoving, the actress stared at herself in the mirror, lovingly trapped in her own reflection. Grips, resigned to their few moments of inactivity, stared at one another like lumpy statues. A dapper actor sat in a chair, poised forever on the moment of turning a page in *Daily Variety*.

Only the camera moved. In a brightly lit corner it rolled silently on its tracks, like a giant insect, toward the bare back of Victoria Moor.

"Action!"

Victoria spun around, her blond hair flaring like the opening of a white silk fan.

"You have no right to tell me what to do!" she defied the camera.

"I have every right," a bored male voice answered from somewhere in the darkness.

Claire moved uneasily, her walking stick tapping the cement floor. She drew a scolding look from a woman dressed as a nurse — or maybe she *was* a nurse.

Victoria undulated closer to the camera, tilted her head back, and parted her lips as if she were going to kiss the giant eye that burrowed in on her. "You forget I own you."

"Only forty-eight percent of me," the voice without a body said.

"As of this morning I own fifty-one percent of you . . . baby." She slowly, reluctantly moved away from the camera.

"No. No. No," the voice droned.

A gunshot rang out. I leaped. The nurse gave me the nasty look. Victoria fell into a chair, her head tilted backwards toward the camera. Blond hair cascaded down. I could see her forehead . . . the tip of her nose. She looked exactly as she did in the photograph. And I knew Claire was wrong: it *was* Victoria Moor in that photo.

"Cut! Print!" a harried voice commanded.

The hairdresser began to comb the actress's hair. The grips started to move and lift. The actor turned to the next page. Victoria, followed by a woman carrying a robe, another holding a comb and can of hair spray, and a man grasping small face brushes as if they were a bouquet, hurried from the cluster of lights toward a large trailer.

"Come with me," Patricia said, moving toward the trailer.

When Victoria saw us, she stopped. "Wait here," she commanded her followers, like a general commanding her troops.

We went into the trailer. It was as large as the room my mother had built onto our house, which she loved to refer to as the "Family Room." Victoria sat in front of her dressing table. The many lights that lined the mirror were dark. In the normal light her makeup looked heavy, tawdry. She peered at herself in the mirror.

"Oh, God! I've asked them repeatedly to leave these lights on. Some frugal bastard is trying to make points with the producer."

She flicked on the lights and was transformed from a hooker into a beauty queen.

"With whom were you acting?" Claire asked.

"The camera. There's not enough room in television to act with other actors."

"Did he kill you?" I asked.

"Slightly wounded." She turned on Patricia, who was sitting nervously in the corner of a sofa. "What is this all about, Mother?"

"They know," she said.

"Know what?"

"Where the picture was taken."

"Why don't you just give us back the photograph and get the hell out of here."

"Victoria . . . please . . . talk to them . . . " her mother begged.

"Talk to them about what?"

"About . . . *it*. Please."

"I don't have much time. They'll be asking for me soon."

She paused and studied herself in the mirror. It was as if she were sucking in strength from the warm, glowing lights surrounding her reflection.

"All right. The photograph was taken in the garden. I wanted to take Ellis on his own territory — or should I say Eleanor's territory? Seduce her son — my father — right under her nose. But that strange man-child wandered in. He had a camera — he was just holding it down by his side. He didn't look as if he were taking pictures, for God's sake."

"Why did you lie and say the photo was taken at the beach?" Claire asked.

Victoria didn't answer.

Patricia leaned forward, her long fingernails digging into the sofa. "They say Brian owns the house where that child came from."

"How do you know that?" Victoria turned in her chair toward Claire.

"A Mr. Erwin told us. He manages the

house for Waingrove."

"You're going to believe him?"

"The records are easily checked. I'll be doing that tomorrow. In the meantime, I have no reason not to believe him. I think Erwin showed Waingrove the photograph. I think Waingrove is blackmailing you."

"We're not asking you to rescue us from our blackmailers. Mother and I can handle the situation."

"Why do you persist in protecting these people? Does it have anything to do with this?" Claire nodded to me, and I took the pink box out of my purse and opened the lid.

"Where did you get that? You stole it from Rebecca!"

"Miss Hill found it in Erwin's — Waingrove's house."

Victoria slammed the lid down.

Claire said, "Ellis gave one to Rebecca and this one to somebody in that house. Who do you think it would be?"

"How the hell do I know? Some poor creature he felt sorry for. He felt sorry for all of us poor creatures. I have to change. I want you to leave."

Claire and I moved toward the door.

"You said you'd give me the photograph!" Patricia stood.

"That reminds me." Claire looked at Victoria. "Your daughter doesn't think this is you in this picture."

"You showed her that? How dare you! Get out!"

She picked up what looked like a very expensive bottle of perfume and threw it at us. It broke against the wall over our heads and poured down on us. We were drenched in Joy. I'd often sniffed it at the perfume counter at Neiman's. That's all I could afford to do there — sniff. Now I knew what it felt like to wear it. We ducked out of the door before she could throw something else.

People stood on the sound stage as if another disembodied voice had yelled for quiet — except this time they were all frozen into silence watching us. Claire and I made our way out of the building, trailing a disgustingly high-class odor behind us.

We drove back to the cottage with all the windows open. Claire had the light on in the car. She never spoke. She only stared at the photograph.

As we headed toward the front door I said, "Did you see Victoria when she got shot and leaned her head back over that chair? She looked exactly as she does in this photograph."

"Dead?" Claire said, pounding on the front door.

"She was slightly wounded."

"Well, you'd never know it by her acting." Claire stopped and looked at me. The dark eyes shone. "That's it, Miss Hill!"

"What is?"

"I need to think."

Gerta opened the door. Her face scrunched up when she got a whiff of us.

"I'm taking a bath. I suggest you do the same." Claire marched off to her room.

I took a bath. But Joy is the best you can buy, and you just can't wash off the best so easily. In that respect the most expensive perfumes and the cheapest perfumes are the same.

I was sitting on my bed wrapped in my pink kimono when Claire strode into the room. She had on a black velvet robe and was looking very judicial — Supreme Court judicial.

"Sit down here," she demanded, pulling a chair up to the dresser mirror.

I did as I was told.

She laid the photograph on the dresser. "Re-create Ellis's expression in the mirror."

"What? I'm no actress!"

"Just do it."

I studied his face and then tried to get mine to do the same. I half-closed my eyes . . . opened my mouth in a sort of sexual passion. I tilted my head and moaned sexually.

"Who asked you to make those awful sounds?"

"It looks as if he's moaning."

"Do it again, and no improvisation."

I did exactly what I had done before.

"Scream," Claire said.

"What?"

"Scream!"

I screamed.

"Keep on screaming!" she demanded.

I kept on screaming, and my expression began to look more and more like his. All the sexual passion I had seen in his face, my face, slowly turned to anguish and despair.

Boulton burst in through the door with his gun drawn. He stared at the two of us.

"Everything all right?"

"Excellent, Boulton. Just excellent," Claire said triumphantly.

"Right." He left the room.

"There is more than one kind of passion, Miss Hill. There is the passion of grief . . . of loss. Ellis Kenilworth is holding a dead woman in his arms. And by the look on his face, he did not kill her!"

I looked at the photograph. There was no way to see it now except as a picture of a man grieving over the woman he held in his arms.

"But they all agreed it was Victoria."

"We have been played beautifully. Victoria Moor is a very clever woman, and I'm afraid I've underestimated her ability as an actress.

Tomorrow, Miss Hill, I want you to drive up to Rosewood Hospital and get whatever information you can about that house and Waingrove. And find out how many patients are usually there. You said there were two twin beds in each room. Only three beds were being used. Find out if there was ever a fourth patient. A woman to whom Ellis gave a child's jewelry box. A woman who is in that photograph. A woman who looks very much like Victoria Moor. A woman he loved — past tense. A woman who has been murdered."

"How do you know?"

"Why would they all go to such lengths to cover up, including protecting their blackmailers, if she hadn't been murdered?" She grabbed the photograph and strode out of the room.

That night I went to bed thinking of an elegant, quiet man passionately pressing the body of a dead woman to his. Who was she? Whoever she was, he had to let go of her eventually. What happens to the people we let go of? What happened to her body?

20

I struggled over my bridge of melancholy . . . groped my way to consciousness. My morning sadness was back. I thought of Ellis Kenilworth. He had given up struggling with his melancholy, given up fighting for light.

I sat on the edge of the bed. Toenail polish was still chipped, legs still unshaven. Again, there wasn't time. Rosewood was on the other side of Bakersfield. I had something to do before I drove up there.

Today was Friday.

Claire was all in white, sipping her coffee, reading the *Los Angeles Times*. I sat down at the table. Boulton poured me coffee.

She peered at me over the top of her paper. "You look more determined than usual this morning," she said, then continued reading.

Boulton leaned down and whispered in my ear, "Do you have your gun?"

"No. I saw enough guns yesterday to last me a lifetime."

357

"Whatever madam wishes." He retreated to the kitchen.

"While I'm at the loony hospital, what are *you* going to be doing?" I asked her.

"Thinking."

"Wonderful."

"And checking records. This young woman looks so much like Victoria that she must belong to someone in the Kenilworth clan — either by marriage or by birth."

I finished breakfast, then went back to my room and got my purse. Claire met me at the front door. She was holding two crisp one-hundred-dollar bills in her hand.

"Money is almost as good as a gun when you need to get people to talk."

"Great. I tried to bribe somebody once and it didn't work."

"Experience, Miss Hill." She shoved the money into my hand. "You will be careful — not only on your drive up to Rosewood but when you attend the wedding."

"How did you know?"

"I'm the detective."

"Maybe you used your female brain."

I went up the steps to the street. Boulton was washing the Bentley. The sun was out, but the sky was the color of Humphrey Bogart's trench coat. I shoved the money in my purse and felt the pearl handle of the gun. I stared at Boulton. He wouldn't look at me.

The Little Brown Church is on the busy intersection of Coldwater Canyon and Moorpark Boulevard in the Valley. This quaint piece of shabby architecture is nestled between condominiums and law offices.

I parked in the red across the street from the church and waited. At ten twenty the doors to the church opened and they came out into the sunlight. Married. Neil was dressed in gray. She was dressed in blue. She carried a small bouquet of white flowers. Two friends threw rice. Neil and his new wife lowered their heads, clinging to one another, laughing. Her hair was the same color as mine, but she was younger and shorter. Still, we were the same type of woman — whatever type that is.

Suddenly she threw her arms around Neil and kissed him. The others laughed. She was pert. I was never pert. The other couple started down the sidewalk. She yelled. They turned and she threw her bouquet. She was wearing white gloves. Short white cotton gloves. So female. So proper. So vulnerable. I swallowed back tears. The blond man with a mustache caught the bouquet. He got a big laugh and gave it a backhanded toss to the woman he was with. She dropped it. This got another laugh. Neil helped his new wife into his car. I had sat next to him in that very same car, resting my hand on his thigh. After a while he would stop helping her into the car. I had stopped resting my hand on his thigh. Walking around to the driver's side, he dropped his keys. He leaned over to get them and raised himself up slowly. Stiff. Tired. He would cry out in his sleep tonight. He unlocked the door and got in. They drove off. Damn those pert white gloves. I shut my eyes, wanting their images to blur and fade.

I opened my eyes. A much younger couple walked toward the church. I put my car in gear and pulled out into the traffic. I blended with all the other cars.

I was doing eighty-five on a highway cut through plowed fields. The sun roof and windows were down, and I could feel the warm, dry air wrap itself around me. I was glad to be back in my car, alone, in control, driving far away from a small brown church and a man I should have given up a long time ago.

I hit Bakersfield about twelve fifteen. Bakersfield reminds me of a certain kind of woman who, no matter how fancy she tries to dress, always has a dirty bra strap showing. I made it through the city, trying not to look at it too closely.

According to my map, Rosewood was about ten miles outside of Bakersfield. I followed the highway past a turquoise-and-orange coffee shop and a field of peach trees. The road started going up into the mountains, and I saw the sign ROSEWOOD STATE HOSPITAL. I turned off onto a road that led into beautiful park-like grounds. Low governmental-looking buildings were spread among pine and eucalyptus trees.

I parked the car in the visitors' lot and got out. I had expected a foreboding Dickensian atmosphere, not a peaceful, camp-like surrounding. It felt good to stretch and walk. My feet crunched pine needles. The air smelled green and was so clear it hurt my lungs when I took a deep breath. Earnest-looking men and women in white uniforms sat at picnic tables eating their lunches. I had timed it just right. I had learned that if you want information, go to the secretary, not the boss. And the best time to do that was when the bosses were out to lunch and the poor secretaries were usually in their offices, brown-bagging it or dieting.

I made my way down a path toward a building marked ADMINISTRATION. I opened the screen door and went in. I heard the rustle of the brown paper bag before I saw her. She sat at one of three desks, behind a Formica counter, under the glare of fluorescent lights. She was fat and had stringy brown hair pulled back with a plastic green bow.

"Hi!" I leaned on the counter.

She looked up at me, popping the last of a white-bread sandwich into her mouth. She chewed and swallowed. "Janet's gone to lunch. Be back in a half-hour." She was probably all of twenty. She already had a double chin.

"What's your name?"

"Ginger."

She stuck her chubby hand into the paper bag and pulled out two Hostess cupcakes. She stared at them in loving amazement, almost as if she were wondering how they ever got into her brown paper bag.

"Good. You're the one that Janet told me to see."

She forced herself to look at me instead of the cupcakes. "She did? But I'm temporary."

"I know the feeling. I talked to Janet this morning and told her it was the only time I could get up here. I just need some information. I'm from the Pasadena Public Health Agency." I opened my wallet and flashed my library card at her. "We're checking on a residence at 1345 Beech Street in Pasadena."

"You are?" She had the Hostess cupcakes out of their cellophane wrap.

"Rosewood has some of their patients staying there. We've had a few minor complaints in the neighborhood. Nothing serious, but we just wanted to check out the patients and the owner of the house to make sure everything's on the up-and-up."

"I think all that would be on the computer. Janet doesn't like me to use it without her being here." She swiveled in her chair, facing me, and I saw the delicate gold cross shining on a thin chain around her pudgy neck.

"Where is the computer?"

"In there." She nodded toward a closed door, then swiveled back to her cupcakes. I knew she wanted to be alone with them.

"It'll take five minutes — then you can eat your dessert without me hanging around. They look real moist."

"I'm still not supposed to work the computers. Janet said she'd fire me if she caught me practicing on them. I take lessons at night school. But you can wait for her."

She turned her back to me and picked up one of the cupcakes.

Oh, hell.

"All right. I guess I'll have to tell you who I really am. I'm a private detective working for the actress Victoria Moor."

She slowly turned around, her mouth full of half a cupcake. I flashed her my library card again. "This is really my P.I. license."

"P.I.?"

"Private eye."

"Victoria Moor? Really?"

I took one of the bills out of my purse. "She told me to give this to the person who helped me. She's very thoughtful. She's not stuck-up like most big stars."

"What does she want to know?"

"Usually that's confidential. But I guess I can tell you. She thinks she might have a family member — a cousin — at this house on Beech Street. And if so, she'd like to look after the cousin. Help her out."

"She sounds real nice."

I moved the hundred around on the counter. "And she says she hopes the person who helps me will take this money and do some good with it in a Christian kind of way."

She pushed herself to her feet. Brown stretch slacks were stretched to the limit. A brown-and-white polka-dot blouse shaped like a tent covered the top of her. Chubby feet were shoved into pink rubber thongs. She waddled toward me and stared at the hundred bucks.

"Did Victoria touch this money?"

"Oh, yes," I said, looking at the clock. If Janet was punctual, she'd be back in fifteen minutes.

"I guess it won't hurt. I mean, this is a kinda unusual situation, isn't it?"

"Victoria Moor just wants to do a good deed."

"It's nice to know that big stars like her

have love in their hearts." The thongs slapped against her fleshy feet as she headed for the computer room.

I came around the counter. She opened the door and turned on the light. I was in! The computer sat on a table in the middle of the room. I could hear the hard disk whirring. Filing cabinets lined the walls.

"I'll be sure to tell Victoria how nice you were about helping me."

She sat down in front of the computer and began to punch in some commands with her flat, short fingers. I stood behind her, watching the monitor.

"What was the address?" she asked.

I gave it to her.

She tapped the keys, then said, "Beech Street house is owned by Waingrove Enterprises, and we have a Jerry Frant, Penny Thomas, and Oliver Basscom residing there."

"Thank you. Aren't there usually four people in that house?"

"I don't know."

"Could I see if there was anyone else there recently?"

"I don't know how to do that."

"What does this mean?" I pointed to a line that read "Access D\M6009."

"I don't know."

"Call it up."

She shrugged and punched at the keys. Up came a list of deceased patients.

"Scroll down to the *K*'s," I said.

"Why not 'Moor'?"

"No. It's a stage name. Oh, hell . . . Excuse me — Victoria doesn't like me to talk that way. Give *K* a try."

She did. There was no Kenilworth.

"What the hell, try 'Moor.' "

She scrolled down to the M's. Up popped the name "Victoria Moor."

"Look — they have the same name!" she gasped.

"So I see. That code after her name starts with the letter *M*."

"I think that means 'missing.' "

"Missing?"

"Sometimes they wander off. We always find them."

"Call up that number."

The door banged open. A woman with pimples covering most of her face snapped, "What are you doing, Ginger?"

"I was just helping."

"I run the computer. Not you!"

"I know. But she's a private eye."

Oh, Ginger. The pimples turned toward me. Some had been freshly picked. "A what?"

"She's helping Victoria —"

"Let me see your license."

It had worked so far. I flashed my library card, but Pimples grabbed it.

"You idiot!" She turned on Ginger. "The only thing she can do with this card is check books out."

I stuffed the hundred in Ginger's hand and started toward the door.

"Thanks, Ginger. I've got to be going — "

"I'm calling security!" Janet cried.

I ran. Janet yelled at Ginger, complaining about not being able to get through to security. The screen door slammed behind me.

As I unlocked the car door, I heard the rubbery, sucking sound of Ginger's thongs flapping against her feet. She lumbered up the path.

"She fired me! You lied and got me fired."

"Look, I'm really sorry. But it wasn't a lie — exactly. Here, take this." I shoved the other hundred at her.

"I can't."

"For night school!"

She opened her hand. Two hundred dollars fluttered to the ground. Big, plump tears rolled down her cheeks.

"I can't take it. Jesus wouldn't like it." She waddled away.

Earnest people watched me. I looked down at the two hundred bucks on the ground. The wind scattered the money like leaves. Oh, hell. I got into the car and drove away.

The radio blared. The warm wind pulled at my hair. I headed back toward Bakersfield trying to figure out why there were two Victoria Moors. I felt something men have been feeling for centuries — the excitement of closing in for the kill. Getting closer to that moment of truth. God knows, I wasn't getting closer to virginity. I had just gotten a good Christian girl fired and then tried to pay her off. Maybe wind could purify.

21

I left the car in front of the house and ran down the steps. Gerta let me in.

"Where is she?"

"At the library."

"Where's the library?"

"Who has time to read?"

"If she comes back here before I do, tell her to wait. I have important information." I hurried out of the house and back up the steps to the car.

I assumed she was at the Pasadena library. I stopped and asked three different people. Not one knew where it was. Too bad I wasn't looking for the nearest video store. I got on Colorado Boulevard and headed toward the Civic Center. I turned north off Colorado and drove around City Hall and various municipal buildings before I saw it — a graceful old Spanish building in need of paint and a good gardener.

I turned into the parking lot. The Bentley was there. I parked next to it. I hurried through wrought iron gates into a tiled court-yard. A brown cement fountain, which looked as if it hadn't bubbled water in years, was spray painted with the words MASSIVE MISFITS 1989. Carved in the stucco façade of the library were the names of Homer, Virgil, Dante, Milton, Goethe, Shakespeare, and Pindar. Who was Pindar? Under this list of names sat a young Asian girl and a Chicano boy. They kissed with teenaged passion — new American sweethearts.

Inside, the lobby was as cool and almost as dark as a cave. I stood for a moment trying to figure out what part of the library Claire would be in. A young woman, her skin the same color as her mahogany desk, asked if she could help me.

"I'm looking for a tall, silver-haired woman with a butler."

She stared blankly at me. I didn't blame her. A middle-aged man, dragging a blanket and swinging a lunch pail, wandered in chanting, "Hello! Hello! Hello!"

She ignored him. I didn't blame her.

"Where do you keep records like births, marriages . . . ?"

He swung the pail down onto her desk. "Hello! Hello!"

"It sounds like you want the Hall of Records."

"No. She said 'library.' "

"Hello! Hello! Hello!"

"You might try upstairs in the microfilm library — where they keep documents and newspapers."

"Hello! Hello!"

"Good idea."

"Library closes in ten minutes."

"Thank you." I turned to the man with the blanket and said, "Hello! Hello!" His mouth dropped open in surprise. He turned and ran.

I headed for the stairs. I went down a narrow, dimly lit corridor. A woman with tangled hair made a large circle around me, watching me furtively. Leaves and dirt were stuck to the back of her stained coat.

I peered into a well-lighted room filled with reading tables and chairs. Schoolchildren studied and stared into space. A young, still handsome wino slept it off; his bottle, in a paper bag, rested at his feet like a faithful dog. An old man and woman sat contentedly reading, feeding each other grapes.

I continued down the corridor and turned left into a small room jammed with books. A goateed man dressed in jaunty tweeds looked up from his studies.

"Do you know where the microfilm library is?" I asked.

"Sorry, darling, I spend all my time with

the Romans. February is the month they talk to the dead."

"Glad it's April."

I backtracked and came out into another room. Newspapers hung over wooden racks. A sign on a desk read, PLEASE PRINT YOUR REQUESTS — sounded like a very organized piano bar. There was nobody behind the desk. I started going down the aisles of books. As far as I could tell, I was the only one in the room. I got smart and decided to go outside and wait by the Bentley.

I started back up the aisle. The lights went out and the room was swallowed up in darkness. A door closed.

"Hey! Wait a minute! I'm still in here!" I yelled, bumping into a table. I tried to get my bearings, feeling as though I'd fallen into a vast black lake and I didn't know which way was the shore. I could hear someone breathing. I held my own breath, listening. A shoe squeaked.

"Is someone in here? Do you know where the light is?"

No answer. And I knew, with extraordinary clarity, that I was going to be murdered.

I edged along the side of the table, hoping I was going in the direction of the door. I stumbled over the leg of a chair; it rattled against the table. I held on to it, listening. Warm breath brushed my cheek. My body went cold. I screamed and threw the chair. Running wildly, I tried to get the gun out of my purse. I collided with a bookcase. Books fell on my head and shoulders. Stunned, I grabbed hold of a shelf for support. Hands gripped my throat. He breathed like a hot lover into my ear. I jammed my elbow into his gut. I kicked. I tore at his hands. He pressed harder and harder. No air. No shore. Only the spinning, suffocating darkness and his soft words: "I'm not my own man, Maggie."

A dark shadow hovered over me. A white shadow hovered over the dark . . . I opened my mouth. No sound.

"Don't talk, Maggie." Boulton's voice.

"Get her to the car." Claire's voice.

Boulton picked me up. What else are big arms for? Strangers gawked. The girl with the beautiful mahogany skin asked, "What happened to her?"

"Fainted. Seven months pregnant," Claire said.

We moved past the curious group. I tried to open my mouth, tell them who it was, but nothing came out.

"She doesn't look seven months pregnant."

"Of course she does!" Claire said imperiously. "Give or take a few months."

We were in the hall. The woman with the leaves on her back stared at me, giggling. The public library looked more like a mental hospital than Rosewood did. I tried to tell Boulton this.

"Don't talk, Maggie. Your neck and throat are bruised."

He carried me down the stairs. I leaned my head on his shoulder. It was a nice shoulder. Strong. Hard. The way a man's shoulder should be. I could see Claire carrying my purse and using her walking stick to poke her way through the transients and the school kids.

Outside, I shut my eyes and let the cool night air blow softly against me. I was alive.

Claire opened the door to the Bentley and Boulton sat me down in the backseat. He poured me brandy from a crystal decanter. Claire got in the other side.

"Would you like one too, madam?" he asked.

"Please."

The brandy burned all the way down.

"Sutton!" I gasped.

"Following Mother's wishes, no doubt," Claire said.

"How did he know I'd be here?"

"Probably following me. Couldn't do much with Boulton around. We left. You appeared.

He must've gotten away by going down the back stairs to the back parking lot. It's a good thing you parked your car next to ours — otherwise we would not have gone looking for you. What a tedious day I've had going through three years of newspapers!"

"Why did he want to kill me?"

"Because we're getting too close."

She turned on the overhead light and began to read from a Xerox copy of a newspaper story. "This is dated about eight months ago. 'A retarded woman wandered away from her home at 1345 Beech Street Wednesday night. Pasadena police have searched the area and are now widening their search to other parts of the city. No kidnapping or foul play is expected. The woman's name is being withheld. She is a ward of the state and had recently been transferred here from Rosewood State Hospital.' "

She put the paper down. "There are many such stories on and off for about a month. Then I found this small item: 'The investigation into the disappearance of a retarded woman has been scaled down. There are few clues, but the case remains open.' Before I went to the library I checked the Hall of Records. No births or marriages listed for Judith. No marriages listed for Sutton Kenilworth. Of course they could be listed in other cities or states. One birth was listed for Patricia Kenilworth. Child's name not given. The year was 1952. Now, I was under the impression that Victoria was born in some city other than Pasadena. So I'm assuming Patricia had two children."

"Victoria Moor."

"Yes. The actress. But there is another — "

I shook my head. "Victoria Moor was the name of a missing patient on the Rosewood computer. Ginger's a good little Christian girl who wouldn't take your money."

"Bless her. Boulton, drive to Victoria's house."

"Why the same names?" I asked.

"Revenge, Miss Hill, revenge. When Victoria stared at her father's casket, she said she was born out of her mother's anger." She poured me another shot of brandy.

I leaned back and watched the lights of oncoming cars smear yellow and thought about Sutton. He didn't kill me. He had the chance. He didn't kill me.

"By the way, do you have my two hundred dollars?" Claire asked.

"I left it there. On the ground."

She sighed and closed her eyes.

In twenty minutes we were driving up the long drive to Victoria's house. The gate was open. The house sparkled with lights. The garage doors were open, and the white limo was gone. So was the creamy Mercedes convertible. Only the Jag and Waingrove's silver Mercedes remained.

We got out of the car. The front door was ajar. Boulton had his gun in his hand. We went in. I heard Victoria's voice coming from the pub room. We moved toward her voice.

Patricia sat on the floor, video cassettes scattered around her like tiny coffins. She looked up at the image of her daughter on television. Victoria shimmered like a silver shadow.

The French doors to the garden stood open. A cool, damp breeze, sweet with the smell of cherry blossoms from Shangri-la, chilled the room. The garden was drenched in light. Every important tree had its own spotlight. Even Waingrove, in his pin-striped suit, floating on the pink candy-striped raft, was illuminated by the pool light. His blood spread from an open wound in his chest through the baby-blue water, turning it as brown as dirt. His empty eyes stared up at the moon, which shone as bright as a new silver dollar. Boulton went out to the pool. Claire and I kneeled down next to Patricia. I could see the barrel of a gun half-hidden in the folds of her caftan.

"Hello, Patricia," I said.

"Look," she said, staring at her daughter's

image. "Look how small she is. I could hold her in the palm of my hand. Keep her there forever." She held out her hand, palm up, toward the television, as if she were holding a small, precious object.

"Where is she?" Claire asked.

"At a very prestigious dinner. They're giving her an award. Most popular — "

"Where is the other Victoria?"

She reached for her drink. Ice cubes tinkled as her shaking hand brought it to her mouth.

"I don't know. I thought Brian knew. But he wouldn't tell me. I kept firing the gun and he still wouldn't tell me."

I reached for the gun and carefully moved it toward me. It felt warm.

"It wouldn't fire anymore," she said simply. "Eleanor must know where she is. She knows everything. She knew I didn't belong." She tried to smile but didn't make it. Her lips went slack and her mouth just hung open. She stayed that way for a few moments, staring at the television, then slowly she began to speak.

"I thought if I had a baby . . . a beautiful, perfect baby . . . I would belong to the Kenilworths. But I created imperfection in a perfect world. A monster. No!" Tears formed under heavy lids. "Sweet . . . always innocent . . . always a child."

"And Eleanor wanted you to give the little girl up to the state? To commit her to Rosewood?" Claire asked.

"Yes. So did I. Only Ellis wanted to keep her." She placed her hand on Claire's wrist in a conspiratorial gesture. "Had I kept her, Ellis probably wouldn't have divorced me. But I didn't see that. I was trying to please Eleanor. Eleanor saw it. Eleanor knew. "

"You named her Victoria?"

"Victoria Kenilworth!" She slammed the glass down, slopping amber liquid onto the floor. "Eleanor made me change it. She didn't want the Kenilworth name tainted. Moor is a pretty last name. It has class, doesn't it?" Desperate green eyes looked up at us.

"And when Ellis divorced you, you knew you were pregnant?" Claire asked.

"He had stopped loving me. But God, he desired me. I was very desirable then. Having another baby kept me going, kept me from killing myself. I prayed every night my baby would be a girl."

She looked up at the television. The moving reflection of her daughter cast flickering shadows across her ravaged face as she took another drink.

"I used the name Eleanor had given my other daughter. I created a beauty. I made her famous — so famous the Kenilworths could not deny her existence!"

"How did your first daughter die?"

"Dead. Just like Brian."

"You shot her?"

"No. Eleanor knows. She called me one day."

"When?"

"Eight, nine months ago. Said how proud she was of my Victoria's success. Said she wanted to make amends. I was so damn needy. I believed her. All those years of pain and I still wanted to be accepted by the Kenilworths." She sat her glass on the floor, almost knocking it over.

"Did she invite you to the house?" Claire took the glass and sniffed it.

"We had tea on the patio overlooking the garden," Patricia said, watching her intently. Claire set the glass back down. "On the table was a pink jewelry box. Eleanor opened it and smiled. I didn't understand at first. Then I saw . . . her . . . in the garden. From the back she almost looked like my beautiful Victoria. But her face . . . so imperfect."

"What did you do when you saw her?" Claire asked.

"What?" Her eyes closed and she rocked back and forth.

"You saw your daughter. What did you do?" Claire's voice was firm.

Opening her eyes, Patricia blinked, trying to focus. She looked at Claire, then at me. The cat-green eyes were no longer clever or coy. They were filled with self-hatred and fear.

"I stood up," she said. "And she ran toward me — as if she knew I was her mother. Over *thirty years* had passed. She didn't really know . . . did she? Did she?"

"She ran toward you, and what happened?"

"My baby wanted to put her arms around me and I shoved her away. I pushed her hard down the stone steps. She fell. She broke her neck." Tears streaked her face and hung from her chin like drops of diamonds. "I ran out of the house. Later, Eleanor told me they had taken care of her. I wouldn't have to worry about police or publicity. Eleanor took care of it."

"And then the photograph of Ellis holding his dead daughter arrived in the mail."

"A month later . . . I thought it was the Kenilworths trying to blackmail me. They thought I was trying to blackmail them." She began to laugh, but it sounded more like a cry of pain. "You were right. It was Brian," she gasped.

"And when Miss Hill discovered Ellis's body, you thought she'd seen the photograph."

"Yes." She looked up at the image of her

daughter. "Victoria realized how much she looked like her sister in that picture. She thought if we told you that story you'd leave us alone." She swayed from side to side. "But you didn't." She slumped to the floor, breathing heavily. "I had to get rid of her," she groaned softly. "She could never grow up. She could only grow old." Her eyes rolled back. The whites glistened; the lids closed halfway.

"She's passed out," I said.

Claire stared at her, saying nothing. Patricia's breathing slowed to a rasping rattle, then stopped. Claire felt her pulse.

"She's dead."

"What?"

"She put something in her drink. Cyanide, I think. Can't smell it. The death is almost peaceful. You just stop breathing."

"You knew it was poisoned? You let her die, just like Sutton let his brother die?"

"I let her execute herself, Miss Hill."

I stood up and walked out into the garden. Boulton kneeled by the pool. His handsome face reflected a ghostly shade of bluish white from the pool light.

"He hasn't been dead long," he said, looking up at me. "She unloaded the gun on him. But it looks like only two hit their mark."

"How come the bullets didn't deflate the raft?" I asked.

"You see, Miss Hill, you do get used to it," Claire said, moving beside me.

"Waingrove was standing," Boulton said. "It looks like he staggered back with the force of each bullet and fell onto the raft."

I stared down at Waingrove. Even dead and floating on a silly raft, he still managed to look debonair. I took a deep breath and almost gagged. The air was too sweet in this garden.

"I want to get the hell out of here," I said.

We made our way to the front door. The governess stood at the top of the stairs, looking down at us. The two maids stood behind her.

"Who are you?" she demanded. "We've called the police!"

"Make sure the child does not come down here. And you had better contact Victoria Moor," Claire said.

As I quietly shut the front door, I looked up. Rebecca stared out of her turret. I thought I saw tears glistening on her cheeks. But then, maybe I didn't.

As we drove away, Boulton asked, "Our destination?"

"The Kenilworths'," Claire said.

22

Again I knocked on the mahogany door of the big white house. Aiko answered. He looked pale. Nodding toward the library, he hurried away. The chandelier scattered golden drops of light on the marble floor. The hall clock chimed discreetly, breaking the heavy silence of the house.

Claire turned to Boulton. "Check upstairs."

He moved swiftly up the stairs. My heels made their tippity-tap sounds as we crossed the foyer to the library.

Judith sat on the silk damask sofa. When she saw us, she pulled her gray cashmere cardigan tighter around her shoulders and stood.

"Get out!" she said defiantly. "Get out of our house!"

"We know the woman in the photograph is dead. She was Ellis's first daughter. Victoria Kenilworth," Claire said.

Defiance faded. She was back to being the hurt little girl. "Moor. Her last name is Moor," she said.

Claire sighed and started to sit.

"You haven't been invited to sit down."

"I'm a very tired woman. I've been dealing with a lot of people I detest, including you. I'm sitting down."

Boulton came into the room. "No one's upstairs."

"Not even Eleanor?" Claire asked, surprised.

"No one."

"Where are Sutton and your mother?" Claire tapped her walking stick impatiently on the carpet.

"I can't tell." Lips pressed white.

"Judith, it's all over," I said. "Waingrove is dead."

"No ... no ... he can't be ... he can't ..." Her body sagged onto the sofa. The cardigan slipped off one shoulder. Her arms hung limp.

"Get her some brandy, Miss Hill. Get us all some."

I poured the brandy and handed it around.

"How did he die?" Judith asked in a flat voice.

"Patricia shot him," Claire said.

"She's destroyed our family. And now Brian."

"Come off it, Judith," I said. "The Kenilworths have destroyed the Kenilworths. And

Brian was a hustler. A blackmailer. The perfect friend for your kind of perfect family."

"I loved him!" Her hands kneaded the hem of her skirt. "I caused all this, you know. I was so tired. I wanted to sleep at night. That's why I told Brian about what happened in the garden. You're supposed to be able to tell all your secrets to the man who loves you. I just wanted to sleep. Mother couldn't understand that. But then she can sleep at night."

"Where did you hide Victoria's body?" Claire asked.

She didn't answer.

"Boulton, go to Erwin's house. Find out if he knows — "

"He doesn't know," Judith said softly. "Erwin really thought Victoria had wandered off. That's what made it so easy with the police investigation. Then the photograph arrived in the mail. At first we thought it was Erwin blackmailing us. But we weren't sure, because Patricia got one too. How could he know about *her?* He wasn't there in the garden when it happened." She pulled the sweater back over her shoulder. "So Mother thought Patricia might even be the blackmailer. That's when she got Bobby to spy for her. And then you told me Brian owned Erwin's house and I knew."

"Where did Sutton and Eleanor go?" Claire asked.

"To get rid of her. Forever."

"Where?"

"Where Ellis and Sutton took her."

Claire stood. "Where is that?"

"The hotel," she whispered.

We hurried out of the room and across the foyer. Judith followed us.

"It was all Patricia's fault. We told Ellis that. She never should've been part of the family. Never!"

I closed the big mahogany door and never looked back.

The carcass of the hotel emerged from the night.

Boulton maneuvered the Bentley down the cracked asphalt road. The islands of brown grass floated like dark pools. He turned onto the circular drive. The white limo was parked at an angle. Its doors gaped open. Boulton got a flashlight from the glove compartment and handed it to Claire. We got out of the car. Boulton took out his gun. He peered into the limo.

"Nothing."

We moved slowly toward the hotel. The padlock was broken, the doors open.

We entered the black, cavernous lobby. Our feet scraped on the grimy marble floor. The three of us moved in a strange choreographed unit as if the darkness had made us one. Something slithered. Insects and rodents had taken over the hotel. Damp, thick air clung to my shoulders like a moldy shawl. I smelled decayed leaves, rotted wood. Death. The beam of the flashlight darted around the lobby. It cast icy white circles on the walls, the floor, then far away into the squalid blackness.

"If I remember correctly, there are stairs just over here," Claire said.

The flashlight located a grand, sweeping staircase. A rat, momentarily paralyzed by the bright beam, stopped descending. He stared at us. Claire banged her walking stick on the floor. The rat ran, its naked pink feet scratching at the floor.

We moved up the stairs. Floorboards sighed and wheezed like old sick people. At the top Claire stopped. She moved the light around. We were on a large landing overlooking the lobby. Long, endless corridors extended from each end of the landing. To the right, about halfway down, a thread of light shone dimly under a door.

We moved down the corridor. The wind whipped through, slamming and opening doors as if the hotel were filled with ghostly, angry guests. Each time a door banged against its frame, Boulton whirled around and pointed his gun, like a cop gone berserk. Claire stopped. The light glowed beneath carved double doors. The flashlight caught a tarnished brass nameplate. The Kenilworth name was engraved on it.

She put her hand on the doorknob and quietly opened the door.

The room smelled of gasoline mixed with a sour, rancid odor. Two lanterns, placed on a wooden box, lit the shabby, foul-smelling room with an absurdly intimate dinner-for-two glow. A large can of gasoline lay on its side. Eleanor sat in a chair that had one arm missing. Sutton and Alt whirled around, facing us. Alt held a can of gasoline in his hand. Sutton held a gun.

"Drop it," he said to Boulton.

"For God's sake, do as he says!" Alt cried.

Claire looked at Boulton and nodded.

"Kick it across the floor near my feet," Sutton said firmly. Boulton did. The gun gave Sutton the authority he always lacked.

"Continue your work," Eleanor said to Bobby.

"The smell . . . I'm going to be sick," he whined.

I followed his furtive glances to a pile of canvas tarps on a wood-framed bed shaped like a sleigh. Dirty white stuffing gushed from the mattress — except it wasn't mattress stuffing. It was long blond hair. Matted. Filthy. Lifeless. A nest for spiders. A little something for the rats to nibble on. It was all the pretty things little girls . . . Bobby poured gasoline over it. He started to move away.

"Stay where you are," Eleanor commanded. "Now, the rest of you stand next to him."

"Do as Mother says."

We moved next to Bobby. I could feel gasoline soaking through the bottoms of my shoes.

"Haven't you destroyed enough people?" Claire stared at Eleanor.

"I've destroyed no one." Aquamarine eyes shone maliciously. "Patricia and her child did not belong. All these years and Victoria comes back into my life. I'd watch Ellis play with her in the garden day after day." She leaned forward, gnarled hands shaking. "Now take out the matches I gave you, Bobby, and light one."

"We're too close. We'll burn up with — "

"That's right, dear."

"No . . . no! I won't!" He lunged toward the door. Sutton fired once. Bobby turned; his desperate virgin eyes came to rest on me. "I didn't do anything," he gasped, blood spurting from his mouth. He crumpled to the floor, head flopping to one side. Lifeless virgin eyes continued to stare at me. I looked at Sutton. He was smiling. It was a beautiful, youthful smile.

"The codicil," Eleanor said. "I would like to know where it is."

"Miss Hill has it," Claire said. "In her purse."

I looked at Claire. I didn't have it. It was locked in her safe in the cottage. She knew that.

"I want to see it," Eleanor said.

I looked at Claire, then at Boulton. "Show it to her, Miss Hill," Claire said in a hard, firm voice.

"Go on, Maggie," Boulton urged.

"Carefully, Maggie," Sutton said.

"Yes. Carefully, Maggie." Boulton's eyes met mine. And I knew what he and Claire wanted me to do.

I reached slowly into my purse. My hand was damp and shaking. I felt the pearl handle of his mother's gun. My hand gripped it. I curved my finger around the trigger.

"What are you doing, Maggie?" Sutton's eyes studied me.

"You know me . . . I carry everything . . . *Madame Bovary*, Filofax . . . " I released the safety catch with my thumb. "Tampax . . . rosary . . . it's in here somewhere . . . here it is."

"Slowly!" Sutton said.

I slowly pulled my hand out of the bag. As I came up with the gun, Boulton yelled. Sutton's eyes darted to Boulton. I fired. I missed. I fired again. So did Sutton. I could hear the smack of a bullet in the wall near my head. Sutton's gun fell from his hand. He grabbed his stomach and went down on his knees as if he were going to pray. He slumped onto his side. Boulton and Claire rushed to him. Eleanor stood.

I leaned against the wall, shaking. The room was quiet. Only the wind banging at doors made any noise. Then Eleanor began to scream and moan. I shut my eyes. I felt something brush against me. I opened my eyes. Eleanor was standing next to me, staring down at the decayed hulk on the sleigh bed. The lantern in her hand tipped dangerously.

"I am so cold." She swung the lantern and smashed it against the bed frame. The gasoline-soaked tarpaulin exploded. I leaped away. She didn't. Flames crawled up her back. She never cried out.

"Get the bloody hell out of here!" Boulton yelled.

The fire greedily lapped at the paths of gasoline and up the walls. I couldn't move. I stared, transfixed, at the funeral pyre. I smelled burning female flesh.

"Miss Hill!" Claire said. "Miss Hill! Please, come with me!"

The flames licked and grabbed at the long

blond hair. It curled up as if trying to escape.

"Miss Hill! I do not want to burn to death in a hotel room!"

I looked into Claire's steady, dark eyes. "I don't either."

"Then why don't we get the hell out of here?"

Boulton grabbed my arm. We ran down the long corridor. It glowed a sickly yellow. The building creaked and moaned, as if it could feel the pain of the growing flames.

23

Three days later, Neil stood in the living room of Conrad Cottage, going over his report with us.

Claire and I had spent most of the last two days talking to the Pasadena police, explaining how the deaths of Waingrove, Patricia, Bobby Alt, Sutton, and Eleanor were all connected to the reappearance and disappearance of a retarded young woman. Judith was interviewed and corroborated our story. Erwin had skipped town. The poor souls were returned to Rosewood. Claire was making arrangements to give the coin collection to the Pasadena Museum.

She would not talk to reporters. She asked me to do the same. Somehow the story of incest surfaced in the newspapers. There were breathless hints of Ellis Kenilworth and his famous actress daughter. Never a mention of the other daughter.

This was the first day we'd had with no police sniffing around — that is, until Neil showed up — so I had been packing my belongings and putting them in the Honda. Claire wasn't talking. She just sat in her Queen Anne, legs extended, staring languidly at the tips of her black shoes. Now she stared at Neil with the same lack of curiosity. I sat on one of the sofas. Boulton stood next to Claire.

"Where's the proof that Sutton killed Valcovich?" Neil asked her.

"It was the way he shot Bobby. He did it too easily. I knew it wasn't the first time he had killed," she answered in a bored voice. "Have ballistics run a check. They'll find that the bullets in Sutton's gun match the one found in Valcovich."

"They're checking right now. That fire was pretty intense. I was a little surprised the gun was in perfect condition."

"You really should talk to the Pasadena police. They have all this information."

"I have. They don't say why the gun was in such good condition. I want to hear it from you."

"The fire destroyed the Kenilworth suite and a few surrounding rooms, but not the entire building." She gestured toward the windows. "As you can see. It still stands — a perfect façade. I think the gun would've survived the fire, but I couldn't take that chance. I picked it up with one of my gloves and put it in my pocket. I knew it was the only connection we had between Sutton and Valcovich."

"Something bothers me . . . bothers me deeply." His dark, calculating eyes came to rest on me. Then, slowly, he looked at Boulton. "What about this other gun that Sutton was killed with?" He made an elaborate search of his notes. "Here it is — a Navy Colt with a pearl handle. Small. Two-and-a-half-inch barrel."

"What is so troublesome about that?" Claire asked.

"Says here your butler shot him." He smiled at Boulton. "Butler did it." The smile disappeared. "You don't strike me as the kind of guy who uses pearl-handled guns." Boulton remained impassive.

The one thing we had not told the police was that I had killed Sutton. Claire decided that since I didn't have a license to detect or to carry a gun, we would get bogged down in "bureaucratic pomposity." She decided Boulton would take the responsibility. After all, that was what he was paid for.

"It was my mother's gun," Boulton said. He sounded a little too proper.

"And you just happened to have it on you."

"Very fortunate. Since I was forced to give up my other gun."

"Where did you hide this gun?"

"Taped to my ankle."

"So this guy's holding a gun on you and you lean over and rip off the tape and come up with your gun and he doesn't bother to shoot you."

"I distracted Sutton, giving Boulton time to get his gun." Claire stifled a yawn.

"I'm real good at detecting bullshit. And right now I think I'm up to my ass in it."

"How very graphic," Claire sighed.

He turned to me. "You're unusually quiet."

"Congratulations," I said.

The eyes narrowed. "On what?"

"Getting married."

"Oh, yeah. Thanks."

"Quick honeymoon."

He ignored me and studied his notes. When he looked up, it was at Boulton. "You must've worried about Maggie running around unprotected. I would've. I probably would've given her a little gun. Like my mother's. If my mother had one."

"The death of Sutton Kenilworth is not in your jurisdiction," Claire said.

"If he murdered Valcovich it is. I'd like to know who really shot this Sutton. They say here the first bullet missed." He eyed Boulton. "I have the feeling you don't miss. And you," he turned on Claire, "I bet you never get your hands dirty. Hey, I don't have to put this in my report. I just want to know what Maggie's capable of."

"Then why don't you ask me?"

He turned slowly toward me. He nodded his head, looking very sage. "Killing a man must make you feel real liberated."

"That's right, Neil, I feel real liberated. A woman either has to fuck a man or kill him to be truly free."

"You said it. I didn't."

I shot up off the sofa. "Listen, you son of a bitch — "

"That's right, Maggie. I'm the villain. Maybe I should be careful. You might have a gun on you."

Claire rapped her walking stick on the floor. "I will not have this eternal bickering between the male and female species in my house! Show him out, Boulton."

"Don't bother." Neil sauntered toward the door. "Honeymoon starts tomorrow, Maggie," he said, without looking back at me.

I went to my room and grabbed my phone machine, slammed it on top of the monitor, and lugged them out to the car. It was back to perfect weather again. My soul couldn't take it. Boulton leaned against the Honda.

"Thank you, Maggie," he said, taking my monitor and placing it on top of my suitcase.

"For what?"

"Saving my life. Miss Conrad's life." He took the phone machine and placed it in the car.

Tears formed. What the hell was I crying for?

The brown eyes studied me. He brushed my cheek with his fingertips. His thumb followed the curve of my lips. I stepped back out of his reach. No. No more big shoulders for me.

"What's wrong with Claire?" I asked, changing the subject. "She's not speaking to anyone."

"Languors," he replied.

"What?"

"Languors. She has them after every case. I'm surprised she's not in bed."

"Why can't she just be depressed like the rest of us?"

Gerta ran up the steps, apron fluttering. "Please," she panted with the effort of the stairs, "you think again about leaving."

"Gerta, I told you. I told *her*. I have my own life!"

"What is your own life?"

I decided not to answer that — mainly because I didn't have an answer. I went down the steps and into the house.

She was back in the Queen Anne, poking aimlessly at the floor with her black walking stick.

"I'm all packed and ready to go."

"Oh, yes. You have your own life to live. It's an adolescent response, Miss Hill. How could you not want to write about me? What are you afraid of? Being a writer? Or me?"

"You may not understand this, but one morning I woke up and my radio told me that virginity was making a comeback. Ever since then I have bribed people, hit people, stolen from people, lied to people, and . . . yes . . . killed. Now, for some silly reason I thought it just might be possible for virginity — "

"Miss Hill, I'm sure where you are concerned there are more obtainable goals."

"Oh, hell, never mind."

Gerta came in and began to put sheets over the furniture.

"What's going on?" I asked.

"I've decided to go to London. But first I will stop in New York to see a man who always wears bow ties. He usually has a financially rewarding job for me, if not a stimulating one. I need money."

"You could've had four million dollars."

She raised herself from the chair and stood facing me. "I didn't want it. I hope you have what *you* want — a very safe life. Of course, you will have to say no to many opportunities to assure that safety. But you will. You're very stubborn." She extended her hand. "It has been a pleasure knowing you, Miss Hill."

"Same here," I said, taking her hand. It felt like a dead fish in mine. "That's the limpest handshake I've ever received."

"It's all I can offer at the moment." She turned and went into her bedroom and closed the door.

"Goodbye, Gerta."

She looked like my mother had when I left for Los Angeles eight years ago. I waved quickly and got out of the house. God, women give women a bad name!

Boulton opened my car door for me.

"Are *you* mad at me, too?" I asked.

"Never, Maggie." He took my hand and kissed it.

I could've sworn I felt his tongue slide over my knuckle and gently probe between two of my fingers.

"What was that?"

"I beg your pardon, madam?" The discreet butler was back.

"My mistake, I'm sure," I said, smiling.

"Does madam make mistakes?"

I spent the afternoon looking for an apartment. I found nothing but depression. My own. Thinking temporary work was what I needed, I drove over to the New Woman Agency to see Phyllis and Corinne.

Corinne was at her desk talking to a young, purple-haired woman. "Maggie! Phyllis, Maggie's here!"

"I don't *have* to know what I want to do," the purple hair said defiantly.

"It would help us to place you," Corinne said sweetly.

I waved and walked back to Phyllis's office. In the clutter of her desk was a portable TV. She was blond this week — Victoria Moor blond. Her nails were fake and blue-red. She was missing the thumbnail. I sat down in the chair and saw the fake nail lying on the floor.

"You looking for this?" I picked it up.

"Oh, God, yes! Isn't it awful?"

"What?"

"Victoria Moor."

"Terrible. Do you have anything for me?"

"A job in Downey. I mean, to be abused by your father . . . Can you imagine doing it with your father?! Yecchh! — It's back on. Shhh!" She turned the television louder.

I got up and took a look at it. Victoria Moor, dressed in black, sat in a chair, facing an audience of mostly women. Phil leaned close to her.

"We know this is a very difficult subject to be discussing on national television."

"If it will help another young woman . . . well . . . that makes it less difficult." She was

402

the woman of unimpaired morality.

Applause.

"Now, Ellis Kenilworth," Phil said in an insinuating voice, "was straight-line Pasadena. I mean . . . we don't think this can happen . . . in *those* places."

"Where's the truth?" I said out loud.

"What?"

"Where the hell is Downey?!"

"I don't know. Listen!"

I headed out the door. "See you later, Phyllis."

She never looked up from the television.

As I said goodbye to Corinne, I heard Phyllis yell in recognition, "Ellis Kenilworth! He's in our files! You worked for him!"

Going down the hall, I thought about a hank of blond hair. Matted. Dirty. I thought about a weak man who killed himself . . . a man who wanted a detective to straighten out his life for him. I thought about Victoria Moor. She was only acting. It was all she knew. It was all she had left. I thought about Patricia Kenilworth saying, "She can never grow up, she can only grow old." I thought about the blond hair curling away from the flames. I thought about the truth. Oh, hell, I'll let television take care of the truth. It was going to anyway.

The girl with purple hair was in the elevator.

"Are they going to get you work?" I asked.

"Look, I didn't come out here to be a frigging typist for some jerk. I got my own life to live."

"Yes."

I sat in my car in the parking lot, searching through my purse for my keys. I pulled out the dove-gray envelope. My name was written on it in Ellis Kenilworth's handwriting. I opened the envelope and took out a first-class airline ticket to New York. The departure time was four thirty. I stared at the ticket, thinking that maybe virginity had made a comeback after all — in the form of a tall woman who on every other day wore black.

I put the car in gear and made my way down Hollywood Boulevard to the freeway. I might just make it.

But what about my car?! My possessions? My life!

Oh, hell.